exactly where they'd fall

a novel

Laura Rae Amos

Copyright © 2012 by Laura Rae Amos

Drew's status update is excerpted from "The Love Song of J. Alfred Prufrock," by T.S. Eliot. 1920.

For inquiries, contact:
Laura Rae Amos
PO Box 150006
Alexandria, Virginia 22315
lauraraeamos.com
laura.rae.amos@gmail.com

ISBN: 0615696074

ISBN-13: 978-0615696072 (Laura Rae Amos)

For all the sisters I've had,
whether for a moment or for life,
whether by blood or by choice.

~

And in memory of my daddy.
I wish you were here.

"Suffering has been stronger than all other teaching,
and has taught me to understand what your heart used to be.
I have been bent and broken, but – I hope – into a better shape."
– Charles Dickens, Great Expectations

SEPTEMBER

1.1: a fraction of a sliver of a moment

JODIE HATED ADORABLE THINGS: HAPPY COUPLES, CHILDREN, puppies, hugs. Jodie hated favors, she hated generosity, she hated having to say "thank you." But Jodie couldn't hate Drew, with those kind, dark eyes, rich as coffee. He was positively adorable. Sweet, even. She didn't even ask him to help, but here he was in her apartment with his laptop, going through his Facebook friends (all five hundred of them) trying to find her a new roommate.

"You really don't need to bother." She glanced over his shoulder as he scanned through the names, face after face of beaming smiles. Smilebook, they should have called it. Fakebook. Jodie hated social media. She hated social anything. She was certain he wouldn't find anyone for her in there. He finally landed on his profile page, his status reading: *That is not what I meant at all; that is not it, at all – updated 14 hours ago*. Other mysterious notifications Jodie didn't understand: *Drew kicked a sheep at Amelia, Amelia poked Drew*. A virtual gift he'd received, a pixel pig holding a heart. Jodie scowled. "Why the *hell* did you kick a sheep?"

"Heh," he chuckled, clicking away from the page. "It's a game, Jodie. Get yourself a profile, and I'll kick a sheep at you too."

The whole idea of it just sounded half vulgar and half like animal abuse. "No, really, that's just wrong."

"Or there's Scrabbler."

"That's not fair, you were an English major. What's wrong with you people?" By people, she meant English majors. "You can't get a job with your degree, so you vow to spend the rest of your life beating people at Scrabble?"

He laughed absently, still clicking away at his laptop. "Go log into your email," he said. "You need to confirm something."

"What?"

"I made you a page. Password's your name, for now. You can change it."

"A Facebook page? Why? No! I don't want one." She backed away from his laptop with her hands held up, fingers spread, as if the internet might jump from his laptop and attack her. "Why did you do that?"

"Really, it'll help you meet people." There was such genuine concern in his voice, she couldn't stand it. She went to the other side of the room and sat in front of her desktop computer. She refreshed her email. There was a confirmation link to click, and she clicked it. A Facebook page with her name on it, and he'd already requested four friends on her behalf: himself (already accepted), and three others still pending, Amelia, Piper, and Tom.

"Refresh your page," he said.

She did. *Drew kicked a sheep at Jodie.* She turned back to gape at him. He leaned back in his chair, arms folded over his chest and a beautiful, accomplished smile on his face. She never liked the color blue, but he wore it so often, and in so many shades – ocean, navy, steel – all of which seemed to highlight the bronze he'd accumulated over the summer on his cheekbones and forearms, and all of which only brightened that generous smile. "I feel so violated," she said.

She was mostly kidding, and he seemed to know that. She was quite sure that would be the first and only time anyone had ever been violated by Drew Weston in any capacity. He grinned, so friendly she thought he might wink, so precious she thought she might sigh, so corny she felt inclined to laugh. But instead she only coughed a stifled "heh," and she didn't know if she was laughing at him or herself.

"But this is easier," he said, turning back to his laptop. "Now I can send you links to these girls."

Somehow it disappointed her that it had all still been about the list.

Jodie wanted him to give up, but she didn't say so. Truth was, she hadn't had any luck finding a new roommate for herself. Piper was getting married in a few months, and now Jodie would have to find someone clean, tolerable, smart, responsible, not too old, not too young, not male, no dogs, no fish (no animals period would be a good rule of thumb), not too sweet, not too boring, not too pretty-pretty. Ugly was okay. Jodie didn't care if she was ugly.

Piper wasn't ugly though. She was perfect. Irreplaceable. And now Jodie had to try to replace her.

Jodie took an empty water glass to the kitchen, the clacking sound of Drew's keyboard carrying on behind her. A flurry of words, all those profiles, one after another after another. How could anyone manage to know so many people? Did he remember how he met each of them? Would he be able to tell two of them apart if they happened to be standing next to each other? Had he ever met them in person at all?

Jodie washed her hands, scrubbing the backs, the cracks in between, scraping her fingernails against her own sudsy palms as if she were scrubbing in for a delivery, though she was only making some sandwiches for lunch. By the time she turned to see what Drew wanted in his sandwich, he already had Amelia on the phone. Of course. Jodie always knew it the second those two connected – he would go positively starry-eyed. "Come on over," he said into the phone, leaning against Jodie's kitchen table as if in a dream. He turned to her then. "You don't mind if Melie comes over."

It wasn't a question in any form, but Jodie answered anyway. "Of course not. I don't mind. Why would I mind?"

Amelia. She was his girlfriend, but it was so much more complicated than that. Longtime friends who happened to be sleeping with each other, nothing alike yet strangely complementary, always side by side. Like salt and pepper.

The kitchen alcove of Jodie's apartment was small. Piper didn't cook, and Jodie was too busy to cook, so they had no use for anything bigger. Piper made salads and Jodie could do sandwiches, but beyond that, the two of them were hopeless. They just stocked their freezer with frozen pizzas and Lean Cuisines. Back before the boyfriends and the real jobs and the grown up lives – it was Amelia who always cooked for them. Amelia hosted their parties. She was the one who made the cocktail snacks, the savory tarts, vegetable trays, and cheeseballs with gourmet herb crackers. She decorated for Halloween, Christmas, the Fourth of July, and even Veterans Day. But it seemed like forever since they had those parties together – now Amelia hosted most of them at her own place, which was roomier than Jodie's tiny apartment, and had a large spacious kitchen for Amelia to work in. Amelia's kitchen was something straight out of *Better Homes & Gardens*.

Drew's phone beeped softly as he hung up. Stepping beside Jodie in the kitchen, he announced his presence by taking a lock of her hair around his finger and flipping it. The hair flopped back down, thick and heavy, the shoulder-length tips brushing across the back of her neck as they landed. She froze. He continued talking about Amelia, roommates, lists, lunch, while Jodie could still feel the tingle he'd left on her skin. He probably couldn't have known how infrequently anyone ever touched her.

When she began moving again, she asked him, "Is ham okay?"

"Yeah, sure. Thanks," he said.

Jodie found it ridiculous how many people were getting married. It was just an ordinary September, but if this was normal, it was something Jodie had never noticed before. What was it about being almost thirty that made everyone want to pair up and breed like the world was coming to an end? At least Piper wasn't getting married until the spring. "Everyone's getting married," she mused out loud.

"Yeah? Amelia's dragging me to her cousin's wedding this weekend."

"See!" Jodie shrieked. "And next week, my brother's getting married."

Jodie's brother, Amelia's ex. Drew looked up, seeming both surprised and relieved. Then, like an afterthought, he shrugged it off – not even Drew was that selfless. "Oh? Good for him."

Jodie laughed. "Don't worry, you've got her all to yourself. You guys will probably be next."

He shook his head. "I already asked. She said no."

"I don't think she thought you were serious."

"She knows I'm serious," he said. "She doesn't even want a live-in boyfriend. I'll go ahead and guess that means she doesn't want a husband either."

"I don't blame her, actually." Jodie twisted her lips into a smirk. If he took offense, he didn't show it.

Jodie finished three sandwiches, and by the time she'd placed them on the table, there was Amelia's knock at the door. Drew let her in. The two of them kissed at the doorstep, smiling at each other for just a moment, and then Amelia turned to Jodie. "Hi Jodie." Amelia took in the scene from the doorway and then offered up a guarded smile. Amelia was all legs and freckles. She wasn't that pretty, more graceful than she was glamorous. She walked like a large bird, slow and poised. She made Jodie feel ordinary – or maybe it was the way Drew looked at her that made Jodie feel ordinary.

"I have three more girls for you to look at," Amelia said, pulling her notes from a paper folder under her arm, placing them on the table. Her list was written in black ink on a yellow lined legal pad, each name numbered and broken into several fields of data – age, occupation, hair color, favorite food, hobbies, habits – as if she were collecting specimens for a scientific study. She took the seat next to Drew at the table and began to narrate the women out loud: "Amy, divorced but with grown children."

"No," Jodie said. "Grown children means grandchildren visiting. No thanks."

"Molly, employed, she's a DJ?"

"No, I hate music. I can't live with a DJ."

"Emmy, single, she's an actress."

"That just means she doesn't work," Jodie said.

Amelia shook a finger at her. "She does work. I promise you she does."

"Is she pretty?"

"Sure," Amelia said. "What does it matter if she's pretty? Piper's pretty."

"Right, but she's Piper. That's different."

"Jodie," Amelia chided. "You should lighten up a bit, or you're going to end up alone." She paused. "Not that there's anything wrong with that. I like living alone." Amelia held her head high when she said it, but Drew took notice, looking up from his ham sandwich, not chewing. Jodie tried to swallow the snark on her tongue, but it was hard. Amelia did *not* like living alone – evidence the fact that she'd quickly moved in with every boyfriend she ever had since she was old enough to leave home. Another reason Jodie was so surprised Amelia and Drew hadn't already shacked up together.

When they were finished, Drew reached out to touch Amelia's hand. "Are you heading back soon?"

"Actually," Amelia said, tilting her head to him as if anticipating his disappointment. "I can't. I have an errand to run out here." They made frown faces at each other, pouting like sad fish. Jodie leaned her cheek to her hand, waiting for them to finish.

"No problem," he said to Amelia. "Call me later then." He gathered his things. When he bent over the table to kiss Amelia goodbye, Jodie became flushed with a wide-eyed and terrible shock. It wasn't a very long kiss, and it certainly wasn't pornographic, but Jodie couldn't bear to watch it. She felt herself melt into a mound of jelly, staring ahead at a blank wall, the two of them coming apart slowly in her peripheral vision. It was just a simple kiss goodbye, yet impossibly deep without even the hint of open lips or tongues. She didn't even know what part she was jealous of; whatever it was, its absence overwhelmed her.

"See ya, Jodie," Drew said, already en route to the door.

Amelia started talking again, and it took Jodie a few seconds to snap out of the shock. Amelia's tense and structured chatter – something about her mother, the bank, phone calls and needing stamps – the tension in her eyebrows reflecting the priority of the task as she counted them off on her fingers.

They were never meant to be friends. Amelia dated Jodie's brother for three years; the friendship was meant to be temporary. It was meant to be one of those tangent friendships, strung together with loose ties so that it could untie again when the time was right. Instead, when her brother broke up with Amelia, they didn't untie. Their little group only became more intertwined and complex, and here were the two of them left over, stuck. It was hard to remember all the previous lives they shared, where they started and where they stopped – Jodie hadn't thought not to mention her brother when Amelia mentioned a wedding she had to attend. "I know, my brother's getting married next week too."

"Eric," Amelia said, her fingers coming to a stop. The tension between her eyebrows went slack, weighted with nostalgia and some sort of accepted sadness.

"I mean," Jodie added, softer then. "I have no idea who to take to the wedding."

"That came up fast," Amelia said.

Jodie nodded, though it hadn't been that fast. Not terribly fast. It had been two years since he and Amelia broke up. Jodie had known Amelia for a long time. Seven years now, since the day her brother first introduced them. She'd known Amelia longer than Piper, and longer than Drew. She knew Amelia back when they were just girls – twenty-two, undergrads and clueless, grasping at the world and trying to create brand new lives from it. She tried to remember before Drew came into the picture. Did she and Amelia always have this quiet tension between them that bordered on resentment?

Jodie began laughing out loud at the joke she had in her head. "So, you mind if I borrow Drew for this wedding? You know how he likes them."

Amelia raised one eyebrow, her lips twisting into something that looked less like a smile than just confused and conflicted – over which part, Jodie didn't know. There was such a careful consideration in Amelia's eyes, Jodie had to glance away. Amelia finally sighed and offered up a strained smile. "No, Drew likes the open bar at weddings, there's a difference. Why don't you take Berges? Don't you like Berges?"

Passionate hate was a better description of what Jodie felt for Berges.

"Can you ask a divorced person to a wedding? Isn't that bad luck or something?"

Amelia didn't answer that. While the tension in her face melted, she seemed to drift into a thought. A deep one. Jodie wasn't sure she'd buried her secrets well enough.

SOMETIMES YOU KNOW OF A PERSON FOR YEARS, SHARING OUTINGS as friends of a mutual friend, bumping into each other at parties but never speaking, never exchanging more than a nod, or a hello, or a goodnight. Jodie could still remember the first whole conversation she had with Drew. He and Amelia were already tied up with each other in that momentous but stunted way, but there was a moment – and Jodie wasn't even sure if it was real – where she thought Drew might have actually been interested. She felt honestly ridiculous to think such a thing, to even consider it in the private cavities of her own head. Interested in her? No, it was unlikely. It must have been all in her mind, that moment when Amelia was still an impossibility to him, before she was dating him, or sleeping with him. That inescapable night Amelia had dragged them all along to their cocktail bar, and left them there with smoke on their clothes and neon lights in their eyes. One fraction of a sliver of a moment when Jodie thought Drew might have considered her an option.

Jodie's martini glass glinted pink light over her blunt-cut fingernails. Drew took the bar stool next to her, bringing in a breath of crisp fall air from outside, almost overpowering the smell of cigarette smoke in the room. He exhaled heavily as he sat. "Why do you think she won't date me?"

Jodie looked him up and down. "Because you look like you're twelve?" The venom spewed from her mouth like a reflex. She didn't know why. She didn't find him unpleasant, and she didn't know him well enough to hate him. He hadn't even said anything to annoy her in the two hours they'd been out that night. In fact, truthfully, he didn't even look like a twelve year-old at all, but maybe eighteen, twenty on a good day, clean-shaven and gentle-faced as he was. He seemed so untouched by the world.

"I'm twenty-seven, thanks," he said.

"Maybe grow some chin hair then?"

His hand moved to rub his chin. "Believe me, I can grow plenty of chin hair if I wanted to." He had to lean toward her, scooting his bar stool a bit closer to avoid shouting over the noise, couples out on dates, a group of girls shrieking with laughter around one boy wearing white sequins.

"Let me guess," she said. "You want to get married?"

He shrugged. "Sure."

"Did you tell her that?"

"Probably. But in a general way. I didn't pop the question or anything."

Jodie shook her head. "What's wrong with you freaks?"

He just stared at her. "What's wrong with *you*?"

She huffed. "Wrong? Nothing's wrong with me."

"You're so angry."

"I'm *not* angry." She folded her arms over her chest. "Tell you what – I just tell people the truth. People don't like to hear the truth."

He pointed at her, his finger wagging slightly. "You're so bitter, jaded. You're statuesque almost, a strange approximation of a woman. Like you're stiffened by your own spite."

She laughed out loud. "Who talks like that?"

"I'm going to write a poem about you." He smiled then, which was both inquisitive and genuine. The unimaginable grace it must have taken not to hold the hostility against her. How could he stand it? It crossed her mind then to ask him why he thought nobody wanted to date her.

Didn't she know the answer already?

He bought her a drink – martini, dry, with an extra olive. He drank an imported beer. They stayed for a while, and wherever Amelia had gone that night, why he'd stayed and Amelia hadn't, Jodie didn't know. It was some drinks, some conversation, a night of company. She was quite sure he hadn't meant it as a date. They were friends, or at least, they would begin to be from that point.

But still, there was a future that might have existed, spawned from that night, those drinks at the bar, with music thumping in their chests and neon lights in their eyes, and those few perfect hours that followed. A man like him – sensitive and tender – he would want a wedding, as much as he liked them, and maybe even a family. Children, in the plural. None of it – the man, the wedding, the children – was anything Jodie had ever wanted, but for that one moment, she allowed the possibility to enter into existence. Maybe she also scowled at it, but it had existed there just the same.

And would anything have ever come of it? Nobody would ever know because just days later, Amelia finally kissed him. She changed her mind, took him in, swept him into her arms, into her bed, into her heart, which was everything he'd always wanted. Just like that, whatever possibility might have existed with Jodie was wiped clean away with that kiss.

But Jodie had no plight to argue. She couldn't say she liked him first. She couldn't say she liked him better, or even that she liked him more. As much as she loathed to admit it, she just liked him. To a ridiculous degree. That was all she knew.

THE APARTMENT WAS BIG AND EMPTY WITHOUT PIPER. SHE WAS a tiny, bubbly woman with hair cut sharp and dyed bright. Like candy, she caused toothaches. She was fully grown but the size of a teenager – an explosion of energy in all forms, including the mess she left around when she was there. Jodie would miss it, in a way, her pillows and pink furry blankets, slippers shaped like purple elephants, her syrupy soda in the fridge and the sticky rings it left on the countertops, a sort of fingerprint she left behind. Piper wouldn't be married for seven more months, but lately, the only time Jodie saw her was when she stopped by to grab some clothes or a DVD, and ran back out to her fiancé's place. The idea being that she should wait until the wedding night to move in with him – the wholesome little Catholic girl that her grandmother thought she was – but that was more a formality than anything. She already had most of her things packed.

Jodie was reading on the couch when Piper burst into the apartment, bringing the wind with her, the scent of fallen leaves and a hint of rain. Tom followed behind, tall and nervous. Jodie made men nervous. It was always a wonder to her – and a little amusing – that she could make such a burly, giant of a man nervous.

Piper ran up the stairs, leaving Tom in the center of the room. He nodded and Jodie nodded back, the mutual acknowledgment of each other's presence. This was the part she hated. Was she supposed to stop reading? Was she supposed to entertain him? Make jokes? Her roommate's fiancé – it was an odd, forced kind of friendship. The walls of the apartment were paper thin. She'd even heard them having sex before. Once you'd heard someone having sex, you could never really get it out of your mind when you saw them again. It was never as appealing or amusing as one might imagine. People always sounded stupid having sex, and looked even more stupid, with their faces all contorted and expressive. On the occasion Jodie actually got into bed with a man, she had to close her eyes to keep from being distracted by the faces, the odd look of so much pleasure it was painful. Jodie hadn't had actual sex in a really long time.

Tom shifted his weight, cleared his throat. "You mind if I steal your girl for the night?"

Jodie shrugged. Did she mind? Didn't she mind? Didn't he already have her? "Sure, have at her," Jodie said. She didn't try to make jokes with Tom like she would Drew – he wasn't the joking type. But he was a good enough guy, and Piper adored him. Jodie was going to be maid of honor in their wedding, next to Amelia and Piper's dozen-or-something sisters. Piper was making the dresses herself – both her own and for the wedding party, clouds of tulle in yellow and purple. They'd all look like Easter eggs.

Piper came downstairs then, a pink tote slung over her shoulder with her pajamas stuffed into it, one pant leg trailing from the back. She dropped the bag on the floor and plopped onto the couch, wrapped her little arms around Jodie's neck, her warm cheek pressed to Jodie's cheek, the overpowering smell of florals and candy lip gloss. Jodie stiffened first, but Piper never made it a choice. She hugged – you didn't get to decline them. She hugged until Jodie relaxed the little bit that she would.

"See you tomorrow, babe."

Jodie hated being called "babe", but Piper never gave her a choice in that either.

And then Piper and Tom were gone with the same quick gust they blew in on. The apartment was far too quiet without her. It was almost worth having him sleep over, at the risk of hearing their animated and eager sex, just to have the presence of human life in the apartment for a night. But even so, how long could it last? They were getting married, starting a family and a life of their own. Jodie had an email from Drew with names and links to Facebook profiles, and on the kitchen table was Amelia's yellow notepad with lines of women and their painfully detailed descriptions. Dozens of faceless strangers sat there demanding a response, a decision, and Jodie didn't want to live with any of them.

Jodie put the news on for background noise, to block the sound of voices echoing through the thin apartment walls. She picked up a magazine, pushed back cushions to fall into – Piper's big, fluffy cushions. Jodie imagined she would probably take them with her eventually.

She flipped open her magazine – celebrity divorces, how to wear leggings, what to eat for four-hundred calories. Wasn't she happy enough alone? She certainly wasn't lonely enough to need just anybody here. And she took that as a good sign. Alone, but not lonely. It was quiet, sure, but it could be nice. Not having to share the shower in the morning. Not having to debate what they'd watch on TV.

She worried though, if she didn't find a new roommate soon enough, would she start talking to herself? Would she run dialogues of conversations out loud to no one? Maybe she would get a pet. A goldfish? No, something sentient, so she could pretend she wasn't really talking to herself. Maybe a cat.

A cat? Seriously? When did she start liking cats?

And then, as she sat in her own empty living room with CNN rattling on in the background, her magazine flopped open on her lap, and a whole conversation in her head, she saw it stretched out ahead of her. Every town had that weird old cat lady, the angry woman sitting on her front porch swing, wearing a nightgown and socks, waving a rolled up newspaper at random children to get off of her lawn. No friends, no family, and way too many cats.

Was this how it started?

1.2: things to do before forty

THE DOG DIED. AMELIA HAD HER MOTHER'S DRY-CLEANING in hand, helped herself into the house to drop it off, and there was the animal's body, lying still between the stove and a chewed up gnawing bone, dead on the cold ceramic floor. Amelia couldn't tell at first, so she crouched down low to watch for its breathing. Nothing. She stood again, looked around her mother's empty kitchen, watched for movement, tapped the animal with a gentle toe. Nothing.

She was an old dog, having joined the family when Amelia was fourteen. Amelia never liked animals much, and never cared much for this dog in particular, a chubby Labrador with a mottled beige coat. But death was still death, abrupt and unsettling. Her mother was alone now. Her father was fine; they'd spoken to him on the phone just days ago. But he was working thousands of miles away in Afghanistan. As a retired Air Force mechanic, they hoped he might be finished with the Middle East. They hoped he would be home to stay until the company he worked for started picking up government contracts. This time, he told them it would be a year. He said he could come home for the holidays, though they both knew he couldn't afford that much travel. Amelia could still remember all of his deployments when she was a girl. During

Desert Storm, she had been twelve – her seventh grade class sent care packages with handmade cards, magazines, beef jerky, eye drops, and socks. Now she was a full grown woman and every day there were the news reports. You didn't need to be in combat – didn't even need to be a soldier at all – doctors, reporters, translators, travelers were killed all the time by children who looked ordinary but had bombs strapped to their chests, or in helicopter crashes, shot down, spinning out of the sky like pinwheels gleaming in the sun. She tried not to think about any of it, until death with its abrupt and unsettling persistence showed up right there at her feet. An old dog, dead.

Amelia started to cry. She set the dry-cleaning over a dining room chair and wiped at her eyes furiously with the back of her wrist. Her mother wasn't home yet from The Lotus, so no one was even home when it happened. The poor thing had died alone. Suddenly Amelia felt guilty for not spending more time with her, for being too self-involved as a teenager, for not taking her on more walks, for not playing fetch. She never liked dogs, but still, she could have played fetch a time or two.

She didn't know what to do, so she called Drew. "Can you come over to my mom's?" She gasped and sniffled into her cell phone. "Lady is dead."

Drew's apartment wasn't very far away. She'd heard him rustling into his jacket before even hanging up his phone, and minutes later he showed up, jacket undone, shoes untied and hair unbrushed. In fact, from the pillow creases on his face, it looked like he'd been napping. She wasn't sure if he had the smallest clue about what to do with a dead dog, but his being there was a form of help in itself. "Oh, Melie," he said near her ear as he slipped his arms around her, pressing their bodies close.

They sat down at the kitchen table, as far away from the dead dog as they could while still being in the same room. Drew sat beside her, held her hand, and she turned away from the dog to look at him instead. His gentle brown eyes were narrow and inquisitive as he stared at it, a fingernail between his teeth as he thought. Amelia figured he was probably composing a poem about the fragility of life, or the arresting poignancy of death. Or maybe he was just wondering what to do with the body.

They had a wedding to go to that evening. Her mother had planned on finishing up paperwork at the spa and leaving Mindy in charge for the day. Amelia still had to shower and do her own hair, and she wondered if they had the time to take care of the dog and still make it to the wedding. She tried her mother's phone, but there was no answer, which likely meant she was already driving.

It wasn't very long before Claire made it home. As she stepped into the house, Amelia broke the news. "Mom," Amelia said. "Lady is dead."

Claire went straight into the kitchen, heels clicking on the stone tile. She stood over the dog for approximately forty-five seconds, a blank expression on her face. "She was so old," Claire finally said. They were all silent then for another moment, as if they were each wondering if they should say something. A prayer? Should Drew recite a poem? But Claire just pursed her lips into a slight frown, nodded her head once firmly, then turned to the coffee pot, pulling out a filter full of old, wet coffee grounds. "Will you call Corbin for me, sweetie? Only if he's not busy. Tell him I'll pay double his regular wage."

Corbin. Amelia cringed a little.

"Well, we can't leave her lying here while we're gone," Claire insisted.

That wasn't the problem. Corbin worked for her parents, offering massage therapy at The Lotus, though in the years he'd worked for them, he'd become more of a family friend than an employee. Amelia couldn't say she was angry with Corbin. He didn't exactly do anything wrong. It had been a couple of years now. She never said she cared about him – she wasn't even sure what she felt for him at all, except taken aback most of the time and overwhelmed. No one had ever presented it so openly before, and so earnestly – the way they'd gotten together, exactly two times, and then he casually went into some metaphysical discourse about how his life was his own and his feelings for her were separate and undefined. He'd said, "I'll always be honest with you, Amelia, but I don't want to possess you. And I don't mind if you want to keep seeing your little friend." They were at the spa, on his massage table, their second and last time together. Her panties were still around her ankles and she was so blindsided by it all, the only response she could offer was to come to Drew's defense. First, she and Drew had not been seeing each other yet back then, and second, Drew was not *little* – he was perfectly average-sized for a man, and while he might not have a rock hard yoga body, he did keep himself healthy. He played golf.

Honesty, when presented with it in all its stark nakedness, only felt harsh and unpleasant. And the most outrageous thing about it was that her parents were right about him. Corbin was completely honest, to the core. He meant every single word of it, metaphysical bullshit and all.

Amelia hesitated, but finally did pick up her phone anyway and scrolled through the names. She could see Drew fidget in her peripheral vision. "You have his number stored in your phone?"

Drew never liked Corbin. Amelia had never even told him about the mistaken tryst, but she wondered if maybe he suspected it anyway. It was so slight a thing. She hadn't even known his name the first time they were together. They were a disaster, and it was so long before she and Drew had gotten together that she just didn't know how to bring it up. She shrugged. "He works for my parents."

When Claire left the room, Drew said, "Your mother hates me. Why wouldn't she just ask me to do it?"

"You need to get ready too." Amelia reached out to his hand. "She just doesn't want you to go to a wedding having just buried a dog."

They both knew that thought hadn't crossed her mother's mind in the least.

"No," Drew said, standing up, sending a ripple across the surface of an oil candle on the table, his eyes alight with both complaint and purpose. "I can bury a dog." He took off his jacket and hung it on the chair, taking stock of the room. In his striped polo shirt and jeans, he looked more like Clark Kent than Superman, but his assertion was impressive. Amelia didn't know what to say. She set down her phone.

"What can we wrap her in?" he asked.

Amelia went to get Lady's blanket, which happened to be one of Amelia's old childhood blankets, a cotton weave in blue and white, worn ratty over the years.

Drew laid out the blanket on the floor and rolled Lady inside it. He picked up the eighty pound dog in both arms, and Amelia went to get the door for him.

Amelia picked the spot, in the back corner of the yard, underneath an apple tree. Drew got a shovel from the shed and started digging, stomping his heel down on top of the blade and ripping up the ground. The midday sun was strong, and even Amelia began to feel dewy in the heat. Drew swiped the back of his hand across his forehead. Amelia went to get him a glass of iced tea.

When Claire came downstairs, Amelia was still watching him work, the sharp drive of the shovel into the ground, the leverage to pop the dirt up, two capable arms tossing the earth away. The hole was about five feet long and two feet deep already.

"You know," Claire said to her in a hushed tone. "We only have four hours until the wedding."

Amelia shrugged. "He's almost done. And he won't take as long to get ready anyway."

Claire stared at the hole, taking slow, steady breaths. If she was upset, Amelia knew her mother wouldn't show it. Claire walked off quickly, and returned with a Frisbee, a mangled one with tooth-marks in it. "Put this with her, will you? I need to curl my hair." Claire turned to go back inside.

When he'd finished the hole and placed Lady's body inside, Amelia knelt down with a small gardening trowel and helped him scoop some of the dirt inside. When they were finished, Amelia placed Lady's Frisbee on top of the dirt mound, a headstone.

They stood together at the foot of the grave. She placed a hand on Drew's back, his shirt moist with work, smelling of salty sweat and the earth. She leaned her head to his shoulder. "Let's go get you cleaned up," she said.

THEY ALL MADE IT TO THE WEDDING ON TIME. THE THREE OF THEM sat at their appointed places around a large round table, family of the bride. The hall was decorated in white lights and ivory. Stringed miniature Chinese lanterns were drawn across the room, crossing each other in a glowing web. Glass bowls sat in the center of each table with floating candles in them, ivory rose petals scattered around. Amelia wore a dress that Piper had made for her, just as strange as any of Piper's creations, ocean blue, with material so airy it somehow managed to lift and float when she moved.

Somehow it turned out that Amelia was the last of all her cousins to remain unmarried. She and Drew sat with her mother, enduring her nostalgic engagement and wedding stories. Amelia's parents were the perfect couple. Alan and Claire Bradshaw – they were so happy together, everyone said so. They'd known each other since they were fourteen years old, high school sweethearts, married for twenty-nine years. And here they were at yet another wedding, recounting the story of how her parents got engaged. "When your father proposed to me, we were at a bonfire..." Claire started the story with her head held high and her hands folded in her lap – there was no dreamy haze in her eyes. It was just history, and she delivered it not like a whimsical memory, but like a classic text that everyone knew. "It was four weeks before graduation. I wasn't going to college, but he was going off for basic training in a few weeks, and after that, we had no idea where. I remember everything about it – the cinders in the fire pit. He said to me, 'I can't do this without you. Come with me – marry me, Claire.' I remember exactly what we were wearing. I used to wear so much color in those days." She glanced down at her dark navy dress. "Now it's all dark, isn't it?" She turned to Amelia then, laying her palm on Amelia hand. "I'm so glad you wear color, sweetie."

Amelia knew this story by heart, the cinders in the fire pit, the very modest chip of a diamond he'd worked odd jobs for months to buy, her father down on one knee. It was the kind of story a woman could let live for generations.

Claire wasn't drinking wine, just a glass of water clutched in both hands. Drew had brought Amelia one glass of wine already, and Amelia sipped it slowly, though she knew she was going to be far too sober for this. "Drew, honey, can we have another?"

At least her mother waited for Drew to leave the table before she started. "Don't you think you two might like something like this?" She waved a hand at the room. The twinkling candles in water, the bad wedding music, nobody dancing except the very old and the children – it was too early, and the rest of them weren't drunk enough yet. The tossed rose petals were already starting to wilt. Amelia could buy all of this at Pottery Barn if she wanted it. "He's a nice enough boy, Amelia."

Nice *enough?* Amelia raised her eyebrows. Sometimes Amelia wondered if there was anyone her mother would oppose her marrying as long as he agreed to provide grandchildren quickly. "Mom, we don't even live together yet."

"I know," Claire said. "Believe it or not, there was a time people got married before they lived together. It's just that you're our only child." Claire tilted her head. "And you're nearly *thirty* now."

"Not *nearly*," Amelia said. Though close enough. It was starting to sink in. Amelia had gray hairs. Two of them. They aged her before her time. One was near her part line, and any time she tried to tuck it underneath, it only rose up again to stand above the rest, pale and defiant.

Claire tapped her fingertips on her water glass, making ripples on the surface. "You know there's a time limit on some things."

Amelia grinned. "You know, Mom, they've got drugs for that now."

"Out of all my siblings, all your father's siblings, we're the only ones without grandchildren now."

"Or there's sperm banks too. You don't even need a man at all to have a baby."

"Well," Claire huffed. "You're just being stubborn."

Drew came back with Amelia's wine, and placed a soft kiss on her cheek. He pointed at the bar. "We were just talking a bit – do you mind?"

Her cousins' husbands, challenging each other's manhood with shots of whiskey – she could smell it on him. "No, go ahead," she said. She didn't want to draw attention to the idea; her mother didn't need another reason to dislike her boyfriend. Claire tapped her fingernails on her water glass, a perfectly polite smile spread across her lips as Drew left the table.

"I'm a big girl," Amelia continued, before her mother could speak first. "I can take care of myself. You'll get your grandbaby someday."

"I know you think it doesn't matter. We just don't want you to be alone is all."

"There's nothing wrong with living alone," Amelia said.

She shouldn't have said it so blunt like that. Her mother flinched. Without the dog now, she was well and truly alone – and Amelia knew she didn't like it. Her mother had been a military wife for the whole of her youth and Amelia knew she measured the time in months and years, units of deployment breaking up the forward momentum of her life. But Amelia couldn't change any of that for her, and Amelia was happy now. Two times before she'd lived with a man, and neither time worked out very well. Now she had friends – she had a best friend who was also her boyfriend and who was plenty more than just *nice enough*. She glanced to Drew at the bar. "I'm not alone," Amelia said.

Drew saw her looking, smiled, and started to walk back then. Amelia looked at her mother, an inhale, a whole conversation with her eyes. *Enough.* Amelia's hand rested flat on the table and her mother reached over to pat it. It made her feel like a child.

"Okay," Claire said, nodding to Drew as he took his place beside Amelia again, rising from her own seat with a sigh. "Well," she said. "I'm going to turn in early, I think. You two have a good time then."

Amelia felt bad – too many bad jokes about sperm banks? Was it the dead dog? Was it being on her own at a family wedding when everyone else had a sweetheart at their side? Amelia wished she could be the daughter her mother hoped for. Why couldn't she just go and marry her sweet boyfriend whom she loved? Many worse things had been asked of women before. "You don't have to go, Mom."

"I do, sweetie." She waved her hand at the room. "This is all making me tired." She stood and leaned down to kiss Amelia's head. "But you have a good time, okay?"

Claire waited for an answer.

"We will. Goodnight, Mom."

When her mother had gone, they both went to the bar. Amelia had seven cousins, and they were all girls. All of them married already apart from Amelia. They all had babysitters for the night, and Amelia caught up with them while Drew did a few more shots with their husbands. Amelia knew he wouldn't remember being so drunk in the morning. He turned back to her occasionally, giving her another glass of red wine and a kiss. The guys all had their suit jackets off, ties undone, cheeks flushed with whiskey. Amelia's cousins were eager to drink too after so many years of babies and breastfeeding. Amelia hadn't intended to get drunk, but she had enough to relax.

Drew slid his hand around her waist and nuzzled his face into the curve of her neck, his other hand holding a shot glass in front of her, mixed tones of brown and beige. He spoke into her ear, "It's called a screaming orgasm, you want one?"

Her head was already buzzing, and her pulse warmed at the thought of a screaming orgasm. She turned around to see him grinning. "Yes, thank you." She didn't mean the drink, but she took it anyway.

She giggled as his placed sloppy kisses over her collar bone, but her laugh was stunted as she caught sight of her cousin Bella doing shots with all of the guys. It didn't surprise her that Bella could hold her whiskey with the men, but somehow, after all these years, Amelia still bristled with contempt at the sight of her. Especially in that curvy black gown, and standing so close to Drew. Bella had given Amelia's high school boyfriend a blowjob in the back seat of his car after their senior prom. That hadn't been the first time Lenny Hutchins cheated on Amelia, and it wouldn't be the last, but as far as she knew, that had been the only time Bella ever betrayed her. Even though it happened over ten years ago, Amelia wasn't sure that was the kind of thing a person could ever really get over.

Bella came closer, looping her arm through her husband's arm. They were all packed in closely near the bar, and Bella had taken a place right next to Drew. She raised her glass to them all, and Amelia couldn't hear what she was saying to them over the noise. Bella had two children now, and for all Amelia knew, she seemed happily married. People grew up, people changed, people moved on. It had been a lifetime ago. They were all happy now, weren't they? Amelia took a deep, cleansing breath and exhaled it. Before she'd started studying yoga, she hadn't been so aware of how insufficiently she breathed sometimes. *Pranayama*, life force, the body's need for nourishing oxygen. It calmed her. Before turning back to talk to her other cousins, she slipped her fingers into Drew's hand.

He was a good find, her cousins told her. Amelia already knew that. She'd never denied it. How many of these family weddings had he been to now, and they still weren't engaged yet themselves? He knew almost everyone by name. He'd been invited to their bachelor parties and weddings, he'd met their children, been to their babies' first birthday parties. The things Amelia's mother wanted from her were no different than the things any of their mothers wanted. Parents did that – they imposed their wants on their children, like their children should want those things already themselves. Amelia's cousins told her the truth – it wouldn't appease her parents if she got engaged. Sure, maybe for a little while. But next, they'd want a wedding, they'd want a grandchild, and after they got one, they'd want another. And what comes next? After one grandchild, two, three? Her cousins hadn't gotten that far themselves, but they were all scared to find out.

Amelia couldn't remember when she'd lost hold of Drew's hand. They'd been standing back to back most of the night, his hand on her shoulder occasionally, a whisper in her ear, or his laugh among the chorus of drunken laughter. Then another voice spoke from behind her, and when she turned, Drew was gone.

"Your man just threw up in the bathroom." Amelia turned to find another husband of yet another cousin – she didn't even remember his name.

"Where is he now?"

"Outside," he said.

"Oh, Lord." Amelia sighed hard. She was tipsy herself, balancing on sharp heels and holding her floaty dress to her thighs as she stepped out the front doors of the reception hall. Across a large grassy lawn, speeding headlights flashed past on the highway. It wasn't very late yet but the sky was dark already, the way fall starts to steal light from the evenings more and more each day. It was chilly, having dropped fifteen degrees since they left the house. September did that. But she hadn't grabbed a jacket because she'd planned to steal Drew's suit jacket later. She should have brought it out with her – and then it came to mind that she'd put her wallet and phone in her mother's purse at dinner.

She stopped walking. "Crap," she said, balling her fists up and groaning at the sky. A man smoking a cigarette against a stone pillar looked over at her. She tucked her arms around her body and continued.

Drew sat on a stone bench a few feet down the sidewalk, where cars pulled up to let guests out or pick them up. He leaned forward heavy on his hands and took deep inhales of the cool fall air. "You look spent," she said.

He nodded. "Sorry, I don't know what they were giving me."

Shots were shots, and he'd done too many of them. It probably wouldn't matter what kind. Maybe he hadn't eaten enough? Maybe he was trying too hard to impress them? That seemed more likely a reason.

He held out his keys to her. "Can we go? I'll make it up to you, I promise."

She'd been drinking all night too. "I can't drive yet, I just had three glasses of wine."

He groaned, wrapped his arms around his stomach, and rocked.

"Let me borrow your phone?"

Drew handed her the phone. She sorted through numbers in her head. She tapped the screen, and it brought up his call list. Pacing the sidewalk, she scrolled through names in his phone book, but she didn't know any of them who weren't at the wedding already. She didn't want to ask for a ride and ruin anyone else's night. She didn't want to call her mother back out again, and she especially didn't want her to see Drew in such a condition. Piper would be all the way out at Tom's, and Jodie would give them the biggest stink about making her drive all the way out there.

It didn't make sense that Jodie's name stuck out from the list, but somehow it did. Amelia counted the calls from Jodie. There were dozens, listed several times a week, incoming and outgoing. And one missed call notice from just a couple hours ago. No message though.

Jodie. Her name on that call log set heavy in Amelia's gut. She didn't like it, for no real reason she could pinpoint. Maybe it was the time they spent together, without her. She just didn't like it. The envy, the fear, it welled up through her body, to her fingertips, hovering over the "clear" button, and she pressed it.

Gone.

It was like Jodie had never called at all.

Amelia had never done that before. Not even with Lenny. Amelia turned back to Drew, still sitting on the stone bench, except now the groom had come out to join him, with his tuxedo jacket off and his shirt untucked. All the undone tuxedos and women in bare feet, standing outside a function hall in the late hours of the night – it reminded Amelia of that senior prom. That time, and all those other times. If she'd have checked up on him sooner, maybe he wouldn't have fooled her for so long.

But Drew wasn't Lenny. And this wasn't her phone. And Jodie was their friend. So Amelia exhaled, her bare arms starting to shiver. There was one person she could try. It surprised her that she actually remembered Corbin's number after all. He lived so close to them anyway, and if she didn't call a cab, or bribe someone else to leave the wedding early, it was the only number she could think of.

Corbin, this time of night, would either be grading essays from his philosophy lectures, or out screwing. He didn't do relationships, exactly, so you couldn't call them "girlfriends." But Amelia also knew that Corbin was the only person on the planet without a cell phone, so if he was out screwing, he wouldn't answer.

He answered. "I'm so sorry to bother you," she said. "My mom left, and I'm drunk, and Drew is trashed, and we kind of need a ride."

"Don't worry about it," he said. "I'll be there as soon as I can."

When Corbin finally arrived, Amelia felt conflicted about where to sit. Drew didn't like Corbin enough to want to sit up front, so he slid straight into the back seat, rolling his woozy head against the headrest. It would have been impolite to sit in the back with Drew, and leave Corbin up front alone like he was their chauffeur – that was not how she'd meant it at all – and yet it seemed just as impolite to leave Drew alone in the back, especially as sick as he was. She stood outside the car long enough that Corbin glanced over to her. She got in beside Drew, leaning forward between the seats to say, "I should probably make sure he doesn't throw up."

Corbin nodded, and they went.

Drew crossed his arms and slumped. Corbin's car was a rusty white Chevy Cavalier that must have been fifteen years old, stick shift which he drove roughly, and suspension that felt like being pulled over potholes in a kiddie wagon. Amelia reached over to squeeze Drew's knee. "You're not gonna throw up, are you?"

He rolled his head – no.

"Your place or his?" Corbin said from the front.

"Mine," she said, then realized that her mother had her keys too. Drew had a set of her house keys though. "You have keys, right?"

He rooted through his pocket and pulled them out.

Corbin pulled up at the street in front of Amelia's townhouse. "Thanks for the ride," Drew mumbled, quickly, and got out of the car.

"Thank you for that," Amelia said.

Corbin turned himself in the front seat to glance back at her. "No problem," he said. "It wasn't that far."

"Well I'll owe you one."

"You don't owe me anything," he said.

Why was he so generous? It wasn't natural – people weren't like that. It only made her feel like he wanted something. She pursed her lips. "Fine," she said, breaking into an anxious laugh.

He bowed his head lightly. "Namaste, Amelia."

Drew was inside already, upstairs in the master bathroom. She came up to the closed door, not because she wanted to hear him puking, but to make sure he didn't die. Was that possible? That in his drunkenness, he might stumble and knock himself out, end up choking on his own vomit? She shivered. "Are you okay?" she asked through the closed door.

He opened it a crack, and she let herself in. The faucet was running, and he splashed his face, looking up at himself with disappointment as drops of water hung from his nose and chin. He smelled like toothpaste.

"You feel better?"

"No, not really," he said. "I bet he got a kick out of seeing me like this."

"Who, Corbin? He doesn't care."

"He's probably mocking me."

"Corbin doesn't mock people."

"Well isn't he a saint?" Drew slumped slowly to the tile floor, his back pressed against the wall, cornered between the sink and the toilet.

"Corbin is *not* perfect."

"I know how your parents like him."

She sat next to him. The tile was cold on her bare legs. "They like you too," she said. At least, she figured her dad did.

"I'm sorry, Melie. Never mind. Did I do anything really stupid?"

"Not that I saw," she said.

But had Amelia done anything stupid? Erasing Jodie's call? She felt so petty for it. It was worrying how often Jodie's name came up lately. Amelia worried about how love could be so changeable, that she could be so adored for a time and then just as easily forgotten.

She was sure he hadn't started the night with two shirt buttons undone, though she remembered he hadn't worn a tie. Now the collar of his shirt hung open, just a peek of chest hair showing. It made her want to touch him there. But he reached out to her face instead, running a thumb along her cheekbone. "*I tuoi occhi sono dolci come il miele,*" he said to her.

He rarely spoke Italian – only when he was drunk, or trying to woo her panties off, or both. But when he did, it reminded Amelia of a story his mother told her once after having had a little too much champagne, of the summer of 1978 and a mysterious Italian man with an accent that made every conversation feel like a song. Drew would never meet his real father, but it must have been genetic why he'd become a poet, or why he felt inclined to study three languages in college, or how he pulled off the charm without sounding too pompous or too false. Otherwise Amelia might have suspected that he only remembered the lines he could use to coax her into bed. "I bet that doesn't sound as good in English."

"Your eyes are sweet as honey."

Her heart fluttered a little, against its better judgment. "Well, I guess that's alright too."

She didn't trust charm. His smile melted her heart, and she wanted to believe. She really did. But they were all charming, weren't they? And she fell for it, again and again and again.

But she shouldn't have cleared that missed call. Her conscience felt the weight of a million lies, even though there was just this one. Amelia hated lies. "Jodie called for you," she said, in one solid exhale.

"Oh, what'd she want?"

Amelia shrugged. "It was just a missed call. I pressed the wrong button and it was gone."

Drew grinned at her. "She wanted to say she'd marry me, you know, since you won't."

It was a joke, but she tensed anyway. "She'd eat you alive, you know. You're too sweet for her." She took his hand and held it still in her lap.

"I want to marry you, Melie," he said. His eyes were heavy and half closed.

She wasn't ignorant. And she wasn't oblivious. It wasn't like she didn't know that this was what he'd been after for as long as he'd known her. It felt different when he said it, like he was actually talking about marrying her, specifically, and not just picking an item off some generic checklist: Things To Do Before Forty. But did he really know what he'd be getting himself into? Once they believed in it, it would fade into something ordinary and taken for granted. He would lose interest and move on. They always did.

But sometimes, it felt so clear and real that she almost started to believe in it herself.

He smiled with his eyes closed. She knew she needed to get them to bed before he fell asleep on the tiled bathroom floor. She sighed. "Why don't you say that again some time when you're sober?"

1.3: likely to fail

IT HAD BEEN A LONG NIGHT, A MIDNIGHT LABOR BLED INTO an early morning delivery. Jodie reached the parking lot with a blinding sunrise in her eyes, harsh and golden, as she dug through her bag to find her car keys. She was tired, and in the glare, she could barely make out his shape, but she knew that walk anywhere: Gary Berges, striding with force, with purpose, like he owned this whole parking lot.

Or maybe he was just angry. "Jodie," he bellowed. "What did you do?"

"Oh hell," she said with a slanted smile, "What *did* I do?"

"The fucking spot. Your name is on my fucking parking spot." And then she knew what he was talking about. Their parking lot had been repaved, and Jodie had run into the building's owner that day. She stood there with the paving crew for a moment as they took notes on how to divide up the assigned parking spaces. She might have mentioned which space she wanted. That spot, the one away from the oak trees, the only spot in the whole lot that didn't get shat on with sap every fall. She hadn't even considered anyone else might want it, that anyone else even noticed that it was a good spot at all.

"Dammit, Jodie," Berges said. "You're twenty-nine and you drive a piece-of-shit Taurus. I've been parking in that spot for ten years. What do you care which spot you have?"

"I hate washing my car just as much as anybody." She put a finger to his shoulder, a tap. "And besides, I'm not stealing it. It was nobody's before, and now it'll be mine. That's not stealing."

She began to lean against her car, but stopped before the dewy windows soaked her back. Other cars filed into the parking lot for early appointments, people carrying coffee and rubbing their eyes. Berges folded his arms across his chest. "I can't believe you did that," he said, pausing. His strong, angry features softened and he laughed. "No, actually, I can believe it."

She'd known Berges for five years now. She first met him at the hospital, in the cafeteria. She knew him before he was divorced, before he got old. He was old now, or at least older. His eyes had become lined and his hair was starting to speckle with gray, thinning a bit at his temples. Maybe divorce did that to people?

She threw her hands up in the air and felt a smirk spread across her lips. "You don't have to get your panties in a twist about it. I really didn't. It just fell in my lap."

He looked down at her lap, then back up with a doubtful squint in his eyes. "I bet it did."

"You're still coming to my brother's wedding with me?"

"Are you asking me or telling me?"

"What's the difference?"

His laugh was like a bark.

She smiled. "Free bar," she said.

Jodie drove home, stumbled up to her bedroom, set her alarm, tossed her scrubs onto the floor – not bothering to shower – and fell into bed in her underwear and a thin white tank top. Three hours passed in a blink. She closed her eyes and opened them again, that dreamless state of semi-consciousness, and then her phone was ringing. Piper sang downstairs in the kitchen. Jodie put a pillow over her head but that didn't stop the phone from ringing or Piper from singing. The cracked blinds let in too much bright afternoon sunlight, and outside the window some bird chirped a shrill song. She grabbed her phone. She couldn't even read the caller ID, but answered anyway. "What?"

"What are you doing?" Her brother. Eric had almost unbelievable timing, that his calls came so early on those mornings she had been up all night. She had her alarm set. She could have slept for thirty more minutes, but he stole that from her. She was awake now. She held the phone to her face, her hands still smelling of surgical soap.

"Doing? I'm sleeping," she said. "Long night."

"Oh, sorry," he said. "But you're coming? Right? You know what day this is?"

"Yes I know what day this is."

"Are you bringing somebody?"

"Oh geeze, yes, don't you worry. I found some stupid idiot to come to your wedding with me."

Eric laughed merrily. "Did you have to pay him?"

Jodie wanted to reach through the phone and hit him. She wondered if Ruth was there. Was she laughing too? Jodie hadn't met her future sister-in-law more than three times, and she didn't know if she liked her much. "Oh, shut up already," Jodie said to her brother.

THE WEDDING WAS NINETY MINUTES AWAY IN LANSING. SHE and Berges drove together, and it never occurred to her that they had so much to talk about, or that they knew so much about each other. Their acquaintance was formed in the hallways and parking lots of the medical complex they shared, or grabbing lunches in the hospital cafeteria, or meeting for a candy bar from a vending machine. She'd known him when she was still in her residency, since before his daughter was a teenager. She'd known him in the months after the divorce blew up, and she'd seen it turn him disillusioned and jaded. The divorce hadn't been his idea.

They had the afternoon to kill before the wedding. Jodie wore jeans and a gray cardigan, and felt too plain for the hair that Piper had done for her before she left, half a French twist with an explosion of curls erupting from the back. Jodie knew she wouldn't be able to do her hair on her own later. As they sat down for lunch in the hotel restaurant, Jodie noticed Berges had gotten a fresh haircut for the occasion. She felt honored, but she didn't say anything.

"I've never been here before," Berges said. The room was mostly empty. Nearly two in the afternoon, and most people had eaten lunch already. The waitresses were dressed in black and white. There was a standing wood stove in the middle of the room that wasn't being used, and stone statues in each of the corners with large, bulging eyes. Berges sat in front of one, and it made her feel like there was another person sitting behind them. But Jodie got the feeling Berges meant that he'd never been to Lansing before, and not just the little hotel restaurant specifically.

"Oh, it's a hole really," Jodie said. "Hell if I know why he wanted to move here. Why does everyone move to such holes? I never see Piper anymore. Her fiancé, he lives out in the middle of nowhere. He lives next to a goddamn field of *cows*."

Berges chuckled. A waitress brought their food. Jodie unrolled a cloth napkin and started in on her salad. She was talking too much. "Shouldn't you talk about your child or something?"

She was half kidding, but he started anyway. "Hazel, she's good. She finally got her braces off last week. Braces I paid for, but of course her mother wouldn't acknowledge that much..." He went on about Hazel, how she placed second at her track meet last weekend, how she was getting a C in algebra, and how her bitch mother didn't stop yapping the whole meet about how he never

36

kept up with Hazel's homework when he had her. He went on about their house which, which he had picked out when they bought it, but was granted to her in the end because it was closer to Hazel's school. He talked about visitation settlements and lawyers and bitterness, going on almost solidly until their food came. And then while they ate, all through the meal, to the point she imagined even the statues sitting behind him had become bored.

AFTER LUNCH, JODIE SLIPPED ON HER GOWN AND CLUMSY HEELS, and since her hair was already done, she went to find her brother. She rapped lightly on the door of a small conference room before entering, and Eric was inside, standing at a window, already dressed in a black tuxedo. "Okay, let me look at you then," she said. She turned him around. His tie was neat enough. She inspected for lint – there wasn't any. She squinted at his face. He'd started growing a little goatee and she wasn't sure what she thought of it. It startled her how much she missed him now that he was so far away.

"You look nice, Jodie."

"Eh," she said. It was just a simple black gown, with a wide, scooped neckline that hung lower than she'd imagined it would when it was still on the hanger. Piper had begged to make her something to wear, but Jodie declined. She'd seen some of the strange contraptions Piper had dressed Amelia in before, and Jodie had no intentions of being Piper's fashion experiment. Jodie went to Kohl's instead.

"But you should get some sun," he added. In all that black, Jodie's pale skin appeared so white it cast a bluish tint.

"Sun gives you cancer," she said.

Seeing the two of them, all grown up and dressed for his wedding, with their degrees they'd earned and paid for themselves, with their careers, you never would have guessed they came from such a screwed up family. Whatever dysfunction that caused Jodie to swear off marriage and children indefinitely only seemed to make her big brother want it more. Like he had to prove he could make it work. It was going to be a very small wedding – neither she nor Eric were close to either side of their mangled family anymore. Their parents would be here with new spouses – third for their mother and fourth for their father – but none of the half or step siblings had been invited. Hopefully nobody would argue.

Jodie didn't understand what the fuss was about with all this wedding stuff, but she wasn't going to stomp on his dreams either. She was proud of him, just as he had always been proud of her. He was the only stability she'd ever known.

"So, your guy seems alright, are you seeing him?" Eric's voice was entirely too optimistic.

"No," she said. "Absolutely not. He's just a friend." Friend was an odd word for their arrangement. It was more like playful adversaries.

"You should bring him over for dinner sometime."

"Ehhh," Jodie said.

"And you should try to get to know Ruth. She's nice. You might like her."

He really liked Ruth – Jodie could tell that much. There was a zest about him with Ruth that was never there with Amelia. Ruth was nice and didn't have much of a sense of humor – neither did her brother, really. They suited each other. He'd told Jodie how they met, the very same week he moved away. It must have been only days after he broke up with Amelia. "I'll know her eventually," Jodie said. "Give me time, it was fast."

"It wasn't that fast."

"Fast enough. Did you meet her and propose the next week?"

Jodie chuckled out loud. But he wasn't laughing. They stared at each other. "I knew her already, when Amelia and I broke up."

Jodie mulled over the information. "Wait, what? Back up the train. You mean, *knew her*, knew her?"

Eric didn't answer.

"Holy shit!" Jodie slapped her brother's arm. "You cheated on Amelia?" Jodie waited for some clarification, some gesture from him that she'd misunderstood.

"Cheated? I don't know." He stalled, shuffling in his place. "That sounds worse than what it was. We were falling apart already. It was just a matter of saying it out loud at that point. Don't tell her though. You know how she is."

Jodie wasn't sure what he meant by that – how was she? Unlucky? The wrong one? Jodie shook her head. She wouldn't tell his secret.

"But that doesn't matter," he added. "She's happy now, right? With that poet? Does he wear a beret and carry around little quill pens?" Eric's hearty laugh filled the room, which caused a little ball of offense to rile inside Jodie.

"It's not like that. He's Drew, he's okay."

Eric was still laughing. "Are you part of his fan club or something?"

She huffed at him. "Fuck you, nobody's talking about your scrapbooking hobby."

"I don't scrapbook, little sis. I'm a historian." Eric slung his arm around her shoulders and led them out of the room. "No worries – they're happy, I'm sure. We're happy. Everybody's happy."

Jodie nodded, full of truth. Drew and Amelia, yes, they were indeed happy.

So Eric got married. Jodie knew it was something her brother had wanted for a long time. He held his new bride's hands on the cobblestone patio of the hotel, with fountains sputtering nearby and the hot September sun setting in their eyes. It was more foreign than Jodie could even imagine. She hadn't ever wanted to get married, never really had the patience for a long-term boyfriend, she never even had a date to the prom.

After the ceremony, she sat with Berges on the patio drinking free wine. The sun had set and the heat dispersed, moist fabric along her back turning cold and sending a chill through her body. She clutched her arms.

"You cold?" Berges said. "I'm not wearing mine." She didn't answer him, but he moved behind her to slide his suit jacket over her shoulders, hanging loose around her. He took a deep look at her breasts as he stood over her for that moment. She didn't care. It made her laugh more than anything. She hardly felt like they were even her breasts at all, in that dress, with her hair all wound up on top of her head and curls that were starting to lose their spring. Jodie could hardly walk in the heels she wore, and she wasn't in the habit of being gawked at by her dates – what few dates she had.

She always found it uncomfortable knowing a cosmetic surgeon. When Berges looked at her, did he wonder what he would fix? Would he soften her nose or lipo some jiggle out of her thighs? He was someone who quite literally fixed broken people, misshapen people, and because it paid his bills better, a lot of people who just weren't as perfect as they wished they were. What did he think when he saw her, a gold mine of work? Or was she beyond repair?

His smile was more eager than it had any right to be. "Jodie, you have tits, who knew?"

Bullshit he didn't know she had tits. He'd been sizing up her chest for five years.

"You're starting to bald a little," she told him.

His hand shot up to his forehead. "I am not."

"Here." She pointed.

"I am not," he said again.

"Do you use hair product?"

"No. And this is my hair."

"Does it work? The hair product? Can it really grow new hair?" His rusty brown hair was short, but he wore the inch-long tufts combed forward to cover the receding parts. She ran her fingers underneath one tuft of hair. His scalp was warm.

"Get your hands out of my hair," he said. He leaned back away from her in his chair. He scowled, distinguished lines creasing over his brow, and she just took them in. There was something admirable about this point in a man's life, the point he first started to show his age, the point he was indisputably no longer a boy. Those lines were new on him too; she couldn't remember them there when they first met. He must have been in his early thirties then. "Scientifically, no," he said. "It just strengthens the living follicles to slow loss."

"Okay then," she said. "Shut up and let's get this dance out of the way already." He'd insisted the whole drive that since she brought him all this way, she at least owed him one dance. Berges loved to dance. He danced to grocery store muzak while picking up frozen meals for dinner. He danced through hospital corridors in his surgery scrubs. She'd never asked him, but she was quite sure he imagined himself John Travolta while he did it. So she led him through the guests, trying to find a spot not too near where her brother was dancing with his new bride. It was a slower song, and for that, Jodie was grateful he wouldn't have a chance to whip out any of his more elaborate moves.

She hadn't had a chance to say much to either of them after the ceremony besides a quick congratulations as the wedding photographer corralled them in and out of groupings for the photos. As they danced now, she noticed Eric was significantly taller than Ruth, so that when they stood together, her head fit right underneath his chin. It was still strange for Jodie to see him with a new woman. She always thought Amelia, tall and delicate as she was, seemed a more natural fit with her gangly brother. Ruth was so different – a mousy woman, small and sturdy with wispy hair and breeding hips. How long had her brother known that Amelia wasn't what he wanted?

As she and Berges settled into an empty space on the patio, Berges took her into his hands. One hand held hers and the other snuck underneath the large jacket to hold her at the small of her back. She held her breath for a moment. She didn't expect to be so stunned by his touch – confident yet gentle, so sure and so precise. Of course it was; he was a surgeon after all. A surgeon who danced. They kept just a little bit of space between them, so that when they moved, her chest would sometimes brush up against his. Among so many foreign things, there was this closeness, this invitation into her personal space. It set her nerves on edge. The music burned her ears, some crooner, a whiny voice like he had a clothespin on his nose. "What *is* this?"

"It's Rufus Wainwright," Berges said.

"Oh God, it's *awful*." She sneered, shaking her head. "I have to hate you just for knowing who he is. And for knowing it so *surely*."

"Heh," he chuckled. "I only know because Kate liked him."

Jodie tilted her head. "She would, wouldn't she?"

He wasn't looking at her then, his gaze falling somewhere in the background, unfixed. "I never actually cheated on her, you know?"

As he returned to her, Jodie was caught in his muddy brown eyes, stunned for a moment. There was a small twinkle left there sometimes, as if he hadn't been completely destroyed yet. Jodie nodded. She knew, to some degree. Or at least she knew he'd never crossed that line on her behalf. Sometimes he seemed saddened by it all, and other times he seemed not to care. She wondered, when

Berges saw people getting married, did he think they were making a mistake? She tilted her head toward her brother. "So you think they're doomed then?"

"Nah," he said. "You have to hope not, right? I'd do it again, I think. Some day."

"Get married? Don't you know they say the second is more likely to fail than the first?"

He laughed, bold, like a bark. "You're a ball of sunshine, Ms. Jodie Larsen, you know that?"

She grinned at him. "Well, we can't all walk around with our heads in the clouds."

They drank some more. They danced again. She only owed him one dance, but she gave him a few. After four glasses of wine, Jodie's head was spinning in the clouds. She sometimes forgot how handsome he was, despite the obvious mess he'd made of his life, and despite the abrasive exterior he maintained. It was easy to forget, but he could be lovely sometimes, in the right light. He had strong features and wide, soulful eyes. She always took him for granted, all their play flirting, their verbal sparring. It was never meant to be any more than a game. But she wasn't an eager young med-student anymore. And he wasn't married anymore either.

Jodie was never the type to assume things – especially *romantic* kinds of things. First, because any time they'd blurred those lines before had only been in fun. Second, because he was a pathetic, wreck of a man, even if a handsome one. And third, because she hadn't been wanted for a very long time. So she stayed up late with him, sitting long after most of the other guests had retired to their rooms or gone home, after her brother and his new bride took off to start their new life together. Jodie and Berges stayed out drinking more wine just to avoid that awkward walk back to their separate rooms. She wanted him to say he was tired, or that he'd see her in the morning.

"Last call," the bartender said.

It was even later than she'd realized. Berges tipped up what was left of his wine and swallowed. "Looks like they're kicking us out, Sunshine."

So they got up, and she followed him into the elevator, stood beside him, not quite touching in the quiet space as they traveled up three floors. She felt like she was assuming way too much. She knew she didn't owe him anything, but she hadn't yet decided if she was going to give it anyway. Her nerves were on fire. As they stood in front of her door, across the hallway from his, she fumbled to speak. "Thank you, you know, for coming," she said. "It's not the kind of thing you want to come alone to."

"Coming alone is never as much fun," he said.

She hardly had time to roll her eyes at him before he was kissing her, pressing his mouth to hers, then as she relaxed, gently slipping his tongue inside. It had been so long since she kissed someone that she was sure she'd become rusty. He was thankfully too drunk to notice it. Or maybe they were both too deprived of it to care, two romantic outcasts, fumbling around in the bright hotel hallway until they finally stumbled backwards into her darkened room.

She fumbled with a light switch, which flooded the room in too much light, so she turned it off and left the bathroom light on instead. He slid a hand up her back as he continued to kiss her, tracing the long zipper to the top, then paused there as his fingertips met her skin. "Your skin," he said, barely pulling his lips away from hers to speak. "It's freezing." He didn't seem appalled by it, just surprised.

"Bad circulation," she said. But he had already resumed kissing her neck and unzipping the dress. She went on anyway. "It's not an uncommon condition. I'm taking medication for it."

He breathed near her ear. "Hmmm." He let go of the gown and it fell to the floor. He looked into her eyes. "Relax, will you?"

They moved to the bed, stripping off layers as they went. She tried to recall the last time she'd had actual sex. Two years? Really? Had it been that long? She didn't know where to put her hands, while his hands were fearless, full of her flesh, her breasts, her butt cheeks. He grabbed a handful of thigh and raised her leg around his hip as he leaned her back over the bed.

Berges had taken off all of her clothes as well as most of his own, apart from cotton boxers which she guessed he was waiting for her to do. He held her in his arms. She clung to him out of modesty more than the desire to be intimate. Stripped down to nothing. Her skin might have been cold, but her blood was warm, and her heart still pumped, and she hadn't been touched in so long she might have forgotten she was still a woman at all. But she was, and not just a strange approximation of a woman, but a real, actual woman, who hadn't been made to feel like a woman for a really, really long time.

"Okay," she said out loud. An answer to his long-past question. A green light. Game on.

"Alright then," he said.

She lay on her back with her eyes closed, so not to see what faces he made, if he made them. He took her legs and held them in his hands. It reminded her of how he always asked, *So tell me, any of you girls ever do it in those stirrups?* Which she thought might have turned her off, but instead, with her eyes closed, she imagined them in an examination room on the crackling exam bed paper, her knees spread wide and feet in stirrups. The sex was foggy and rather fast, but not unpleasant. He rolled off of her when he finished with a deep groan.

She turned her head to him. He had a victorious grin on his face. It looked good on him; it reminded her of the spirit he used to have. "Don't look like you've won me over or anything. You just want me to give you that parking spot back."

"That's not why I did this."

"Why then?"

"Because I was wondering what your tits looked like naked."

Jodie threw her head back laughing.

He rolled onto his side, perched on one elbow. "But why do you care so much? With that thing you drive."

"What, like you don't care so much about your stupid car?"

"My stupid Mercedes costs four times as much as your Taurus."

"That's very compelling," she said. "My heart is breaking for you." She held her hand over her heart. "But if you'd have kept even half of your spine when Kate left you, it wouldn't be all you had."

The grin on his face fell, slowly, like it was melting. "You're serious?" He sat up, cross-legged, not hiding a thing. He wasn't shy, and had no reason to be. It made her blush. He just looked at her, desperate, reminding her of the wreck of a man he really was. It was almost enough to make her feel bad for him.

"Oh come on, really?" She propped herself up on her elbows. "You didn't *do* anything. *We* didn't do anything."

"That wasn't the point."

It was Jodie that Kate caught Berges flirting with, that day, that final straw before the separation. Jodie refused to take any responsibility for that, for their flirting, if that was what did him in. Jodie wasn't the only woman his wife caught him flirting with. Not by far. But that didn't count, and they never did anything. It wasn't an affair, and Jodie knew what real affairs looked like. Kate should have met Jodie's parents and all the broken relationships that followed, the mess that they made, the sneaking around and suspicions, the lies, the accusations, the throwing bottles and domestic dispute visits from the cops. Those were affairs – those were fights. She and Berges with their silly angsty play-flirting in the hallways, that was a joke. "She needs to lighten the hell up if she thought that was an affair. It was a joke. She's a joke! And you're still taking it from her. She gave you custody of that damn car and not your daughter."

His face flushed clean of emotion, his mouth hung agape. It was true – and he knew it, didn't he? Ten seconds he stared at her like that. Then he moved across the bed. He got up, shaking his head, his voice resolved and emotionless. "You know, you're a real fucking bitch sometimes, Jodie."

"Oh come on," she said. He didn't turn, he just dressed himself quickly, not even bothering to button his shirt. "Where are you going?"

"My room." He had his shoes in his hands.

She sat up on the bed, naked still, pulling a sheet up to cover her chest. "Not like I was going to let you sleep in here."

His movement in the room stirred the chilly air, leaving her skin to rise in goosebumps, but her blood pumped with fury and adrenaline. He wouldn't respond to her. They'd been drunk – that's all it was. They'd said things they shouldn't have said, and did things they shouldn't have done. As he went for the door, she searched for something inside her, some venom to spew before he reached it. Something harder, something cutting. But there was nothing sharp enough. As he opened the door, as he walked through, as it closed behind him, all she found was disappointment.

1.4: light at the top of the stairs

AMELIA WAS THE FIRST PERSON DREW HAD EVER MET who had truly sad eyes. Sure, people were sad sometimes, but on the day he met her, she wore defeat with her whole body.

Drew had been coming in from his car, and he stopped across the street pretending to sort through his mail as he watched her through sunglasses. Her front door was propped open and she struggled with a long cardboard box in front of her house. First she lifted the front end up one stair, then up the next. She strained under its weight but she was determined. When the box rested on the slope of the stairs, she heaved up from the bottom of it, bringing it to rest level on the stoop. But as soon as she tried to pick up the front end again to raise it into the door, the back end toppled over and pulled the weight of the box back down the stairs. She was right where she started again.

She left it. She grumbled words into the air that he was too far away to hear. People walked down the street, and any one of them could have helped, had she asked. But she didn't ask. She put the box down for a moment, held her fingers to her chin, serious about her strategy, defeated and yet stubbornly hopeful. How long had she already been trying?

He left his mail in the mailbox. Between breaks in the traffic, he ran across the street.

"Can I help you?" He reached for the box in her hands, but she wouldn't let go of it.

"No, I'm fine," she said. "I don't need any help. I can get it." She only half-glanced at him, keeping her eyes to the ground. She crouched beside the box, not trying to move it anymore, her fingers clamped under the edges and her palms worn red.

"I'm sure you can," he said. "That's not what I meant."

Finally she looked up, considering him. Her eyes were the same honey brown as the freckles on her cheeks and nose, and up close, he could see how tired they were, how they held too much worry for as young as she was. She wore her hair pulled back into a ponytail, which had started to unravel, and her forehead glistened with sweat from her efforts. Her deep V-neck t-shirt hung loose as she bent over. The freckles on her chest faded into smooth peachy skin in the supple depths of cleavage where sun didn't reach.

She'd caught him staring. But instead of being angry or even rolling her eyes, she just sighed, a soft whimper. She was lean but strong, so he knew it wasn't her body giving up the fight with that box; it was all that worry and disappointment in her eyes, surrendering to the box, to being ogled by a stranger, to life.

"I would be able to," she said, biting her bottom lip, finally stepping away from the box. "But it's just too long, I think. I can't get the weight distributed right."

"I know," he said. "It's okay. Here, let me get the bottom."

He hoisted the back end up to his shoulder while she lifted the front up off the ground, and together they walked the box into her kitchen. There were other boxes in her kitchen half-unpacked, and dishes in neat piles, stacked on the counters, ordered by function, by size, by necessity. She had more stuff than he could ever conceive of using: pots and pans, cheese graters, cookbooks, every kind of spatula, slotted spoon, or grilling tongs anyone could ever need. She had a blender, a toaster, a food processor, a coffee machine and cappuccino maker, a toaster oven. On the kitchen table, she had a stack of picture frames without any pictures in them. She seemed far too young to have so much stuff. He couldn't even recall what he had in his own kitchen to cook with – a cookie sheet for pizza rolls, or maybe a wooden spoon to stir his scrambled eggs.

She had cans of paint on the floor and some rollers. He asked her, "Do you need help with that?"

Her lips turned up in an uneasy smile. "I don't even know you," she said. "You don't need to help paint my kitchen too."

It was the first time she'd even cracked a smile in the five minutes he'd known her. It lit up her eyes a bit and sent a pink flush through her freckled cheeks. She swiped a hand over her brow. "But thank you," she said. "I think my mom will help me."

Drew introduced himself. And she told him her name: Amelia.

"I don't want to date anyone," she blurted out then. "Not for a really long time, maybe not ever again. I'm bad at it. I think I break them. Relationships, I mean."

"I wasn't," he started. But yes, that had been exactly what he was thinking, he just hadn't said it out loud yet. "Yeah, I mean, okay."

Her reluctant smile turned into a full-on grin. He didn't care what he meant or didn't mean, or what she thought he meant, he was just glad to see it.

"In case you ever need anything," he said, pointing out toward the front door. "I'm just over there. The one on the corner."

"Thank you, Drew," she said. "You know, wait here, just a minute."

On the counter, between stacked plates and a box of coffee mugs, she grabbed a wicker basket. She took tomatoes from the windowsill and placed them inside, covering them in a linen cloth. She held it out to him. "Tomatoes," she said. "I grew them in my old garden." A quick sadness washed over her face then; whatever happened to this old garden of hers must have been unfortunate. But she went on. "They have Lycopene. It prevents cancer."

He was speechless. What do you say to that? It might have been the very first time anyone had cared whether he got cancer or not, and he'd only known her for a few minutes. "Thank you," he said. "I don't know what to do with them."

Her laughter was a soft sound, not mocking but like something was trying to rise up from the depths of her, striving to break the surface. He'd never met anyone so defeated, yet so stubbornly hopeful. "That's okay," she said. "Try them sliced, on a good, coarse bread. With just a drizzle of olive oil, a sprinkle of salt, and a little fresh mozzarella."

"Thanks," he said. "I will." But he wasn't thinking about food. His eyes were full of her freckles and soft curves; in his head were the tiny fragments of newborn poems. She had him.

THERE WERE PEOPLE WHO HAD HARDER LIVES THAN DREW HAD. There were probably a lot of them. Drew ran errands. It was his assigned place in the family, his penance for being a writer (which none of them saw as real work), and for being a lighthouse tour guide, which they hardly saw as real work either, even if it did have scheduled hours and a paycheck.

On the brink of October, they were finishing up their final tour for the season. For the last time, Drew pointed out the Belle Haven Light with its cream-colored stucco tower, two single windows on its east wall spilling light into the stairwell, its lantern room on top encased in iron and glass. It was built in 1839, still active but now automated. The keeper's house that stood nearby was now used as a bed and breakfast. Drew told them stories about the light keepers. They were men of many jobs, providing shelter from the storms, safety and rescue, or a warm meal and bed to weary seamen. True as it was, what really sold the tickets were the ghost stories, the unfortunate mariners struck down by a sudden storm, the small children who perished to illness or accidents, the lonely wives gone mad, the doors that opened and closed by themselves, the brass that attendants found mysteriously polished every morning, the voices whispering in empty rooms.

Drew never told the tour guests this part, but his grandfather had been Keeper Ferdinand Weston, charged with the Belle Haven Light until 1963. Both Drew's mother and his uncle had grown up on the lighthouse grounds, and Drew had asked them before about the ghost stories, were they true? His stoic uncle denied having ever saw anything, but his mother didn't. Moira would only lean in closer, with a glass of champagne in her hand and a glimmer in her eyes, "Now when I was a little girl," she would start, "I had this imaginary friend, a little boy. And I used to wake up in the morning to find your uncle's toy soldiers lined up on my windowsill like someone had been playing with them..."

The story was always different. Uncle Mitch denied having ever seen anything himself. He was the older of the two by eleven years and spent most of his childhood there. But when the lighthouse was automated and handed over to the Coast Guard – the great tragedy of progress, Uncle Mitch would say – Moira was only three years old. It was unlikely she really remembered much of anything. Everyone knew how much Uncle Mitch loved his baby sister, as much as a grown woman in her fifties could be considered a baby sister, but he'd be the first to tell you how much of a storyteller she'd always been.

They docked the seventy-five foot tour boat near the Fort Gratiot Lighthouse, where passengers could visit the museum or the lighthouse for its guided tour. The crew lined up with the captain to wish them each a nice day. "Thank you, watch your step," they said. Drew held out his hand for the old ladies. When they were clear, they headed back to the marina to close down for the season. There would probably be some private charter work from time to time, but once the rivers froze, they'd have the winter off.

Drew took off his crew jacket, his polo underneath advertising The Fort Gratiot Boating Company, and he flung his cap into the back seat of his Jeep along with it. He took a long gulp of water – the stories and the cool lake breeze got into his lungs and made his throat dry. He laid his cell phone on the front seat next to the mail he'd picked up on his way to work. He slept over at Amelia's place often, and the mailbox at his apartment only built up: spam, spam, spam, poetry rejection, more spam, another poetry rejection, more spam, a postcard from his mother.

Drew started in on one of the poetry submissions, all of which were sent back in his own self-addressed envelopes. The first read (at the bottom of a half-page stock rejection – she couldn't even spare the paper to send a whole page): "While your poetry was lovely to read, and sounded quite exquisite, perhaps you might spend some time defining what this is really about. What is the great tragedy of this piece? Find that great tragedy and build from it," (yes, she'd truly underlined it), "Build around it, and let the reader feel that tragedy in the pit of their very being."

Drew was mystified. Did he even have any great tragedies? Or did he only have the opposite of tragedy – privilege and prosperity and luck. Could he blame his rejection on the lack of great tragedy in his life? Because otherwise, he'd have to accept that he was just a terrible poet. He wasn't sure which was worse.

But then he opened a second letter, and it made the first one sound downright gentle: "Nobody wants to read your love poems but your lover."

"Hell," Drew grumbled, balling the letter in his hand and tossing it at the windshield, where on the other side, two seagulls fought over a McDonalds bag in the parking lot.

He put down the rest of the letters and found that his phone was blinking – a voice mail. He checked it. It was from his uncle's housekeeper – Yi Min was a middle-aged Chinese woman with a tiny sharp voice. "I think you should know, he think he fire me, but I quit first. He is horrible old man. You find someone else." She hung up quickly.

Drew let his head fall heavy against the seat. That had been number six. Uncle Mitch fired household help like it was his mission in life. Drew already knew he'd insist he was capable on his own, but the truth was, he couldn't do his own grocery shopping anymore, or clean his bathrooms, and he'd even started forgetting which bills he'd paid or hadn't.

Drew stuffed the spam aside and picked up the postcard from his mother. She was in Tokyo at the moment, where she'd followed her husband on business. They'd been there for a few months, but she sent a postcard whenever she found one that inspired her, no matter how many she'd sent already. This one was a landscape, with a five-story wooden pagoda rising out of a foggy valley, and on the back she wrote:

Thinking of you, darling. The fog makes everything feel just perfectly mysterious, don't you think? Reminds me of the lakeshore in the spring. Richard sends his love.

XOXO – Mom

He needed to find out why his uncle fired his housekeeper, and he wasn't in the mood for any more poetry rejections. He put his mother's postcard next to his phone in the center console, then he tucked the rest of the mail under his jacket in the back seat so the wind wouldn't blow it around. He started to drive.

It was a thirty-minute drive down I-94 to where his uncle lived in Grosse Pointe Shores. Drew drove with the music loud, butchering the lyrics to every song that came on the radio, whether he liked it or not. He wasn't a poet today. He wasn't sure what he was. What does one do with all that useless knowledge? The twenty-two kinds of knots he knew how to tie, the four languages he could speak and write semi-fluently (including English, he feared sometimes), or all those dates: the first lighthouse built on Lake Erie, the invention of the Fresnel lens, the first solar-powered light? Today, Drew was just an errand boy for his uncle.

So he turned up the radio. First he wallowed along to some Radiohead, then he shouted out some U2, and by the time he reached Grosse Pointe Shores, Weezer's "Island in the Sun" came on, and he was bouncing behind his tinted windows, drumming his steering wheel, and singing along, even the parts that went *"hip, hip"*.

The neighborhood was quiet and tree-lined, just a couple blocks from the lake. His uncle was rich and cheap. In front of his colonial estate, a large lawn begged for a trim, but Uncle Mitch had a reputation for refusing to pay these local boys enough to keep it. When he was still able, he used to mow it himself into crooked crosshatches. All his life he'd been of the type to never pay for something he could do himself, but in his early seventies finally, he couldn't do much of anything himself anymore. Uncle Mitch didn't like to talk about his money. He was a retired lawyer who scarcely spent his lifetime wealth, except on weddings for his two daughters and three college educations. The rest of it he saved for the dire day he would finally need it, while complaining of his aches and pains, or how soon he hoped to die, how much cancer treatments cost (everyone got it – it was only a matter of time), or burials.

Drew stopped at the mailbox and grabbed his uncle's mail before parking near the side entrance. He let himself in at the keypad, which opened into a spacious kitchen. The house was silent except for a running dishwasher. Beyond the kitchen, the hallways of the old home were dark and narrow. The house sat under a thick copse of tall oak trees, blocking almost any natural light except thin beams in the early mornings or late evenings. Instead of illuminating the hallways, the small windows only reflected their shapes off the polished hardwood like it was glass. These were the hallways Drew used to run through as a child, pretending ghosts were chasing him until he got his cousins running after him too – Anna and Leslie would never dare run in that house until Drew started them up. The three of them took off down the darkened, bare hallways, the echo of their voices bellowing against the narrow walls. Until they were shouted at by one of the adults, stern Uncle Mitch or angry Aunt Irene. But Drew's mother never minded – she would only coo back, "Let the children be children. Don't they bring life into this tired old house?"

It was only Uncle Mitch living here now and the big house had never felt emptier. Drew found him in the den, sitting in a stiff armchair with a newspaper in his hands. The room smelled like a library. The books his uncle kept were old – biographies of World War II heroes and battles, picture books about bombers, battleships, and submarines. They mostly just collected dust these days. There were wooden model ships mounted on the walls.

Drew cleared his throat as he stepped into the library. "I'm here."

"I know," his uncle said. "With how you tear up that driveway."

Drew had hardly torn up anything, but he didn't argue. And he didn't move to sit down either. In a moment, when the newspaper page had been finished, folded and placed on the coffee table, his uncle would stand up. Uncle Mitch still had most of his hair, salt and pepper gray, and eyebrows long enough that they curled. He wore navy cable-knit sweaters and loafers without socks.

"You have some mail," Drew said. "Looks like the electric bill is in there. And did you eat today?"

"I had something."

Drew went to the refrigerator. Luckily Yi Min must have stocked it just before she'd had enough of his bullshit. And luckily she'd waited until boating season was finished too. Bless her heart.

Uncle Mitch hobbled into the kitchen after him. "But if you don't mind helping an old man out," he said. "There's that damn light again, the one upstairs."

"Again? Didn't we just replace that one? There might be something wrong with the wiring."

"It's because they've got the chinks making all our shit now."

Drew cringed. Poor Yi Min, she'd been such a sweet lady. Drew wondered what his uncle had said to her. He would have to send her two weeks wages and some flowers.

The light at the top of the stairs had always been a hassle to get to because of the second story stairwell's vaulted ceiling. Even though Uncle Mitch couldn't even reach the second story of the house, he always insisted that the rooms be kept dusted, the linens fresh, and the light bulbs in order in case anyone ever needed to come home. Now those duties were left to Drew, and whatever household help stuck around for more than a few weeks.

"Why did you fire your housekeeper?"

"She's stealing from me," Mitch said, "I just know she is. I don't like that girl."

They didn't have to be actually stealing from him – and never had, as far as Drew knew – but his uncle would think it anyway.

"You can't fire them. How am I going to keep finding new ones? They're going to start warning each other about you. And you're not going to clean the toilets yourself."

"There are six toilets in this house, and I'm only one man. I'm not paying that girl to clean toilets that nobody shits in."

Drew raised his eyebrows at his uncle. "Now don't try to tell me you don't shit in them," he said. "We both know you're full of shit."

Uncle Mitch slapped Drew in the middle of the back and laughed heartily.

Drew went to grab the ten-foot step ladder from the garage. He carried it upstairs to the second floor, propping it up against the banister for extra stability. He opened doors in the hallway – the sun was setting by then, and cast a fiery glow into the dark, cavernous space, giving him just enough light to work with. He climbed up the ladder while his uncle stood at the bottom of the staircase, watching, leaning on his cane and fretting. "Now be careful, son," Mitch chided. "You don't want to find out how much a hospital ride for a broken head costs without health insurance."

"I'm careful, I'm not going to have an accident."

"Don't be a fool," Mitch said. "Of course you are."

Drew turned his head to glare at his uncle so fast he felt the need to grasp onto the ladder's top. "What?"

"What I mean is, everyone makes mistakes. Even if you didn't make a mistake, it wouldn't have to be your fault, and it might not even be in your control. Before you know it you're lying at the bottom of a ladder or have your head through a windshield and blood pissing down your face."

Drew laughed lightly. "Heh, well, health insurance isn't going to help me any if I'm dead."

"It's not a joke, son. There will be mistakes. No one can be that perfect."

"Alright," Drew mumbled. "Alright." He positioned the light fixture over the new bulb with one hand while screwing it in with the other. He had the old bulb stashed in the pocket of his sweatshirt.

"They like you over there," Mitch said. "I bet they'd make you a marina manager if you wanted. Then you could sign up for their health insurance plan."

Even Amelia had told him, placing both hands on each of his cheeks: *Drew, honey, you really should have health insurance.* She even calculated the costs of his dental appointments for him – having been cut off his parents' policy at twenty-four, two cleanings a year out of pocket, $125 a pop, and considering he was likely to live at least another forty years, was that really what he wanted to spend his money on?

Drew enjoyed his job doing the lighthouse tour, and he was good at budgeting his money to last the winter slow season. He knew his uncle didn't understand it. Uncle Mitch had been a lawyer for thirty-five years – a real job. Drew couldn't tell his uncle that he loved the sunshine in the summertime, or being able to work on his poetry through the winter, especially since his poetry had brought him back nothing but rejections. Perhaps he should give it up and become a journalist after all, one of those writers who published emotion-heavy news stories with a lovely poetic flair. *That was a well-written piece,* people would say. *So poignant and so astute.* Purple prose, they would mean, but they wouldn't know one way or the other. It would be writing. But with a by-line. And a paycheck. And maybe even a health insurance plan too.

Drew climbed safely down from the ladder. He flipped the switch and the dark hallway was lit, illuminating the dust on the mahogany banister and the tarnish on the silver mirrors. Drew turned the light off again and carried the ladder down the stairs.

Drew walked slowly beside his uncle as he hobbled back into

the den. "Or couldn't you teach with that fancy degree you got? What do they call that thing?"

"Master of Fine Arts," Drew said. "I might teach some day. I haven't ruled it out." Drew had no desire, in the least, to be a teacher. But his uncle had paid for his degree, and Drew wondered how long it would be before he began to regret that expense. "I don't need help getting a job. I have one. I enjoy it."

"You have half a job," Mitch said, crowing to himself. Drew was mostly convinced the old man was just giving him a hard time. Anna and Leslie hadn't used their degrees either, marrying instead, becoming a stay-at-home mom and an office secretary instead of a doctor and a business executive like they'd meant to.

"Your girl could help you, what's her name again? The stuffy redhead with the tits?"

Drew's eyes went wide. "Amelia," he said.

"That's the one," Mitch said. "She's the kind of girl who'd know about insurance. Got her head on straight."

It was almost the first nice thing his uncle had said about her.

Drew returned the ladder to the garage. When he joined his uncle again in the den, Mitch asked, "Close those windows for me, will you, son?"

It was nearing evening then, and a chill had filled the room. Drew closed the windows. He lit the fireplace and took the chair across from his uncle. He'd wait there long enough to make sure the fire would go out.

Uncle Mitch held out a newspaper, pointing to a headline. "And if you don't mind helping an old man out, could you tell me what this one says? It's those god-forsaken glasses – I can't see for shit. I don't know where the fool learned to write prescriptions."

Drew grinned. "You should fire him."

Uncle Mitch bellowed a deep, full-bellied laugh so contagious Drew had to laugh with him.

Then he began to read the newspaper, and his uncle sat back and listened to the story, turning his head to look out the window, the last warm rays of sunshine for the year, the trees already starting to show their fall colors. Drew read, and his uncle nodded here and there. The ladies at the club would always tell his uncle how much they loved Drew's speaking voice, how charismatic he was, how charming. It was how he landed the job he had, telling stories about the lighthouses, with *that smile* – Drew was a minor local celebrity among the senior set.

So Drew read his uncle the news for a while, until his uncle grew weary of it and said, "Hand me that clicker, will you?"

Drew handed him the remote, and Uncle Mitch turned on the History Channel. He checked to make sure Mitch was wearing his Life Alert, though Drew knew he wasn't allowed to ask that out loud. His uncle wouldn't ask him to mow the lawn, but he'd come back in the morning to do it anyway. In truth, Drew really didn't mind.

1.5: ready to run for it

AMELIA CAME HOME TO AN EMPTY HOUSE. THERE WAS NO clacking of Drew's laptop keyboard, no Coldplay in the background left on repeat, *A Rush of Blood to the Head* that he didn't want to admit he loved so much. There was a whole negative space that a person left behind when they were gone. Amelia and Drew didn't live together, except that most of the time, they did. He'd even taken up a corner of her spare room with his stacks of *The New Yorker* that were delivered faster than he could ever keep up reading, his pens left around the house, his scribble of random poetry on grocery receipts and sticky notes.

She picked up an electric bill payment stub from the kitchen table. *Paid online, 9/25*, she'd written on the front, and then his handwriting was scrawled over the back: *freedom, friction, fiction, fallacy*. She examined it, tossing the words around in her head like a puzzle. She'd asked him once what these random scribbles meant. "Oh, it's nothing," he had said. "I thought it might be something, but it was nothing."

Living together wasn't anything they ever really decided on. First more of his stuff gathered around her place, and then once she was used to him, she made space for his deodorants slotted between hers in the bathroom. She made room for his razor in her medicine cabinet, and he left his shaving hairs in her sink. One day, she told him where her spare key was; she told him to meet her there, let himself in, let himself in whenever he liked. Now he took out the trash for her on Sunday nights. He had his dirty clothes mixed in with hers, and she washed them for him. He brought home her favorite groceries, and she was surprised that he always remembered what she liked: hummus and pita chips, couscous salad (though he had no idea what it actually was), albacore tuna rather than the chunk light. She made room in her cupboards for his Fritos.

She called his phone. "Where are you?"

"Just at my place," he said, sounding sleepy.

Come home, she thought. Then she quickly laughed it off. This wasn't his home, was it? "What are you doing?"

"Just writing a little. There's a submission deadline I want to make, and we didn't have plans. I just thought I'd use the quiet here."

"Oh, okay," she said. "Did you eat already? Are you going to eat?"

"Yeah, I'll eat," he said. "See you in a bit. Love you."

"Love you too," she said before they hung up.

She started dinner. One pound of ground beef, then she diced up breadcrumbs for a meatloaf. It was far too much dinner for even two people, but she had no idea what she'd make otherwise. Then she imagined herself cooking for their little imaginary family. He would play with their children while she cooked – how many would he want? Would they have her curls and his dark eyes? Would they get her freckles? Not likely, she guessed. Then she shook her head at herself. They were officially sleeping together but not officially living together. Part of her liked it that way, and part of her wondered who she thought she was fooling.

She squished the cold meat with her hands, folding it over and into the breadcrumbs. *Beep.* The oven was preheated. Amelia closed the meatloaf inside, set the timer. She went to fold some laundry while watching the Evening World News Report.

So she decided – there while folding his boxer shorts – that she would make him a writing space in one of her spare bedrooms. Her house had three bedrooms: a master bedroom; a second bedroom she used for her treadmill, filing cabinets, and an ironing board; and then there was a tiny third room. He could use the smallest room if he wanted. It had one big, airy window, room enough for a big desk, and space on the walls for shelving. It would work, and besides, it was far too small a room to ever put a child in some day.

Amelia wouldn't dare tell her mother that she'd bought this house with the least concern for which rooms might or might not fit children. It would only please her too much.

Amelia went to the front door, looking down the street between parked cars and people walking to restaurants for dinner. She didn't want to call Drew again; she didn't want to be a nag. She would just wait for him instead. She slipped on a sweater and stepped out onto her front stoop, grabbing her cell phone from her purse, but not bothering to slip on any shoes. The pavement felt cold even through her socks.

She cradled the phone between both hands, watching the couples walk by on dates, hand in hand. She recognized some of her neighbors and waved. She said "hello" to some of the ones she didn't recognize too. She flipped open her phone and scrolled through her contacts list, running down the small list of people in her life, trying to decide who she could call. Piper would be with Tom tonight, and Amelia didn't want to bother them. Her mother was watching a movie she wasn't interested in. And Jodie?

Jodie hated phones – all she ever wanted to know was if they were going to hang out or not, where, and when? Amelia remembered her phone call to Drew the other night, the one she erased. What had she wanted?

Help? Nightmares flashed through her head – Jodie in a ditch, after having drunk herself silly. Had they heard from her since the wedding? Had she ever made it home? Amelia counted back the days, Sunday, Monday, Tuesday. She imagined Jodie lying in wreckage, her leg trapped between mangled metal and probably broken, one last battery bar left on her cell phone. She'd called Drew for help – maybe she'd tried to call Amelia too, but Amelia hadn't had her own phone that night. Jodie had called for help, and Amelia deleted it. "Oh no," Amelia said. She dialed.

Jodie answered. "Yeah?"

"Hey!" Amelia almost said, *You're alive!* But she stopped herself, and toned down her relief. "Are you okay?"

"No, I'm not okay," Jodie said. "I just came off an eighteen-hour labor that ended in a c-section. And I came home three minutes too late for *American Idol*. Why?"

Amelia sighed, the tight muscles in her face relaxing. "No reason," she said.

Before long, Jodie made it clear she needed to go pee, slap together a sandwich to eat for dinner, and make it back to her TV before *Dancing with the Stars* came on.

Amelia wondered if Drew would be back before bedtime. She could never sleep well alone. Her mother had suggested she get a big dog, and though Amelia never really cared for dogs, she did consider it. At night, she heard every creak and groan of the house, drunken footsteps stumbling home, wind rattling the storm door. She might have taken karate, but she didn't particularly want to kick people, or get kicked. She slept with a fireplace poker under her bed, but then she had nightmares about having to stab someone with it. In the nights before Drew slept over often, she used to call him at odd hours of the night, trying to convince him, "I'm fine, I just can't sleep." She was not really fine, but that she couldn't sleep was the truth. He had the most lovely speaking voice, forming his phrases like poetry, and when he was tired, his voice grew low and mellow, sonorous. He would talk to her until she fell asleep.

It was cool enough outside that the concrete steps chilled her bottom where she sat. She hugged her arms around herself. This had been the exact place she'd first met Drew. She knew he didn't believe that she was happy that day, but it had truly been one of the proudest moments of her life – becoming a homeowner. This two-story new-build townhouse, with its tiny yard and narrow hallways, its drafty windows and all the spiders in the basement. It was all hers. Buying her own home was the proudest thing Amelia had ever done for herself. That, and not marrying Eric.

She was brave not to marry Eric because he was a good man, and they cared about each other enough. It would have been plenty for a lot of women. He had asked her. It was a thoughtful proposal too, dinner at an upscale French restaurant a little more expensive than he could afford. The ring he offered her hadn't been impressive, but she wasn't surprised or offended by that. What he offered her was a long and complex list of how he thought they might work together, the facts of their compatibility, their similar life goals, all laid out in order like he was considering buying a house. He was right – about the compatibility, the similar life goals – and after living together for three years, after so much time invested, she seriously considered it.

She didn't want him back. Not at all. What she wanted was what he had – the ability to move on, to fall in love again and land so carelessly.

She heard the timer go off in the kitchen. Had it really been that long already?

She pulled the meatloaf out of the oven and called Drew. She got his voicemail. She called again and there was still no answer.

He'd fallen asleep, hadn't he? She covered their dinner in foil and put it back in the oven. She slipped on her shoes and started out across the street.

It wasn't very late, but late enough that considering it was a weeknight, the streets had gone quiet. There was an older woman walking with a bag of groceries, a man jogging with his dog, a local bar had a few smokers gathered around its front door. Amelia crossed the street to Drew's apartment building. An unsettling tension grew inside her, but she didn't think it was because she felt unsafe. This part of town had always been fine, even at night.

She searched through her key ring for the spare he'd given her. She knocked first, lightly, not wanting to disturb his neighbors at this time of night. She wasn't sure if she should have knocked or not; he didn't knock first anymore before coming into her house. She called him one more time and didn't hear his phone ringing inside the apartment. He left it on vibrate somewhere, she hoped. Or maybe he turned it off so he could focus – though she knew that wasn't true because she'd just called him a couple of hours ago.

It was almost enough to make her turn around, go home, pretend nothing was wrong. Just wait for him to come back, however long that took. She'd eat dinner by herself and save him a plate to heat up later. The last thing she wanted was to walk into yet another scene she was never meant to see – muffled whispers, bodies rushing apart, grasping for cover – she'd been through that too many times before.

She filled up her lungs, breathing out slowly through her lips. Then she shook her head. No, that's not what this was. It couldn't be. She slipped the key into the door.

Being in his apartment felt like being in a hotel room. He didn't keep much here anymore. The refrigerator buzzed and she wondered if he even had any food in it. She couldn't remember the last time they'd actually cooked something here.

She found his cell phone on the couch, blinking with her missed phone calls. Then she found him in his bedroom, napping. She exhaled, only then realizing she'd been holding her breath, and a smile took over her face. He had pages of poetry spread out over the bed and a red pen still held in his hand. She sat beside him.

His eyes fluttered open, and he reached out to touch her hand. "Hey, what time is it? Are you okay?"

"Yeah, it was just too quiet over there. I made dinner, it's finished. Are you ready to head back?" She grinned. "And you have red pen on your face."

He wiped a hand over his face, in the wrong spot, and then stretched, reaching, sweeping her into his hands with a hopeful smile on his face. "Can we take a few minutes?" He took her hips into his hands, a migratory hug that rolled her on top of him. He slid his hands under her shirt, and she leaned over him to rub the red pen mark on his cheek until it was gone. She had the oven turned off, but the heat should keep for a little while.

"Ten minutes, maybe."

"Is that all?" He grinned. "What I have in mind is going to take at least twenty-five."

His hands moved surely over her skin, skimming over the small of her back, slipping down her sides and sending warmth coursing through her body.

"Okay, twenty-five," she said, leaning down to kiss him.

THE WAY THEY HAD FIRST COME TOGETHER WAS MORE LIKE a beautiful accident than it was an actual decision. They were camping, and Piper wanted to switch tents so she could bunk with Tom. "Please, please," Piper pleaded, taking Amelia's hands into hers, while Tom stood behind her by a few yards, quiet but surely hoping to get laid. The problem was, that would leave Amelia only men to bunk with, and most of them were strangers.

Liberal and forward-thinking as Amelia might have been, that was just not going to work. But there was also Drew. "Come on, it's Drew," Piper said. "You guys are friends. He's not going to assault you or anything." She paused then, a very serious consideration, nodding her head. "He might dream about you naked though."

So Amelia bunked with Drew. The first night, they lay awake talking – or she talked, as he mumbled back sleepy responses. He was listening; he promised he was. He'd reached between their sleeping bags to hold her hand, and at some point she realized his dreamy mumbles had stopped entirely. He'd fallen asleep.

The way he slept was so peaceful, so calm, that a part of her felt jealous. It was the first time she'd seen him sleep. She placed a hand on his chest, flat, watching it rise and fall with each breath. It was chilly then, early in the fall, so she lowered herself and slipped her arm around him, rested her head on his shoulder, stole his body heat – no, not stole. It was hers for the taking, if she wanted it. He had always made that much clear. He didn't wake at her touch, but stirred a little, turning to nuzzle his face into her hair. The way he slept amazed her; she'd never been able to close her eyes with so little worry. Not since she was a child – and maybe not then either, with the turbulence of her family's nomadic military life, all that unpredictability.

Drew hadn't tried anything more scandalous than spooning her that night, which she knew he wouldn't. She let him hold her for a while before they both rolled over in their sleep and lost each other.

The second night, there were a dozen of them sitting around the campfire. Some of them Amelia knew better than others: one of Piper's sisters and her husband, a couple of Drew's friends and some random girls they'd picked up at another campsite. Jodie hadn't come – she hated the outdoors.

They'd run out of chairs. Amelia hovered near the fire, holding a plastic cup in her hand, filled with a cheap boxed red wine blend. She didn't see Drew's hands before she felt them on her hips, reaching out and pulling her back to him, mindful not to pull so fast she spilled her wine. "Come keep me warm," he said.

Before she could worry about falling backwards off his lap to collide with the ground, he had one arm behind her back, one arm around her waist, a warm cradle for her to settle into. She'd never sat in his lap before, and it was a sensation she wasn't prepared for. Not because they were too close, because they'd been this close before, leaning in to whisper secrets in each other's ears about their friends, or stealing a sip of his beer to see if she would like it (and she never did). It wasn't because he leaned his lips to her shoulder, as if to kiss her through the polar fleece – there had been countless little play kisses on the cheek or the hand, snuck in between laughs or tickles. It wasn't because of the way he touched her, because she'd felt his hands before, the way he would stealthily feel her up in the disguise of a well-meaning hug, as if she didn't know what he was doing. It was because she had to turn her face away from his lips, so close to hers that she felt an unbearable pull to lean right over and kiss him. If she looked into his eyes, she knew she wouldn't last the night.

At some point people had gone elsewhere, to bed, or to flirt in front of other fires. There were extra chairs now, but she was still sitting in his lap, leaving all those empty chairs unused. She wondered if she should get up to sit somewhere else, but she didn't move. And that was when he looked at her, and she was caught there as he took her hand into his and said, "Your fingers are cold." Her heart swelled so much she could hardly remember how to breathe. She must have looked stunned. Or sickly. He asked her, "You okay?"

Was she okay? She didn't know.

Because there, in the quiet of the woods, sitting in his lap, she knew that she'd finally fallen in love with him. She wasn't sure when or how it happened. It wasn't something she ever decided. She hadn't ever set aside all those precautions, or given those feelings permission to grow, and yet there they were.

So she kissed him. Not on the cheek like she usually did, not playful, not a joke. When her lips left his, he pulled back to look her in the eyes, half speechless and half startled. How long had he been waiting for an actual kiss from her? This was a big deal, wasn't it? *See*, she wanted to tell him, *I told you so*.

But when the shock wore off, he put his fingers in her hair and kissed her back. They kissed with his hand on her cheek and her arms wrapped around his shoulders. They kissed some more, and she worried that his legs might go numb from her weight – if they had, he didn't say so. They sat kissing long into the evening, the firelight fading and growing cold, occasionally pulling back to whisper to each other, or even just to breathe. They kissed for so long that neither of them noticed the rain starting, a fine mist that settled on their hair and clothes, until the sky broke open with a heavy downpour.

Amelia jumped up from Drew's lap. "It's raining," she told him, though it really wasn't something he could have missed. They should have taken cover in the tent – in the dry and dark privacy of his tent – but somehow her feet wouldn't carry her there. It would have meant too much. She started picking up the campsite instead, paper plates and plastic cups, beer bottles tossed beside a trash bag and not into it. She put away all the things their friends had left lying around. She moved quickly, the rain gathering on her head and starting to run into her eyes, and it didn't help that the fire had sputtered out and left them with no light.

Drew stopped her at the cooler. "It's okay, leave it."

"But the animals," she told him. "Don't you know a bear can open a cooler if it wanted to?"

He looked at her, though he was in shadow and she couldn't make out his expression to know what he was thinking. He took a key ring from his pocket, beeping open the trunk of his Jeep. He picked up the cooler. "Open the hatch for me?"

They stowed the cooler in the back and stood under the open hatch as rain fell around them. There was little room under the hatch. They were both already wet, but she nuzzled against his side to keep warm. Their friends scurried back into their tents, some with a wave, or a shout, or dragging back a girl they hadn't known at the start of the night. Casual sex – Amelia had tried it before. Strange as it had been for her, casual sex had been easy and uncomplicated. That wasn't what was happening here. What was happening here, the next logical step, the only direction they had left to go, would have been the least casual thing she ever did. *Break my heart if you want*, he used to tell her, *it'll just make for good poetry*. She'd been there too many times before – it wasn't worth good poetry. But hadn't she been all wrong about it? It was hearts, not bodies, that broke when these things went wrong. And weren't their hearts already in it? Whatever came next was completely out of her control.

The rain only grew heavier – they had nowhere else to go. He nudged her. "Ready to run for it?"

She nodded. She was ready.

He closed the hatch, wrapped his arm around her shoulders and they ran, unzipping the tent and trying not to bring too much mud inside with their shoes.

She zipped the tent flap behind her, letting her eyes adjust in the dark. A nearby trail light cast a yellowish glow on the tent. Drew sat on his sleeping bag, wet in his clothes, taking his phone and keys from his pockets. "Wait," she said, reaching for his hands, her cheeks flushing warm with the intentions she had in mind. "You'll get the sleeping bags wet." She pulled him up to kneeling, slipping her hands underneath his shirt to pull it up, to pull it over his head.

They kissed as they undressed each other, laying wet clothing at the foot of their sleeping bags to dry, carefully at first, then losing themselves to the frenzy, flinging the clothing across the tent – a sock, a pair of jeans, her bra. She pulled his body closer to hers. He lowered his face to kiss her shoulder, his hands pressed to her damp skin, warming her then leaving behind goosebumps and a trail of static. He laid her back across the sleeping bag and moved himself over her, taking slow pleasure in every touch, every kiss. He reveled in her. He touched her like it was his reward.

Her skin became electrified as he traced from her collarbone, down, slowly, finally taking her breast into his hand, her nipple to his tongue. Hands and bodies were tangled, lips and tongues, fingers and hair, and one of his hands finally slid down. She inhaled, a soft gasp. He paused there, where she throbbed at the feel of his fingertips, only separated by the thin cotton of her panties, wet from the rain, transferring all that heat from his skin. He hesitated, as if asking permission. He didn't have to ask, but she answered him anyway, nodding, yes. He slipped her panties down, and she wrapped her legs around his hips, pulling him inside her.

The rain went on steadily that night, a cadence of splattering drops and thrumming gusts of wind. No one could hear their heavy breathing, or the telling crinkle of the sleeping bags they rolled on, moving together, wet kisses and stifled moans. The rain covered them and kept their secret.

And in the morning, when they'd dressed and come out of the tent to join the others for breakfast, with tired eyes and tousled hair, when he kissed her cheek in front of them all, no one thought the least thing about it. It was just Drew kissing Amelia, doting on her the way he always had, that tired old game. It had been so big, so transforming, and yet no one noticed the difference, as if at some point, it had already happened when she wasn't paying attention. As if it had been there all along, and she'd only just seen it with her own eyes.

His bedroom closet was open and mostly bare, holding five empty clothes hangers and a sweater she'd never seen him wear. The sheets smelled stale, and the clock on his nightstand was six months overdue for its Daylight Savings Time update. They lay naked, their bodies still flushed and buzzing, one of the sheets twisted and pulled haphazardly across their legs. They'd taken a little longer than twenty-five minutes. "You should move in with me," she said. "We're never here anymore."

He smiled. "I guess you're right."

"Your bed is better than mine, but I want to keep my couch. You can bring your lamps, but you're not touching my kitchen. Not a single thing."

"What would I know about kitchens anyway?"

"You really want to live with me?"

"You know I do. I'd love to."

"This is going to make my mother happy."

"Well, while we're at it," he said, grinning at her. "I know what would make your mom even happier."

"I can't marry you," she said.

"Oh, I wasn't talking about that," he teased. "I meant I could knock you up."

"Ha," she laughed. He was right.

"But why can't you marry me?"

It gave her pause. Why? "Because my dad isn't here," she said. "Who'd give me away?"

"Ah, right. Good reason." He lay on her chest, his face full of her breasts and smiling. He traced a finger along the curve of one, then let his hand spread over it. "We could just have a really long engagement. And get married some time after he gets back."

That. When she heard it, she stopped breathing a little. It was terrifying in a perfect way, because she knew that was exactly what she wanted. She hadn't even considered it an option. She'd had proposals before, the lines and propositions and promises, but the most honest thing she'd ever heard was her drunk boyfriend saying he wanted to marry her on her bathroom floor. He wasn't just her lover; he was her best and most trusted friend, and there was no turning back from that. She had already fallen much deeper than she ever intended. "Okay," she said.

He lifted his head. "Okay?"

"Okay," she repeated. "Really long. And we can't tell my mom, because you know she'd start planning."

His brow twisted, and he sighed, full of both joy and disappointment. "I would have taken you somewhere. I don't even have a ring yet. I would have made it really nice."

No, she thought, this was nice. It was just what she needed. "It was perfect," she said.

He finally let the shock and surprise fade from his face, and he kissed her. He wasn't scared and she knew he wouldn't be. She willed herself to believe he was right. As she kissed him back, she thought the fear might have dissipated, but it didn't. Not completely. In the undercurrents of her mind, she found herself pleading with the universe or whatever god might be listening, that this love would never become stale or grow into something vague and metaphysical, that it wouldn't become yet another heartbreak to make for good poetry. This was more than hoping. This was a prayer, *Lord, please, let this time be enough.*

NOVEMBER

2.1: what normal people look like

WHEN JODIE SAW AMELIA AND DREW STEP INTO THE bar, it was like seeing a pair of rare barn owls, the kind you might have heard in the quiet of the night but that you've never actually seen. They had become almost mythical creatures, maybe once existing in reality but now extinct, or at least endangered. Two months ago they'd moved in together, finally, and Jodie had hardly seen them since. Now here they were, come out of hiding for the night, holding on to each other as if one or the other might be poached for someone's rare animal collection. "You're actually alive," Jodie said.

Amelia laughed lightly. "Of course we are."

Jodie sat with Piper at a tall table near the bar while Tom got their drinks. It was almost like the old days, but not quite. It used to be the five of them, but now it was two pairs and Jodie. She should have brought a date, Piper had told her. It was hard though, bringing a stranger into a group of friends like this. And Jodie hated strangers as it was.

There was a DJ in another room, playing something electronic, sharp beats mixed with a soft acoustic piano riff. Wordless, just the way Jodie liked it. Words just messed up everything. She tapped a finger on the table to the beat. Tom brought three drinks over, the stage lights twinkling in the liquid, reflecting off the lacquered table top, sequins on shirts, and so many other sparkly things. A diamond on Amelia's finger. Jodie stopped tapping.

She squinted at it. She looked to Piper, who wasn't looking at the ring at all, but instead reaching for the flimsy teal chiffon Amelia wore. "Oh, stand up," Piper said. "Can I look at this?" Amelia stood as Piper turned her around like a living mannequin, examining the cut and seams of the blouse. Drew watched her spin, all curves and freckles. As Amelia turned, the ring caught light, and lost it, caught and lost it again.

Jodie couldn't believe nobody else was wondering about it. Unless everyone else already knew. "Is that–?"

Amelia sat back down, holding her hand still in front of her, turning the ring with her thumb. Drew reached to her leg underneath the table, and she turned her head half-way to offer him a slight smile. She lifted her face to the group of them and spoke. "We're sort of engaged."

"Oh," Jodie said, turning to Piper sharply. "You knew?"

"Only just," Piper said. She took Amelia's hand and held it up to the light. "I mean, how do you miss that?"

"It's not that big," Jodie said, still looking at the ring. "Piper, you wouldn't miss an engagement ring if you were blind."

Amelia blushed. "I didn't ask for this."

"I wish I could have bought you one for each finger," Drew said, picking up her hand to kiss it. Jodie tried to restrain herself from rolling her eyes at them. She didn't try very hard. She buried her lips in her drink to distract herself, swallowing hard, feeling the burn in her throat. "When did it happen?"

"The ring is new," Amelia said. "But the engagement, I guess about two months ago?"

"Two months?" Jodie glanced at Amelia, at Drew, at Amelia again. She wasn't sure which of them she'd expected to tell her, but she never imagined neither of them would.

Amelia had a pained crinkle in her eyebrows. "It wasn't a secret from you, Jodie. It was a secret from everyone."

"A secret engagement?"

"We just wanted a little private time."

"Huh, well I guess I'm happy for you then," Jodie said. She raised her glass to Drew. "We all know *he's* wanted this for a stinking long time." They all watched her, their eyes widening in shock, or horror – she wasn't sure which. She didn't wait for the rest of them to grab their glasses before she drank, slurped back the last sip. She felt her face burn with heat, and over what? All she knew was that she was only embarrassing herself. She stood. "I'm getting another. Anybody want anything?" She didn't wait for any of them to answer. She just started for the bar.

The dark room with its colored lights was full of bodies by then, reeking of sweat and cologne and the hope for sex. She slipped in between two people at the bar and watched the bartender ignore her. The men on either side didn't look over, but she didn't care. She leaned her elbows on the wooden bar top, polished slick and sticky with something she couldn't even see. What did it take to get some attention around here? Squeeze her chest together, those tits Berges liked so much? She wouldn't know how to squeeze her tits together if she tried, and even Berges hadn't looked at them in weeks. She missed the pleasure of being looked at. "Hey," she shouted at the bartender. She'd only meant to speak above the voices but instead, her voice heaved out like a roar.

"Hey, what?"

She held up her empty martini glass at him, tilted it sideways. "Stronger this time?"

The bartender sneered at her and eventually looked away. She didn't know if that meant he'd get her drink or not. But then there was a hand on her hair, pulling twice, lightly. Tug, tug. Drew. She didn't even need to turn around to know it. But she did turn. He lifted his bottle. "Another one for me?"

She took Drew's bottle and waved it at the bartender. Maybe he saw, or maybe he didn't.

"So what's more commitment?" she asked him. "Marriage or moving in together?"

He hesitated, hanging his thumbs in his pockets, his eyes locked on hers until he cracked a slight smile, agreeing to play her game. "Marriage," he said finally. "Unless both names are on the mortgage – then I guess it's a call."

"Is yours?"

"Not yet," he said. She wished he wouldn't look at her. If he was trying to decipher her, she could just save him the trouble – she wasn't that complex. "Okay," he said. "Marriage or tattoos of each other's names?"

"Definitely tattoos," Jodie said, letting her lips curve into a smirk, glancing at Amelia, then back to him. "People get divorced *all* the time."

A dagger. She couldn't hold them back. He squinted at her, a skewed smile and doubtful eyes. Then he looked away. She couldn't even say why she was angry, or at whom. She leaned her elbows against the bar, her silver top pulling tight against her chest, though he wasn't looking at her then, just staring across the endless room of strange faces. She asked him, softer this time, "Marriage or a baby? Which is more commitment?"

He didn't have an answer. Or maybe he had one that he didn't want to tell. Or maybe he wasn't playing anymore. He only smiled, slanted and almost apologetic.

"Hey," the bartender barked behind her. A bottle of beer and a martini, strong and dry with two olives. She considered falling in love with him instead.

Drew raised his beer bottle to her. "Happy Birthday."

Jodie raised her own glass, but stopped short. "What?"

He moved his arm in front of her face, a sleek, steel Rolex reflecting the bar lights. She didn't mean to inhale then, the scent of his cologne mixed with Amelia's perfume, impossibly intertwined and inextricable. "Midnight," he said. "It's your birthday now."

He was right; it was. She let one corner of her mouth twist into a smile. Just one corner. "Well happy fucking birthday to me."

"Hey, you do smile," he said.

"Well, only because you're ridiculous."

"Heh," he laughed – half a laugh, half a sigh. "We better get back," he said. His face had already turned back to their table, Amelia perched on a tall stool, long legs crossed, her pantyhose shimmering in the bar lights. Always back to Amelia. He started to walk. After a moment, Jodie followed him.

JODIE NEVER THOUGHT SHE'D FIND HERSELF HIDING OUT IN THE parking lot of her own workplace. She and Berges couldn't avoid each other forever, but she'd avoid him as long as she could, and seven weeks? That wasn't close enough to forever. She hid her face behind a magazine as he stepped out of his Mercedes, straightened his shirt in the driver-side window reflection. He was torturing her. She sent a text to Piper to meet for lunch, she synchronized her car clock for Daylight Savings Time until he'd gathered his things and made it clearly into the building. Then she waited another five minutes to make sure he'd made it inside his office, that he hadn't stopped at the vending machine to grab a bag of those pork rinds he ate.

She couldn't believe she'd fucked a man who ate pork rinds.

She could have avoided him by using the lot a couple blocks down the street, but she wasn't going to do that now that she had the good parking spot. She had told Berges that was an accident, but no, that wasn't true. She knew exactly what she was doing.

But she hadn't thought the pavers would actually listen to her. They did, and now here was the spot with a "reserved: Dr. J. Larsen" standing proud on a pole. "Fine, you know what? Have it," she finally told him. "I don't even care." But he shunned it. And even though there was a spot – a decent one – with a similar pole, "reserved: Dr. G. Berges" standing right there in the front row, just feet from their mailboxes, he wouldn't park there. Because of the damned trees. "It's sap season," he told her. "It's the principle." It was his stubborn pride. And it wasn't even sap season yet for at least four more months. So while part of her had wanted to make amends with him, she couldn't bring herself to do it. Anytime she saw him, he just looked so smug and entitled that she wanted to smack him for it. Then she forgot that she'd ever felt guilty at all.

Jodie hadn't taken her birthday off work. Her birthday was just a day, like any other day of her life. She was thirty years old, plus or minus a few hours, stuck in a waiting room full of mothers-to-be, swollen and glowing, some of them with husbands and boyfriends to hold purses and fetch new magazines. It was a kind of teamwork she couldn't hope to understand, yet it was thrummed into her every day that she worked – this was what normal people looked like.

Jodie stood behind the reception counter as one of the couples checked out. She held their sonogram in her hands, ten weeks, healthy. It was their first. The dads always showed up for the first. They showed up at the beginning, scared and enthralled, asking their questions of the black and white shapes on the screen. Is that a foot? Is that its head?

"Is that his... you know?" the father asked her, grinning.

"No, that's a leg," she said, handing over the pictures to him. "You can't tell the sex for a few more weeks." She turned to the mother, "We'll see you again in four weeks."

Piper had texted back to say she'd pick up some sandwiches and stop by for lunch. Jodie waited behind the desk for her, pretending to look at the patient forms in her hands, but really just shuffling the papers. She had forty minutes clear for lunch, and here was Piper with fruit smoothies she stole from work, the Beaners logo emblazoned across the front of them, and something that looked greasy in a takeout bag.

She and Piper went back to Jodie's office and closed the door. The room was stark and orderly, even more clinical than the examination rooms themselves. Jodie hadn't ever felt inclined to brighten it up. Piper brought her a plant once, a tiny thing that flowered once but failed to ever do so again. It sat there on the window sill, plain but hearty, and Jodie felt obligated to water it occasionally so it wouldn't die. Besides those few green leaves, Piper was the brightest thing in the room in her puffy, dandelion-yellow parka. Piper went to open the blinds and flooded the white room with light. The light was bold and warm, but Jodie knew it was deceptive. November was cold.

Piper signed a cross over her body, mouthing a silent "Amen" before diving into her cheese steak. Jodie didn't pray – didn't even believe in God – but for some reason, could never start eating until Piper had finished her prayer. Jodie took modest bites of her tuna melt, while Piper attacked her cheese steak with enthusiasm. Jodie wanted to tell Piper about Berges. Piper had asked once, after the wedding, "How did it go?" Jodie hadn't wanted to talk about it then, and now the moment had passed. Weeks had passed, and Piper had other things on her mind, dress materials and patterns, booking reception halls and musicians, and would Jodie mind coming with her to hold fabric swatches against their skin in artificial lights?

On a promo note pad advertising birth control pills, Piper sketched wedding shoes on bodiless pairs of legs. Jodie asked her,

"Is it weird to ask prospective roommates what kind of birth control they use?"

Piper had a collection of paint sample strips, in various shades of purple and yellow, on the table near her plate. She held up one strip after another in the direction of Jodie's face, against her own forearm, then one strip in each hand angled to the sunlight. "Yeah, that's weird." Piper put the paint samples down on the table, and began to think about something. "You know, there's this guy."

"No," Jodie said.

"Just hear me out," Piper said. "He's a journalist."

"I hate journalists."

"When have you ever dated a journalist?"

She hadn't, but that wasn't the point. Jodie hated dating. She especially hated dating people's friends. "I won't like him, and then it'll be weird."

"You might like him."

"But I might not, I probably won't, odds are ninety-five percent I won't, and then you have to explain to Tom – and to his friend – that I didn't like him. Like I told you I wouldn't in the first place."

Piper tilted her head, mumbling, "Hmmm..." Then wagged her finger. "But what if they're not such good friends?"

The idea of this vague, faceless journalist floated in her head, and Jodie sneered at it.

There wasn't much that bothered Piper, so when there was something, a funny constipated look came over her face, and her tiny bright eyes filled with more weight than they were able to carry. "It came," she said.

Jodie knew she meant her period. Maybe it was because Jodie dealt with vaginas all day that people felt inclined to just tell her things. Jodie was the only one who knew that Piper and Tom were actually trying to have a baby, and knowing that two people were having lots of sex in an effort to make a baby was more awkward than Jodie knew how to explain.

The wedding was four months away. "What would you do with your dress if it did happen?"

"I'd just make it bigger," Piper said. "It's just that I have *twelve* nieces and nephews. All four of my sisters have babies now, and one of my brothers. My oldest sister, Carolyn is already a *grandmother*. Her son is married with two kids, and he's four years younger than me."

The sprawling network of Piper's family boggled Jodie's mind. She looked at a desktop calendar, tapping at dates with her plastic fork. "How many months since you stopped taking your pill?"

"Five," Piper said.

"Wait a little longer," Jodie said. "It hasn't been that long yet. Just keep taking your prenatal. And no caffeine."

"No, no caffeine. I mean, I just thought it would have happened by now. You know, knowing my family."

"Maybe the baby is Catholic. Maybe it wants to wait until after the wedding?" Jodie laughed at her own joke, but Piper only gave a sad smile. "I mean," Jodie continued. "What would your grandmother think?"

"But do you think it won't happen? What if we can't?"

"It could be him though."

Piper shook her head. "He got a girl pregnant once in high school. She didn't keep it."

"Oh," Jodie said. "Well hell, don't tell your grandmother that. It just takes time sometimes. You know, they say if you stop trying, it'll happen."

Jodie never understood the appeal herself – this breeding thing – especially when it took so much work. All the women she came across, every day, trying to get pregnant, accidentally getting pregnant, finished with being pregnant. The other doctors at the clinic had framed pictures of their little ones lining their office walls. They often gave Jodie *that look,* the one everyone gave her, well-meaning and sure: *Oh, you're still young. You'll change your mind some day. Just wait 'till you meet the right man!* As if choosing never to pair off and breed wasn't actually a valid life choice. As if it was some kind of betrayal against her biological nature.

Jodie delivered the babies. Wasn't she doing her part?

"So anyway, Tom's friend? Please go out with him," Piper pleaded. "You might like him. Just try?"

Jodie's voice broke out in an exhale, "Eh." Piper wasn't going to let her decline. Jodie hated the idea of a first date. She hated it to death. Especially a first date with a stranger who she already knew she wasn't going to like.

IF JODIE WAS GOING TO SUCCEED AT THIS AVOIDANCE GAME, leaving work was a little bit trickier than arriving. His office was on the second floor, while hers was on the first. So she had no way of knowing when he might leave except to listen for clues.

She peeked her head outside the door. The hallway was long and carpeted, lights flickering. She listened for footsteps echoing in the stairwell. She knew he wouldn't take the elevator; he used to boast about taking the stairs for his cardiovascular health, while carrying a bag of pork rinds. At first, he would shoot her these sad, sideways glares, avoiding the main hallway that led out to their parking lot. But that hadn't lasted long. He'd turned his dejection into anger. He started walking stronger, more sure, as if finally deciding it was time to re-grow his spine. He walked right past the door of Rainbow Women's Care, and he did it slowly. And the few times she neglected to look out for him first, and they happened to walk out at the same time, he only brushed past her, cold as a ghost. It was more than post-sex awkwardness; he seemed to resent her. But for what? For telling him what he didn't want to hear? For telling the truth?

She made it down the hallway to the door, opening out into the cold. The sky was dark and heavy with clouds that threatened snow. All was clear, and she made her way straight for her car. Until one of the nurses caught her there on the way out, talking about her plans for the weekend. By the time Jodie broke free of her, the timing and surveillance had all been shot, because there was Berges striding down the path.

Jodie hadn't meant to back up like she did, pressing herself against the long concrete half-wall. Maybe he might have just brushed past her like he had become so accustomed to lately, but instead, he only looked at her oddly. "Heh," she chuckled, shaking her head at herself. He stopped, silent, staring her down as she stammered to find some words, any words. He'd never been intimidating to her before.

"I've had a bad fucking week," he said. He beeped his car open with the remote – he liked to do that, liked to show off that it was his. It was a nice car. It was something she wouldn't be able to buy herself for decades still, if ever. She wasn't going to mock him again for that car being all he had. She would have been proud to have even that.

"Huh, a bad week?" Try being the last one left on the planet who wasn't engaged, when she didn't even want to be engaged, but she also didn't want to be *not* engaged in a sea of engaged people. But she didn't say that. "What's so damn bad about your week?"

She sat down on the brick half-wall. He stood a few feet away from her, taking a breath as he would before launching into one of his long tirades, except he held it, tucking his hands into his coat pockets as they stared at each other in awkward silence. Like hell if he was going to tell her anything. Sadly, she expected he wouldn't. "Nothing for you to worry about," he said.

There was enough space between them that people passed in between, leaving their dentist appointments, consultations with their lawyer, or pregnant women and nurses and medical supply deliveries, heels clicking and rubber soles scuffing on the pavement. She should just go. She was starting to go. He asked her, "Would you ever date a redhead?"

"What? Why?"

"Just answer the damn question."

She didn't have to answer shit to him – that was the reaction in her head, but in her gut she found herself asking back. "A guy redhead?"

"What, as opposed to a chick? Have you been with a chick before?" He actually grinned. For a split second, before letting it fall away.

Jodie narrowed her eyes at him, darts. "Shut up. I don't think I've ever met a guy redhead before."

He shook his head. "Kate's dating one. Smarmy bastard. He's a real estate agent, and he has a fat head."

"I'm sorry to hear that," she said. She felt the need to clarify – was she sorry Kate was dating a redhead, or that he was a real estate agent, or that she was dating at all? But he didn't question that. He nodded, and they lingered in that for a moment. A heavily pregnant woman passed between them, three children trailing behind her.

"Yeah, well..." he said, flipping his keys in his hand.

It wasn't like they were friends. Not real friends. She didn't like him, she passionately hated him most of the time. What did it matter if they were awkward around each other? They didn't need to be anything to each other at all. Then why was it driving her up the wall that she couldn't fight with him anymore? "Come on," she said.

"What?"

"It's just not a big deal. The wedding, I mean. It was a mistake, okay? I'm over it. You could be over it."

But instead of countering back with a dirty joke, like he would have before, he only gloated. "The sex? You think I'm upset about the sex? Get over yourself, Jodie."

It shouldn't have stung her the way it did. Her heart was pounding hard. "Well you... you... you stick out your tongue when you're screwing." She exhaled. "And it looks really stupid."

She felt like a twelve year-old. He just raised his eyebrows at her and started to shake his head. He stopped to take a steady breath, fuel for his attack. "You're a miserable woman, Jodie. Do you know that? You don't want to be happy, so you just can't stand to see anyone else happy either."

He started to walk away, but she wasn't done with him yet. She wasn't. "What the *hell* do you know about happy?"

People stopped to stare at her – all of them – pregnant women and children and orderlies and couriers carrying samples of blood. But Berges was a void where she knew substance used to be. Maybe they had been friends after all. But now he was a moving piece of the world, the cold, the sun, the people as they started moving again, started talking again. He only kept walking to his car, not a flinch in his step, like her voice had gotten lost in the crowd.

2.2: how not to kill a koi fish

AMELIA STEPPED INTO THE LOTUS ONE SATURDAY afternoon, and the room was hot, closed up, smelling strongly of sandalwood and sweat and someone who wore too much cologne. Her sinuses tightened at the onslaught of such different sensations. She ached for the deep stretch and muscle burn of a Vinyasa Flow class, but for the past couple weeks, she'd been shadowing the prenatal and postpartum class instead. The class was so calm, fluid and relaxing, given the tender and delicate bodies of the women who took it. Amelia could never appreciate that ethereal place some yogis reached in the gentler forms – it only made her want to sleep. She preferred to use her muscles, to find precision and order through the postures.

Corbin sat with another student on their mats, though practice must have ended quite a while ago. His friend was an earthy-looking brunette – clean, sun-kissed face with a full, gap-toothed smile – having a conversation that apparently required wide hand gestures on his part and dreamy admiration on hers. Amelia often found the two of them lost in some deep discussion.

Mindy was the instructor Amelia was meant to shadow, but she was nowhere to be seen. Amelia wasn't sure how any of them could stand this stuffy room, but November in Michigan was too late in the year to keep the patio doors cracked open. There was time still before the next class, so Amelia opened them slightly, taking half a step into the courtyard, breathing the air. Not too much though, nobody liked to do yoga in a cold room. Fresh air poured into the room, dampening the smell of sandalwood. They wouldn't have many of these days left before the real cold set in. In the summer months, many of their guests loved the courtyard, reed flutes piping through the sound system, a koi pond and rock garden surrounded by high, vine-covered walls. The place was partly inspired by a spa they'd visited while they were on base in Japan. Amelia had been far too young to remember most of it. But Claire remembered, the reed flutes, the hanging bamboo curtains, a rock garden and koi pond. She'd spent months reading up on how not to kill the koi fish.

Corbin finally looked up from his friend, likely surprised by the sudden chill in the room. Amelia closed the doors. "Sorry to be a bother," she said to him – the apology meant for both of them really. She dreaded having to break up a conversation as impossibly dreamy as they were having. "Can I ask you something?"

"Of course," he said, patting his friend's arm and whispering something to her. He hopped up from the floor, limber and quick, and bounded over to where Amelia stood.

She pulled some paperwork from her purse. "I hate to bother you, but I need a reference for this workshop application."

"Oh, you're doing the course then," he said. "I'm glad to hear that." He took the paper from her hands. "And I'd be honored to," he added with a slight bow of his head. He was too generous with her, and yet he never asked anything of her in return. It made her feel out of balance in the universe. She made a mental note to bake him some bread sometime.

"Thanks," she said. "No hurry or anything."

There was a faint cough in the hallway, and emerging from the shadows, a lean body in fitted yoga gear. Mindy. She was young, petite but powerful, and was the kind of girl Amelia might have admired were she not so conniving and competitive. Mindy told Amelia once that she was all body and no mind when she taught. She often offered these generous nuggets of unsolicited wisdom. *Your poses – while physically precise, don't get me wrong – are just a little uninspired. I'm not sure you've found your center.*

Amelia knew she wasn't naturally suited to this, but was there anything that couldn't be learned? She wanted to become one of those ethereal yogis who found comfort and contentment in their practice, like Corbin, like his dreamy friend. Amelia wanted to learn to be more at peace in her own mind.

Mindy strode quickly to the patio doors, shaking her head. "Amelia, nobody likes to do yoga in a cold room." She brushed past them both and Corbin excused himself, clearing his throat and ducking his head, all but darting across the room back to his friend. Mindy rolled her eyes, watching him go, riling at the sight of him talking to that brunette.

"Oh Lord," Amelia said, laughing lightly – she hadn't meant to say anything out loud. Corbin had slept with Mindy, hadn't he? Of course he had. It didn't surprise Amelia, and she wouldn't dare say anything – it was none of her business in the least – but it would just amuse her to know if there was one woman on this planet he hadn't slept with. Or who wouldn't sleep with him, for that matter.

Mindy glanced at her. Her voice came out sweetly, though there was heat in her eyes. "What are you laughing at?"

"Nothing," Amelia said.

Mindy clapped her hands together once in front of her, reminding Amelia of a high school cheerleader. "Well then, session number three, how are you holding up?"

It was prenatal and postpartum; it was hardly taxing.

"Good, I think," Amelia said. "I've already done the Vinyasa shadow, so one more form after this one and I should be set. I saw you were doing a meditation class?"

Mindy's smile was more like a sneer. "No offense, Amelia," she started, and Amelia prepared herself to be offended. "But your speaking voice is... well, kind of tense." The way she said these things, with a soft tilt of her head, her tiny palm reaching out to Amelia's forearm, was enough to make Amelia's jaw clench. "I just don't think leading meditation would be your most effective choice."

"Right." Amelia inhaled, exhaled. "Some other form then. Sure."

Mindy didn't like her – Amelia knew this. Amelia had no intentions of trying to replace her. The workshop she was applying for was not only a teaching certification, but an enrichment course too. Amelia hadn't even decided yet if she'd want to teach. But Amelia figured Mindy didn't like the idea of a new addition, even if only a theoretical one. Not to mention that Amelia's mother owned this place, and that probably threatened her too.

Amelia raised her arm, the coat draped over it. "I'm just going to drop this off and talk to my mom for a minute."

"Of course," Mindy said. "Go talk to your mom."

Amelia found her mother sitting in her office on a phone call. When Amelia peeked her head inside the door, Claire waved her through. Amelia set her yoga mat on the floor near her feet, catching a few words of her mother's phone call, an order for bromine for the hot tubs. A small television sat on a filing cabinet, tuned to a news channel – another helicopter crash overseas, seven soldiers dead. As her mother finished her phone call, it caught Amelia's attention the way she might watch a car crash – simultaneously disturbed and transfixed. But it was okay, she told herself every time there was another report. Her dad didn't fly in helicopters anymore. If he'd still been a soldier, they'd find a man in uniform at their door with the bad news; how did one end up hearing about a contractor shot out of the sky?

Claire didn't even look at the screen before grabbing the remote and flipping to a different channel. "You shouldn't be watching that stuff, sweetie." She landed on a financial news channel, no war reporting expected, with its generic scrolling blurbs. A charismatic man with slick plastic hair gave the hourly money report, green and red arrows pointing in their endless patterns of ups and downs. There was a comfortable predictability to it. What was down would someday be up again; what was up would never stay that way for long. At least you could see it coming. You could do something about it, take action, protect your investments.

Claire took Amelia's hand, and gazed fondly at the ring on it. They did well with the secret for a few weeks, but Amelia hadn't been able to keep the engagement from her mother once Drew had given her that ring. Amelia felt bad that they'd been so hurried in bed that night, for spoiling a question that he'd probably imagined asking someone for most of his life. But how else would he have known she was ready for it if she hadn't said so? How else would *she* have known she wanted it, if it hadn't blurted out of her mouth like it did?

When he was ready, he'd gotten that nice moment he wanted, to make up for her hurried question in bed. He took her out on his uncle's boat. It was just the two of them and the cold, choppy waves. He placed a small box in her hands. An engagement ring – she hadn't even asked him for one. She hoped he hadn't had to dip into his off-season savings to afford it, but she also knew he wouldn't have asked his uncle for the money. Her family wasn't rich, and she hadn't seen many diamonds in her life. But he asked, holding the ring over the tip of her finger, "Can I?" She nodded, and he slid it on. She was too small for it; she didn't know how to carry her hand. But she wore it anyway, staring at for weeks until it started to look right on her finger, until she started to convince herself that a man could really think this much of her.

Claire set Amelia's hand down gently on the desk. "I'm glad you're not alone, sweetie."

"You're not alone either, Mom." It was just one of those things to say, involuntary, like blinking when someone's blown in your eyes. Claire reached out to pat Amelia's hand, all but saying out loud, *Yes, dear.* Her mother was alone. The dog was still dead, and she had nothing to do but take better care of the koi fish. "We'll help you find a new dog," Amelia said.

Amelia went to find Mindy before their class started. Corbin was still there, bagging up the trash bin in the lobby, which Amelia was sure her mother had asked him to do. She cringed for him – he wasn't a janitor.

Even so, his friend stood there talking with him in her hushed way, grinning at him like a fool. With his chiseled features, his shoulder-length hair pulled into a slick ponytail, the way women flocked to him, he could have been a celebrity in another lifetime. He could have been a rock star, or a bodyguard, or an actor, the one who played a thug, or bad guy. Except as soon as he spoke, you knew he wasn't a bad guy. He was that kind of guy who didn't even kill spiders. He was just a university professor who moonlighted as a massage therapist and screwed too many women – and even that he did with a conscience.

Sometimes he reminded her of her first boyfriend, Lenny, which mystified her because they were nothing alike in spirit. It was the build maybe, the strong arms and shoulders, the bravado. It might have been the way he screwed around. As much as it had baffled her at the time, Corbin had been clear and open about his intentions to screw around while Lenny only insisted on lying straight to her face. Honesty – it was more than she could say for most of the men she'd known.

Mindy had the room ready and was occupied with another guest. When Corbin's friend left, Amelia walked over. "You should ask my mom for more money."

"What do I need more money for? I can pay my rent, I can buy books. Your mom gives me free classes and spa time."

"A house?" she said. "Retirement? You need to start taking your future more seriously. Even Drew has an IRA, so I'm sure you could do it too." She'd meant this to be encouraging, but then she realized that as a part-time adjunct, with his occasional massage income, he was probably the only person alive who made less money than Drew.

"I don't want to retire," he said. "I love what I do. I'll do it until I'm old and feeble."

"And then what?"

"Maybe I'll give myself back to the earth." He held his hands, fingertip to fingertip over his belly. She couldn't take him seriously; he was like a studly Buddha.

"You know, someday you might want to settle down. Plant roots or something."

"I don't think roots are in the cards for me." There was a resigned acceptance in the way he said it. It aggravated her.

She shook her head at him. "There are no cards," she said. "You make the life you want to have."

"You really believe that?"

She shrugged. In her heart she hoped it was true, even if her life had proven otherwise so many times.

"You know what," he said. "If I ever have enough money to save for retirement, you can help me invest it."

It was the first time, even if theoretically, that he'd ever asked for her help. She stood a little taller. "Okay," she said. And since he seemed to know everything, maybe he knew this too. "So what does she mean by that? I haven't found my center?"

"She said that?"

Amelia nodded.

"Well one thing I've noticed, you don't stay in Corpse Pose long enough. You're too eager to rush into the next thing."

"I am not," she injected. She liked *Savasana* as much as anyone, the relaxing neutrality at the end of a practice. Then remembered the itch of just lying there, like a corpse, begging herself to just move and prove herself alive. No, he was right, she couldn't stand Corpse Pose. "And she said my speaking voice was tense. Is it?"

Corbin paused, considering his words. "Not all the time," he said. "But if you're happy, it doesn't matter. You look happy."

She always found that comment surprising, and it came from people more often than she expected it should. How unhappy did she normally look? But she just smiled. "I am happy," she said. She held up her hand, the diamond sparkling in the light. "We're engaged now."

"I know," he said. "Good for you. I'm happy for you both."

"You know?"

"Your mom. She talked about it the whole day when she found out."

Amelia's lips curved into a wry smile. "Of course she did."

Pregnant women started to gather in the studio, arching their backs and moaning and smiling at each other's bellies. Corbin went to the hallway, opening one of their supply closets. As he moved things around inside, Amelia saw him take out a modest wooden toolbox and set it on the floor. The toolbox was as old as she was herself. It was her father's toolbox, though Amelia had just as many memories of her mother using it, putting up shelves or coat hooks, assembling doll houses, or fixing a leaky faucet. "You should be careful with that," she told him.

He'd been perfectly careful; she knew that. "I mean, you don't have to do so much around here."

"Your father asked me to look after things for you both while he was away."

"Well you don't need to do that," she said. "We're fine here." Amelia and her mother took care of each other. They always had.

He stood solid, monolithic. "I gave him my word."

She didn't want to argue any more, and she didn't think he would relent either. So she just nodded to him once, and he took up the toolbox in both hands. She wasn't watching, but she heard him open the utility closet and slide the toolbox back onto a shelf.

It was time for class to start. This was so different from her day job, managing money, all the numbers and figures, reason, rules, order, standard, form. This part of her day was all release. But Amelia wasn't really sure why she decided to go for her teaching certification. Would she ever be that convincing? Would these women ever think she knew what she was talking about? It was Mindy who told her, "Involve the pregnancy – they want to hear this stuff. *Smile* down at your belly..." She said the word "smile" like it was a whole song in itself. Amelia repeated the words softly, but she didn't even convince herself.

Mindy went to her mat, and Amelia took her place beside her.

Amelia calculated the precise center of her mat and planted her feet there, solid through her legs, through her hips, through her hands folded over her chest. She raised her eyes across the room. "Namaste," Mindy said to the class. "Namaste," Amelia and the class answered back. The ring on her finger caught sunlight and sparkled, so heavy on her hand she wondered if it made her lopsided.

2.3: metamorphosis

"CAT'S OUT OF THE BAG," AMELIA HAD SAID TO HIM that morning. Since her mother knew about their engagement, he might as well tell his family now too. She had even emailed her father, and he'd already responded with congratulations. But Drew knew that a quick email just wouldn't do for Moira Weston-Dyer. He planned it strategically. Considering her excitement, he would try to catch her in the evening Tokyo time, which was early morning for him – she would be calmer, he hoped, having expended her energy all day. Amelia watched him raise the phone to his ear. That he was making a phone call at all was an event, and considering the news, Amelia stood by with a look of both concern and encouragement on her face.

Suddenly their long and comfortable engagement had turned into an onslaught of questions to be answered, dates to be picked, venues to be considered – and that was just from Amelia's side of the family so far. He wasn't quite prepared for this. Part of him hoped the voice mail would pick up, but no luck. It wasn't that he didn't love his mother – he loved her dearly – but to call his mother, it was necessary to take a deep breath of preparation first. It was always needed. She picked up. "Hello, dear."

"Mom, hi."

"Is everything alright?"

"Fine," he said. He didn't tell her about the engagement right away. First he let her talk for a few minutes about a *marvelous* sushi restaurant they went to, and how she'd learned to say a few more phrases in Japanese, and that Richard was very much enjoying his work. "That sounds good, Mom. And well, I guess I have some news."

"Oh? What is it, dear?"

Amelia had been listening quietly as she sliced some zucchini at the counter. He knew she'd been listening, because she knew just when to look over, as he declared it out loud. "Amelia and I are going to get married."

Moira's voice was instantly tight and animated. "Married? My baby's getting *married*? Oh, to hear such a thing over the *phone*. I wish I were there, darling. Oh, I just want to hug you both. That's magnificent! Oh, I'm so happy. I hope you bought her something nice. You picked out something nice, didn't you? Oh dear, how *did* you ask her?"

The lack of faith people had in him never failed to disappoint. But then the fumbling first proposal came to mind – in his dusty unused apartment bedroom, naked, no ring, and it hadn't even been a proper question. It was special in its own modest way, but it wasn't something his mother would have appreciated. "I took her out on the boat," he said.

"Oh, that sounds lovely. Is she there? I want to say 'congratulations'."

"She is," Drew said, glancing to Amelia from the kitchen's doorway. She'd already returned to the lasagna she was prepping, and she'd never looked more peaceful. He didn't want to bother her. "I'll tell her for you."

His mother's excited chatter continued in a flurry of wild squeals, promises, proclamations, the preludes to some grand event. She would throw them an engagement party. She and Richard were going to pop back home for the holidays anyway. It would be *extraordinary, darling*. His mother had grown up watching too much Audrey Hepburn and Elizabeth Taylor. She never got over it.

Drew tucked the phone closer to his ear, as if he could shield escaping sound with his hand. She finally finished with a soft sigh, as if having exhausted herself. "Oh, my baby's getting married," she said. "Richard says congratulations too. Did you tell your brother?"

"No, not yet."

"You have to call your brother. Do you ever call your brother? You should call him, darling. It hurts me that you boys don't talk more."

"I'll call him," Drew said. By "call" he meant email.

"I'll let you go then," she said. "I have plane tickets to book."

Drew ended the call, exhaling so hard that Amelia finally turned around to look at him, her face full of empathy. He wondered how much of it she'd heard. She smiled gently. "Everything okay?"

Okay? His mother was a tornado in pearls and Chanel. Was that okay? "She's coming to visit. She's planning an engagement party and bringing presents."

"Oh wow," Amelia said. "She doesn't have to do that. But I'll be happy to see her again too." People should have only been eager to greet his mother with a warning, a mental health release form, and a Valium – but Amelia only smiled. He was sure she didn't know what she was getting herself into.

It wasn't long before Drew's phone set off ringing again. It was his uncle this time, after exactly as long as it must have taken for his mother to call and share the news. She'd told him everything. "Well why don't you bring the girl around?" Uncle Mitch said. "If you're really going to marry her." It was half playful, and half like a challenge.

Drew avoided taking Amelia over there because his uncle had called her "that stuffy redhead with the tits." He claimed he'd never said that, but he had, at least twice – once while she was there at a family barbeque.

Drew took the sauce pan from her hands and reached his arms around her waist, taking refuge in that warm space between her throat and collarbone. He kissed her there. She smelled like organic lemongrass and ginseng. "My uncle wants us to visit," he mumbled into her skin. Her quiet resolve was comforting, her soft breath near his ear, her fingers behind his neck. She pulled her hand off his shoulder, onto his chest, glancing down at the ring on her finger, then back up to him, letting whatever thought she held disperse. A gentle smile, and she turned back to the lasagna.

"You know, we should bring some of this over for him. I can make some extra, it would be no trouble. You wanna help?"

He nodded, and she handed him a wooden spoon and the handle of a sauté pan full of diced onions.

She laughed. "None of my other boyfriends would ever cook with me. It's nice, isn't it?"

He'd known her for years now, and she still never talked about the men who came before him. It astounded him that she'd done all of this twice before, the long-term relationships, the domesticity. Prior to him, she'd had two other fully formed lives. He'd never lived with a woman before. The thought of her, not in this specific kitchen, but some other, with some other pair of hands helping her serve their dinner, was a strange thing to think about.

"Is that why you dumped them? They wouldn't cook with you?"

She went quiet. "No, not quite." He couldn't see her face the way they stood; he only heard her silence. She finally took a breath that came back out like a soft hum. "Hmmm, I don't know. They just didn't stick."

He waited for her to say more, but she didn't offer anything. So he helped her with the cooking. She handed him things and told him where they went and in what order. She even told him why. He could have lived on french fries before he met her, and now he knew red bell peppers contained more antioxidants than green ones, green tea more flavonoids than bottled beer. He knew what omega-3 was. He never knew he needed it, but she insisted he did. It wasn't about ideals or glamor. It was science. "It'll make you live forever," she said, then she began to laugh at the idea of it herself. "Okay, or at least a really long time."

He had a hot skillet in one hand, sizzling with oil, green peppers and minced garlic, and he had a wooden spoon in the other. "I didn't used to eat that bad, did I?"

"No, it's not that," she said. "I just want you to live a really long time." She turned her face down, smiling, her fingertips stroking his arm. He wondered if she'd ever looked that far ahead into her own future before.

UNCLE MITCH WAS NAPPING WHEN THEY ARRIVED THAT EVENING. Drew went to wake him while Amelia loaded his freezer with freshly-baked and portioned lasagna. She made a whole pan for him, and even wrote out thawing instructions for him to follow. Drew vetoed her idea to make the garlic bread from scratch – his uncle would eat the frozen loaf from the grocery store just fine.

"He'll be out in a minute," Drew told her. They waited in front of the fireplace in the den. He offered her the chair opposite his uncle's favorite chair, but she was busy inspecting the walls, mounted model submarines and battleships, and one large portrait of the sinking USS Arizona at Pearl Harbor, the wreckage of oblique metal and plumes of heavy gray smoke. Family photos were lined proudly along the mantle – they were the only photos Uncle Mitch kept in his whole house. One of Mitch and the girls, holding one by each hand, and little Drew sitting up on top of his shoulders. Drew must have been four or five, skinny with a thick mop of dark hair on his head. Among the bunch of them, with their fair eyes and wheat-brown hair, he might have seemed stolen from some other family. There were just as many of Drew as there were of Anna and Leslie, all of their baby photos, first communions, proms and graduations. One of his ex-wife, Irene, but probably only because his children were in it. Drew at his mother's wedding to Richard, dressed in a miniature white suit. Drew's little brother, Fenton as a baby, being passed around by Anna and Leslie, who were nine and eleven at the time and held him like a toy doll. Uncle Mitch had no pictures of his ex-wife's new husband.

Amelia had found a photo taken at Fenton's high school graduation. "I'll never have a sister," she said.

Drew hadn't been expecting that – not just the comment, but all the disappointment hanging on it. Like it needed an apology.

"Because you have a brother," she clarified, her voice perking up. "So I'll have a brother-in-law. What's he like?"

A half-brother, Richard's real son. He'd been studying abroad for nearly three years now and was the only one Amelia hadn't met. "Ha, he's emotional and moody. Spoiled."

Amelia grinned. "More moody and spoiled than you?"

"Really, you have no idea."

Amelia leaned in to examine some of the photos closer.

"My parents' wedding," he said.

"Your mom and Richard?"

It always felt odd to use the term "parents" at all, but there was no other term for a combined mother and step-father, was there? "Yeah," he said. "It was just a little weird. All the different names. I'm a Weston, my mother's maiden name. Fenton's a Dyer, after

Richard. And then my mom became a Weston-Dyer. And when my Aunt Irene moved Anna and Leslie away, they all took back her maiden name. You'd think none of us were even related at all."

Amelia still poked around the mantle, looking at model submarines and Navy ships. Uncle Mitch's arrival was announced with the soft shuffle of his loafers on the floor and his cane, a single, pronounced thud with each step.

"Hello, there," Uncle Mitch said, standing in the doorway with his cane. He pointed up at the portrait hanging over the mantle. "You know I was just a baby when Pearl Harbor happened," he said. "Still just a boy when we fought Korea." Mitch gazed off at his wall of model ships, and he patted Amelia's shoulder twice and let his hand rest there. "And well, nobody's disappointed they didn't get to serve in Vietnam." She didn't shrug off his hand, though she was tense. Her version of tense looked like poise to anyone else. She listened to his chatter. Hopefully he wouldn't start talking about the communists. "Drew tells me your father is a military man?"

Drew felt his face fall stricken – the inevitability of age, the relentlessness of the toll it took – Uncle Mitch had asked her this question before. But Amelia only smiled politely and answered it again. "Yes, sir, he is. Air Force. He served in the first Gulf War, and he's over there again now. He's a contractor this time though."

Mitch nodded. "And you're an accountant?"

"Yes, sir. I am."

This was a new question. He was going to ask her to balance his bank book, wasn't he? Drew felt inclined to protest on her behalf, but if she wasn't going to, then he wouldn't either. Drew knew it was his uncle's way of accepting her into the family, trying to get her to do work for him for free.

"If you don't mind helping an old man out, would you mind trying to make sense of something for me?"

"You don't have to," Drew said to Amelia. "I could do it."

"Oh, I don't mind," Amelia said. Of course she didn't mind here, to his face. Drew would have to ask her later what she really thought.

"You do enough, son," Mitch said. "And I'll bet she's better with money."

"I don't mind at all," Amelia said, and Uncle Mitch showed her to his study, a small, dreary room off the main hallway. She sat behind his desk, taking a quick inventory of the books and files.

"Has he ever shown you around the house?"

"A bit," Amelia said. But no, he hadn't really, apart from these couple of rooms.

"Well, I'd show you around myself, dear, but this knee," he said, taking his cane and tapping his leg with it. "You know, it was the reason I couldn't join the Coast Guard. Did you ever climb on lakeshore rocks when you were little?"

"No, sir."

"Better you didn't. They're slippery bastards, that wet algae growing on them. It tore the ligaments and cartilage and some other parts I forget the names of. It's never been the same since."

"And then he grew up to become a lawyer instead," Drew added, throwing his arm around his uncle's shoulder. "He says he's miserable, but he made a lot more money than he would have in the Coast Guard."

Amelia smiled politely, and Uncle Mitch roared out a hearty laugh.

Leaving his uncle to rest in the den, Drew led Amelia off to show her the parts of the house she hadn't seen before. He showed her the living room, where large patio doors cast the only natural light in the house, leading out to the back yard and a patio garden where most of the plants were struggling to live. The kitchen and library she'd already seen. He took her to the unused second story, the wooden staircase leading up to it with its fully functioning light bulbs.

"It's a lot of house for one man," Amelia said.

Uncle Mitch couldn't even get to these rooms anymore, but Anna and Leslie had kids and came back to visit once or twice a year. Moira and Richard stayed here too when they weren't jet-setting around the corporate world. The hallways upstairs were dark and polished slick, carrying the ghostly echoes of childhood, running footsteps and laughter.

"You don't have to be *so* polite, you know."

She smiled at him – her lazy and careful smile, the real one. "Of course I do," she said.

"You don't have to do it. I'll find him someone new around here soon." There was a to-do list running in his head that only got longer and longer – a new housekeeper for his uncle, his mother asked him to find a local caterer for the engagement party, and Jodie had declined all of the roommates they'd found for her so far. He had to admit, it would be easier if Amelia helped with the banking. One less thing to take care of.

"It's fine," she said. "He probably wouldn't trust someone new anyway."

And she meant it, he knew. He could imagine her going starry-eyed over the leather-bound account ledger, with all those numbers to be put back in balance. She started to wander down the hallway, stepping first into a pink bedroom with balloons on the bedding. "I'm going to guess this one wasn't yours," she said with a wry smile.

There had been wooden dollhouses in this room until a few years ago, when Anna's daughters were finally old enough to play with them, and she took them back to Omaha with her. "Anna and Leslie shared this one," he said. "They used to make me go to their tea parties, and they'd tie my uncle's neck ties around my neck and make me pull out their chairs for them."

Amelia grinned and he grimaced at himself. He couldn't believe he'd told her that.

"That sounds really fun," she said. "I never had anything like that growing up. My mom wasn't exactly the playful type."

She took his hand and pulled him to another room, and this one was his. "Nothing exciting," Drew said as she took in the bedroom with its generic blue painted walls and a border through the middle of white stenciled sailboats, just as stripped bare as Anna and Leslie's room was. All his childhood things were stored in Richard's house now, having either been passed down to Fenton or put into storage, and all that was left here was what he needed for summer visits, a bed and dresser and a few toys. Drew had stayed here again shortly after college, when he added a few posters and some beer stains to the carpet, and the cigarette burns on the curtains were from Fenton – the summer Fenton was fourteen and Drew was twenty – when he'd lean close to the window so their mom wouldn't smell the smoke. Fenton had still been a little boy when Drew left for college, and then he was suddenly a little man, with a patchy mustache on his upper lip and a cigarette between his fingers.

Amelia knelt in front of his toy box and opened it, picking through some wooden blocks, Matchbox cars, toy airplanes, and an old stuffed rabbit. Every time he stepped into this room, no matter what else had gone on here, he could only think of packing it up when he was six.

He vaguely remembered the weeks after his mother married Richard. He even got to be the ring bearer in their wedding, and he hadn't dropped the rings or tripped down the aisle or anything he was dreading he might do. Until then, Drew and his mother lived with his uncle's family, so when she and Richard went off on their honeymoon, Drew considered for a moment that maybe she was leaving him behind. He was six, and it was a perfectly reasonable assessment at the time.

"She's not leaving you, boy," his uncle explained to him. "But things are going to change."

So after he was assured that his mother wasn't leaving him, Drew learned that he and his mother wouldn't be living here anymore – no more long dark hallways to run through, no more climbing the rocks on the patio (though his uncle always hated when he climbed the rocks on the patio). Uncle Mitch, with his bad knee, could never stoop down low the way some grownups did, to look the child in the eyes as they talked on the same level. Instead he stood beside little Drew, placing his large hand over the top of Drew's full mop of hair, the heaviness of that hand like an anchor. "They're coming back in ten days," he said. "We have to pack up your room so you'll be ready to move your things into Richard's house."

Richard's house was near Chicago, which at the age of six, very well might have been the other side of the planet. Drew remembered that the excruciating four-hour drives to visit him there were impossibly long. He couldn't fill enough coloring books, he couldn't count enough white cars. It had never occurred to him that he'd be the one moving. He just assumed that Richard would move to Grosse Pointe, and they'd all live in Uncle Mitch's big, dark house. There was room enough for everyone, so why not? Drew couldn't think of a happier scenario.

So while his mother and Richard honeymooned in the Bahamas, Drew's childhood bedroom was disassembled, portioned out, sorted and boxed, the shelves and drawers emptied out and dusted clean, like his whole existence was being erased. Anna and Leslie fought with each other over what the room would become next – a doll sanctuary, a stuffed animal farm? "Don't be foolish," Uncle Mitch told them. "It will stay. He'll need a place to sleep when he comes back to visit."

In those days, Uncle Mitch was still a lawyer, so it was mostly his Aunt Irene who had the duty of helping Drew pack his things.

"It's not normal," she explained to him one afternoon as she packed. "A grown woman like your mother, being so dependent on her brother's family. You're going to have a *normal* family now." She said it happily, like it was cause for celebration. The tight wrinkles around her eyes creased with her glee. Little Drew just shrugged his shoulders and glanced away from her, down to the stuffed rabbit he held by its head. But his aunt Irene was still staring at him, the wrinkles around her eyes not gleeful anymore, but slack. "You poor boy," she added, "This is what your mother should have done the first time. Then you wouldn't have to be going through all of this."

Amelia held the stuffed rabbit in her hands, turning it over carefully, inspecting the broken seam on its leg, its stuffing showing. "This looks well-loved. You didn't want to take it to Chicago?"

It had been his favorite stuffed animal when he was little – he couldn't remember having decided to leave it behind, or why. He leaned his cheek to her shoulder. "Ha, who knows. Maybe I got too old for rabbits that year."

She placed the rabbit back inside the toy box, sat upright with its arms on its lap, and she patted its plush head before she lowered the lid.

THOSE FIRST FEW WEEKS OF THEIR ENGAGEMENT, THERE WAS something tender and newborn about the time they spent at home, alone. Home was a delicate cocoon where they'd toss between sheets, lie on couches and kiss, as they transformed over the weeks from one thing into something else. It was a phase that needed privacy and protection, to be kept away from the prying eyes, the judgments, and the skepticism.

The fall weekends were too cold and rainy to spend on the lake, or outside grilling with friends and family, so instead the two of them lay on the couch in front of cable movies they'd each seen a dozen times before. They weren't sure if they wanted to invite company over or not. He'd already taken a few minutes to check his email, and then he fell asleep on the couch while Amelia talked to her mom, for what turned into nearly two hours.

He didn't dream, just a blink of darkness and her voice in the background. Then she'd hung up the phone, and knelt there beside the couch to wake him. Outside it had stopped raining – who knew if it might rain again later? She took the small space in front of him on the couch, leaning over to rest her cheek on his head. "You wanna walk over to the park and get some hot cocoa?"

"We'd have to get dressed," he said. He groaned and stretched his legs hard over the edge of the couch.

"Hmmm," she hummed. "I can make some coffee here instead. We should have some dinner too. You want to invite some people over?"

She had her fingertips in his hair. He could have fallen asleep again like that, but his erection wanted something else entirely. She wore yoga pants that hugged her curves and a tank top that dipped down low as she propped herself up on her elbows. "Nah, we'd have to get dressed."

They'd get dressed some other time. He snuck his fingertips under her shirt and traced circles around her belly button, and they whispered to each other about anything and nothing at all. He pulled her body closer and they kissed, stretched out long on the couch. They made lazy love on the couch, then they fell asleep again, arms and legs entangled, wearing nothing but their t-shirts and socks.

The afternoon turned into evening. They never did get dressed. Amelia ran them a bath, lighting candles to place around the sink and windowsills. He couldn't place the scent, so he picked one up, the label on the bottom reading "spring rain" over the bar code. The laundry baskets were made of hemp and the curtains were made of bamboo.

Drew slipped into the water behind her. He pulled the tangle of her long curls together and swept it over her shoulder. She let him touch her hair when it was wet, or when she was sleeping, when she was least concerned the curls might fluff or frizz. She let her head sway, heavy on her neck, her eyes closed and lips smiling.

"What are you thinking about?"

"Not work," she said.

He touched a wet finger to her nose and whispered near her ear. "I think I'll write a poem about this freckle."

She smiled. "I dare you."

He wanted to write her something beautiful. It would be a poem about that freckle on her left cheekbone, same honey-brown as her eyes. He raced through words in his head, but they stumped him. He leaned to kiss the center of her back instead, there between her shoulder blades, and he composed a poem – not the kind he could ever publish, not the kind he would ever call beautiful – but the kind that rhymed a little and would hopefully make her laugh. "My lover has a freckled nose. / I asked her, 'Are those on your toes?' / She was wearing long socks, / so I said, 'Take them off!' / And that's how I got her unclothed."

She rolled her head back on his shoulder and giggled.

"All that time I was trying to woo you," he said. "I should have tried the limericks sooner."

"You never needed to woo me."

"You told me you were only interested in friendship."

"I still am," she said. She held his hand in hers, twisting in the water to rest her cheek on his chest." You're my best friend in the world. I've never felt loved before you." She smiled when she said it, but the crippling disappointment in her voice proved it was not dramatics, it was no plea for sympathy – it was simply the truth. She'd never really been loved.

He whispered near her ear, "You don't have to worry about that anymore."

She still had his hand in hers, her fingers tracing up and down the length of his. "I think we should make the spare room into an office for you, for some writing space."

"Yeah?" His response was enthusiastic, so much so that he hoped she wasn't insulted by it. It was just that he'd finished moving over the last of his things from his old apartment and finally turned in his keys. It was odd for him, having no place of his own anymore, nowhere to go that wasn't hers. This mossy green bathroom, it was fine, but it was all her, natural earth tones and organic bamboo. The well-structured kitchen with its ordered pantry and French Bistro table set, that was all her. It was everything she loved, and she'd spent the past two years putting it together. His first week there, she let him put some of his magazines on her coffee table in the living room, and it was the only thing in this whole house that he felt had his mark on it. "I think I would like that," he said.

She rolled in the water and turned her face into his neck. The way she held his arms around her body, to her body, was like she was trying to fuse the two of them together. She couldn't look at him the way they sat, and she didn't try to turn. "I never didn't want to marry you," she said. "That wasn't it, exactly." He knew she didn't like to talk about these things. She didn't need to remember, didn't want to remember. She receded into a thought then, a sad one. "Because you wanted to know," she started, keeping her eyes to the water, holding on to him tighter then, whether she realized it or not. "Lenny, he cheated on me, three times. He eventually left me for one of them. And Eric, after living together for so long, he just wanted to get married. A week after we broke up, he met the woman he ended up marrying. Like he never even meant it. I knew he never meant it." She pulled herself up then, her eyes meeting his. "I thought all those second chances would be the death of me."

He'd seen it the first day he met her, all the wounds, all the rejections, all the scars, the doubt, and the fear. "No," he said. He leaned down to her forehead, placing his lips to it, a kiss, a promise that carried more weight and responsibility than he'd ever needed to bear before.

2.4: measuring tape

PIPER'S SEWING ROOM WAS FILLED WITH CHAIRS – DINING ROOM chairs carried upstairs, camp chairs that still smelled like campfire, two rolling office chairs stolen from other rooms. Amelia and Jodie sat on two plastic lawn chairs in the corner as Piper's frenzied sisters and nieces circled the room around them, dresses hanging on door knobs and railings, bolts of lavender and buttercream fabric pulled out and bunched up on the floor. Piper had told them both how much she loved this house. She'd taken the whole sunlit hallway on the second floor for her sewing space, with bright windows and hardwood floors, and along each wall were shelves holding bolts of fabric and boxes of trimmings. Piper said they picked it out just for that space at the top of the stairway, for those bright airy windows that looked out on their yard. Tom wouldn't have known what to do with the space, but Piper had it all planned out. "When we have kids," she said. "I'll gate off the stairs and they'll all run around here, playing in their rooms, and I can be out here working on my designs."

Amelia hadn't asked how many kids Piper wanted, but the way she described it, there would be a whole brood of them.

There were twenty-three women in the house – Piper's sisters and nieces, two aunts and her mother, and Tom was nowhere to be seen. Piper measured the span of shoulders, the circumference of waists, the lengths of legs, writing each onto a single page of notebook paper, and all Amelia could think was, *That page is definitely going to get lost*. Piper insisted on making all of these dresses, which made them wonder if she wasn't just a little bit crazy. "I've had this wedding planned since I was five years-old," she said to them as she measured. "I know exactly what the bridesmaid's dresses look like, and I've never seen these in the stores."

"That doesn't make me want to wear one," Jodie whispered to Amelia, snickering to herself.

Amelia laughed a little too. It was true, and she was nervous to see what the dresses would look like finished. From the sketches, all she could tell was that they'd have wide tulle skirts in the shade of buttercream, with accents of lavender. On the model Piper had sketched in her notebook, the hair had been piled up on top of her head in a mess Amelia couldn't begin to imagine how she'd duplicate. The dress though, from what Amelia could tell so far, would be on the odd side of a standard bridesmaid dress – Amelia had worn much stranger things than that at Piper's hand before.

But Piper's sisters wanted to "see" the dress.

"Okay, I can do that," Piper said. "Amelia." Piper waved her over, gathering up an armful of fabric, buttercream yellow, and held it up against her cheek, nodding proudly at her choice. "Like this," Piper said, picking up Amelia's arms. Amelia was used to this, being picked at and turned, asked to raise her arms higher or lower, or to try something on *just one more time*. She could hardly remember how she became Piper's personal living mannequin, but she knew it started some time back in college. Amelia was never particularly shy or self-conscious about her body, not terribly averse to being touched, and as Piper had told her once, "You just stand well."

So Amelia turned at Piper's prodding, as the fabric was pulled taut around her waist, pinned in the back, and the bolt rolled out. Piper took the length of it into her hands. "Semi-strapless, like this," Piper narrated, wrapping a band of fabric around Amelia's chest and up over one shoulder. "And then imagine this a full, billowy skirt. To the knee?" Piper asked herself the question like she hadn't really decided yet.

Amelia looked down to her legs where Piper held the fabric, trying to imagine that she wasn't wearing pants underneath, and that it was spring. She'd be barefoot maybe, toenails painted gold. "And here will be the lavender belt," Piper said.

Piper stopped then, dropping the fabric from her hands and letting the faux gown unravel. She took Amelia's hands into hers and went bright-eyed, "You're engaged too," she squealed and turned to her sisters. "She's getting married too," she told them, declaring this now as if she'd only just heard the news. Amelia blushed as all those eyes turned on her, echoing soft *ahhhs*.

"Have you picked a date?" Piper asked. "Have you picked colors? Will you wear a floor-length or tea-length gown? Indoor or outdoor? Afternoon or evening? Spring, summer, fall?"

The questions made Amelia's head overload, her breath quickened and her hands went clammy with sweat – was this how people had panic attacks? She hadn't thought about any of it. She was getting married, it was a big deal, wasn't it? Amelia took a deep breath and answered, "We're having a long engagement."

Piper nodded. "Oh, that's *fine*, but it's never too early to start planning."

Piper took the unraveled fabric back and tossed it on a chair, bringing back the measuring tape to finish Amelia's measurements. Piper's sisters came in and out of the room, carrying plastic cups filled with pinot noir, their tiny barefooted daughters carrying slices of pizza in hand. Amelia imagined the greasy fingerprints left all over the banister and wanted to hand them paper towels. Piper's oldest sister, the one with the deep, harrowing eyes and long brown hair left to go gray, began to sort the strewn fabric Piper had tossed onto the chair and the floor. Amelia couldn't remember any of their names.

"Oh, and I bought you all *brooches* to wear in your hair," Piper said.

"Oh no," Jodie moaned. "I hate doing things with my hair."

"You shouldn't have, Piper," Amelia said. "How can you afford that?"

"No worries, Tom gave me one of his credit cards."

"Really? Already?"

"What do you mean already?" Piper grinned, leaning in close to whisper. "My name's on the mortgage already too – don't tell my grandma."

"Oh, I don't know, it just seemed quick. You're right though."

Amelia had been so hesitant to even share the household bills. She'd certainly be keeping her bank accounts separate. They'd only been living together for six weeks – didn't she have time to make up her mind? Did married couples absolutely need to have pooled money? Her mind sorted through the questions of joint living. Would they buy a car together? Have a joint checking account? Should she put his name on the mortgage, and when? After the wedding, or before? When they were married, would they file taxes jointly? She'd lived with plenty of men before, but she'd never been engaged to marry any of them. Close, maybe. Maybe it looked similar, the shared address, shared meals, but wasn't it quite different? Relationships ended so easily, but wasn't an engagement – all those promises made – harder to walk away from in the end?

Piper didn't seem to worry about much of it at all.

Amelia raised her arms as Piper wrapped fabric around her

waist. Piper had a knowing grin on her face. "You're making him sign a pre-nup, aren't you?"

Another thing Amelia hadn't been prepared to consider yet. "We haven't talked about it," Amelia said. "Maybe." Amelia knew full well that she hadn't even consulted Drew in this decision yet. In her mind, she imagined him being offended by the idea. But she also felt herself suddenly very naïve for not considering all that disaster could happen to them too.

Eric flashed through her mind. How stupid she'd been to end up with most all of their credit card debt. At least she'd kept the TV and living room set they bought on an impulse, twenty-two with new shiny plastic in their hands. Any hesitation in her better judgment had been squelched by his eager desire to start building their life together, a matching living room set and brand new forty-eight inch TV. They weren't even engaged. She'd only just graduated from college. Even though Drew was nothing like the others, she heard her mother's voice in her head. *He's a nice enough boy, Amelia, but how does he plan to contribute to this life you're building together?* Her mother was always so stoic, always so practical. Amelia could only hope to grow so wise herself some day. If Amelia had been so practical when she'd been dating Eric, they never would have split those credit cards. If she had been so practical when she was dating Lenny, all those years she dated Lenny never would have happened at all.

"I know the best kind of pre-nup," Jodie chimed in from the corner. "Don't get married." Jodie cackled at herself, a sharp laugh that seemed directed at all their wedding talk.

"Okay," Piper said to her. "Next." She held up the measuring tape with a devious grin.

"Huh? Oh, are we doing me now?"

Jodie stepped to the center of the room with a frown, and Piper held the fabric to her body. With the yellow tulle draped over her shoulder, in all this light, her skin looked deathly sallow. "Oh, Jodie." Piper shook her head in disappointment. "You *can't* wear buttercream."

Jodie turned back to Amelia, and Amelia covered the grimace on her face. It was true. Jodie couldn't wear that shade – not if she wanted to look alive, anyway.

"Wait," Piper said, picking up the bolt of fabric her sister had brought over, a soft shade of lavender. "Maybe if we reversed them?" Piper handed Amelia the bolt as she pulled out an armful of it. It draped between the two of them like a banner.

"Yes," Amelia said. "That's much better."

She and Piper laughed as they spun Jodie up in the fabric. Jodie stood stiff, hands on her hips. Piper raised one corner of it to Jodie's scowling face, holding the fabric against her cheek so they could consider it. The color brought out soft silvery tones in Jodie's skin – not so dark it made her look gothic, not so pale it blended in. Piper looked to Amelia for confirmation. It was true. Amelia nodded. "That looks much better."

"It's so... purple," Jodie said.

"It's not *purple*," Piper said, shaking her head. "It's lavender, and it's tremendous."

Jodie laughed. "It's what?"

"It won't wash you out," Amelia added.

"Right," Piper said. "So I'll do buttercream on most of the dresses, and lavender on Jodie's. That's okay, right? Maid of Honor is allowed to be a little different."

Amelia watched Jodie smile slightly as Piper unwrapped her from the drapery of lavender tulle, feeling a little forlorn sting at how close they'd become in just a few years. Amelia already knew Piper had chosen Jodie to be her Maid of Honor – with all the sisters Piper had, Amelia hadn't even considered Piper might choose her instead. But she couldn't help wondering how far down the list she'd been. Amelia had known Piper since college, but in all that time, as Amelia was falling in and out of love, Jodie and Piper were living together every day like sisters.

In the three years Amelia dated Eric, Amelia had never met his parents, but Amelia remembered the day he introduced her to Jodie. If she ever told him she wanted to meet his family, he'd say, "This *is* my family." There was a quick ease in the way she received Jodie, unlike any other female relationship she'd known. Jodie was her boyfriend's sister – Amelia didn't need to be jealous or fearful of their affections. And not only that, but Jodie actually seemed to like the idea of Amelia and Eric together. Amelia was cynical enough to enjoy Jodie's snarky banter. Jodie seemed detached enough to honor Amelia's need for space. And in that understanding, something was born. Not a sisterhood, but close to it. Not a friendship, but serving the same purpose. They were allies for a time, brought together by their bonds with this one man.

Being alone again had been a strange thing to get used to after having had Eric so fully integrated into her life. Eric moved out fast, taking whatever was certainly his, and leaving her with the credit cards, most of the furniture, and the rent payment she could just barely cover on her own.

There were eight weeks left on the apartment lease Eric had left her, and Amelia should have felt comfortable enough on her own. But instead, she found herself making excuses to stay over at Jodie and Piper's place. Instead of sleeping in the bed they once shared, she watched sappy cable movies with Piper, drinking too much wine as an excuse not to have to drive back home to that empty apartment with all its contents split in half. She would borrow a pair of Jodie's pajamas and a sheet from Piper to lay over the couch, a fluffy pink blanket and extra pillows. She'd set an alarm clock on her phone to wake up in the morning for work. She felt like they were in college all over again, like the life Amelia should have been living in her early-twenties, instead of failing at so many years of "playing house." It felt like this should have been the freedom to rewrite her life all over again.

But instead, some nights, it felt like panic. She'd gotten a call from Eric earlier in the day. He said he was just checking up on her. He sounded so fine. It pained her that he had sounded so fine. And after Piper had taken herself up to bed, Amelia was still awake, alone, with her knees pulled to her chest, a sappy Lifetime movie on TV, and she tried to tell herself the movie was the reason she was crying. She wiped her eyes dry and breathed off whatever residual sadness might be left over. Like the cleansing exhale between mountain pose and the standing forward fold, long and deep. The movie was about a woman going through a divorce. In the weeks it took to separate all of their stuff, their furniture and belongings, their shared photo albums in the meticulous way he kept them, Amelia felt like she was going through a divorce of her own.

Amelia was still sniffling when Jodie came home. "The movie," she said, before Jodie had even mentioned it. "I don't know why I watch these things."

Jodie had been in her residency then, returning at odd hours of the night in her scrubs and dark rims under her eyes. She wore her hair longer then, pulled together in a heavy ponytail that hung straight down her back. Jodie didn't ask her what was wrong, or why – maybe she already knew why – she just sat down on the couch with her, talking absently about the two women who delivered that night. In those weeks after the breakup, the two of them were tense together – when a three-year relationship ended, who got custody of the mutual friends? It seemed at some point, a decision would have to be made, one way or the other. "Eric seems to be taking things well," Amelia said to her.

Jodie shrugged, her body rigid as if she'd been caught doing something wrong. "He's a guy. Maybe that's just how guys are?"

Amelia hadn't meant to burden her with any of that – it wasn't her problem, and it wasn't her fault. Amelia had rejected his marriage proposal first, but that Eric had hardly flinched at their breakup felt like a rejection in itself. "Well, I'm happy for him," Amelia offered.

It was a lie, and Jodie seemed to know it. She shrugged. "My brother's a doofus anyway," she said. "You want some ice cream or something?"

Amelia nodded, and Jodie got up to scoop two bowls of ice cream. A decision had been made. They ate ice cream together, and they finished watching that Lifetime movie, laughing at the melodrama, mocking the bad dialogue, each of them pretending they had no intentions of crying at the sad parts.

THEY HAD FINISHED UNWRAPPING JODIE FROM ALL THAT TULLE, rolling it back up around its bolt and placing it on the shelf next to Piper's sewing machine. Piper's sisters and nieces had gone back downstairs to overwhelm Tom's house, which had probably never seen so many women before.

Amelia had been talking to one of Piper's sisters, but as she ran off after a little girl chasing a scared cat, Amelia noticed how quiet it had become as all those bodies cleared out one by one. Amelia overheard a blip of Jodie talking to Piper about her brother, about how he and Ruth were already trying for a baby. Amelia was shocked at how easily time progressed for others while she felt like every little change in her own life was wrought with such struggle. Eric was married now and trying for a baby. "It's not that fast though, he's known her five years now," Jodie said to Piper.

Amelia's attention perked. Five years? That couldn't be right. He'd told her he met Ruth the week after they broke up. Amelia counted back the years in her head, one, two, three, and a half.

How could he have known Ruth for five years when they hadn't even been broken up for four yet?

There was a hiss from another room, and a little girl started to cry. "Oh no, the cat," Piper said, turning to run downstairs and sort out the scuffle.

Jodie's attention was free then. Amelia hadn't meant to listen so closely, or to stare so intently. Jodie looked nervous. The two of them each waited for the other to speak first, to say something, to change the subject. But Amelia couldn't get this off her mind. "I didn't know he knew her so long," Amelia said. It was always a mystery to her how well he took their breakup, almost too good to believe. Amelia hadn't understood it at the time. They had loved each other, hadn't they? Even if it wasn't meant to be? And as sure a thing as it had once seemed, they were just as soon portioning out their things, dividing up that eagerly unified life they'd started.

Jodie stammered. "Oh, I wasn't going to say anything. It doesn't even matter."

"What?"

Amelia felt it coming. She knew what it meant. She'd been through this before. *Don't worry about it, she's just a friend*, one minute. And, *I think I might love her*, the next.

"Just, he knew her when he knew you – that's all. You guys were practically broken up by then. It was just a matter of saying it out loud."

Amelia caught her breath, searching Jodie's eyes. She couldn't find any words to say. Eric had asked her to marry him – were they practically broken up by then? "Is that how he saw it? Is that how you saw it?"

"You've got Drew now," Jodie added. "You're happy, right? So it doesn't matter."

"What doesn't matter?"

"I mean, it's not the same thing as cheating." Jodie's eyes insisted the statement, but no matter how much Amelia tried, she couldn't buy it. Jodie couldn't take it back. Amelia knew the truth now and it changed everything she thought she knew about the way her relationship with Eric had ended. They hadn't broken up mutually after all. His marriage proposal had been exactly the polite business offering it had felt like; he hadn't wanted her to accept it. And when she'd declined it, he'd left her. He already had someone else lined up to take her place. He'd done exactly what Lenny did, only with better intentions and a smooth cover. Wasn't it all just the same?

Jodie shifted her weight, crossing her arms over her chest quickly, like she didn't know what to do with her hands, the way she did when she was nervous, when she'd gotten herself into more trouble than she could carry. "Hell, it's hot up here," she said, nodding her head toward the staircase, and started off after the rest of them, leaving Amelia to follow.

But Amelia's feet couldn't move from where she stood. Had she known it the whole time? And if she'd been keeping that secret for so long, what else might she be hiding? Of course she would keep Eric's secrets; they were family. Whatever small friendship Amelia might have had with Jodie was trumped by that. Whatever small alliance they once made was cut short. So easily severed. So easily turned to nothing. One minute they were friends, soon-to-be sisters, and then they were just the leftovers of a union that had failed to happen.

2.5: stories about lighthouses

EVEN IN THEIR MORE FRIENDLY DAYS, JODIE NEVER expected a visit from Berges on the first floor at Rainbow Women's Care. He did so only once, and she was there behind the reception window to watch him cringe at the pink floral wallpaper, the embroidered pillows on the lobby sofas, breastfeeding mothers and snotty-nosed toddlers, any of which might be singing songs or crying or both sometimes. It was too much estrogen for even Jodie.

Usually, he would have sent a quick text or called her cell. Especially when he ordered lunch for his office staff – they rarely ate much of it, those pencil-thin Barbie dolls. So if he knew Jodie was working, he'd text her something like:

`You hungry? These girls don't eat food.`

Jodie would text back:

`I think they're actually store mannequins.`

He responded:

`No. Have comm sci degrees. I checked.`
`Right, point made.`

Then Jodie would dash upstairs whenever she found a minute to grab a wrapped tuna sandwich, which he would have autographed with a dirty picture or perverse joke.

The other doctors in her practice hated him, and they looked sternly down their noses at Jodie when she'd been caught talking to him in the parking lot, like studious big sisters, shaking their heads, maybe deciding to take back her place on the team. The nurses hated him too, seething at Jodie, "He won't date you, you know." As if Jodie would presume so much. She wouldn't dare tell them what had happened at the wedding. How many of them had he slept with and not called? Or more likely, flirted profusely with and not taken to bed?

She didn't think she'd ever get another text from him, but one afternoon, he finally sent one:

`I have something for you.`

She chuckled to herself, typing into her phone:

`Let me guess, seven inches and ready to go?`

She wished she could hear him laugh, that sudden and powerful bark of his. Instead she imagined it in her head. He didn't give her any indication whether he found it funny or not, just replied:

`Not that. Come up when you're done. I'll be here.`

Rainbow Women's Care took their final appointments that day at 4:45, and Jodie didn't have one scheduled that evening. Berges's office was usually open later, which she remembered him telling her Kate was never fond of. Many of his clients were working professionals though, and he wanted to cater for them. Jodie stepped up the stairs to the second floor. She peeked into his waiting room through the glass door, semi-frosted except for a few clear squares in the geometric pattern. She could see Dana behind the reception window, a lovely brunette with long, shiny, bouncy hair, an elegant nose, high cheekbones, and striking blue eyes. Berges never really went for the blond and bubbly type. He kept the most glamorous receptionists in there, and Jodie didn't know how Kate ever stood for that. Jodie assumed she'd demand that he keep someone much less attractive.

Though history had also proven that Berges never budged much to Kate's demands – until the day she asked for a divorce.

Jodie leaned closer to the glass, trying to make out whose shape stood behind Dana. She tried to maneuver her head to guide her line of sight around a large woman checking out.

"Peep," a tiny voice spoke behind her.

Jodie jumped back, slamming her elbow on the door jamb as she turned, throwing a scowl at Piper. "Fuck me," she said, clenching her elbow. "What are you trying to do to me?" Piper didn't have a car of her own, but the coffee shop where she worked was three blocks from Jodie's office, and Piper hitched a ride when their schedules matched. So Jodie would usually expect a visit from Piper this time of evening, but not up here on the second floor.

Piper laughed. "What are *you* doing? Surveillance?"

"No," Jodie huffed.

"He'll meet you at the bar then, tomorrow night, seven o'clock," Piper said. He, who? Jodie searched her brain finding no reference. "I told him you'd be wearing black," Piper added. "You probably will, right?"

The date. It was still happening, despite Jodie's hopes that it would have fallen through by now. She sighed. "Probably, or gray."

Then the door opened behind them. It was Berges.

He glanced between the two of them. "Is the party in the hallway then?" He smiled at Piper, and it was an ambitious one at that. "Hi, Piper, how are you?"

Piper grinned. "They have Skittles in the vending machine up here."

"Taste the rainbow," Berges said, sweeping a hand in front of him. "Come on. Skittles all around, on me."

Jodie hated Skittles. She stayed by the door as Piper followed Berges into the small alcove where the vending machine lit up the hallway with its bluish glow. Piper's engagement ring wasn't an obvious one, but Berges did know she was engaged. It wouldn't stop him from flirting with her though, or her from giggling at him like a fool. Was he really handsome enough to be giggled over? Jodie rolled her eyes at the idea of it.

They came back down the hallway, a bag of Skittles in her hands, a bag of Utz BBQ Pork Rinds in his, the fatty flesh of a dead animal, fried. Jodie's stomach started to turn, eying the bag in his hand to the point where he noticed, held it up and inspected it himself.

"You know they're better for you than potato chips? All protein."

All protein and spiced and meaty. She smelled them already, even though the bag was still sealed – or maybe she had an overactive imagination. Her body retched and she needed to step back for air. How many years had she known him and never before recently had she been so repulsed by his foul snack choices? But she'd also never kissed him before recently, and now all she could think of was her mouth on his mouth, and pork rinds.

She felt her face burning. "You said you had something for me?"

They both followed him into the waiting room and Piper sat down with his patients, a fashion magazine and her Skittles in hand – she was in heaven. Jodie followed him back to his office.

He held out her *Entertainment Weekly*. She didn't know what she was expecting, but that wasn't it.

"They delivered it to my box. It's yours."

"You read it first, didn't you?"

"Why would I read this fluff?"

"Did you wank to the lingerie ads?"

He only shook his head. He didn't say he didn't though.

"That's it?"

He squinted at her. "Unless you wanted the seven inches again."

Jodie laughed so loud Dana turned around to glance at his office, the door left open. "You're foul," she said. She turned her face nervously, fighting the urge to look down at his crotch. Her eyes drifted to his wall instead. The pictures were new, but she couldn't remember what the old ones looked like. His wedding photos maybe? The pictures a person hangs on a wall, they blended into the scenery, rarely making an impact. It felt like a lesson. Pay attention, plenty of things would be snuffed out before they ever had a chance to be noticed.

Instead, there were more pictures of Hazel. She was a pretty girl, yet tomboyish. She looked too much like her father. He didn't tell Jodie about Hazel much anymore since they'd been avoiding each other. He didn't talk about Hazel's bitch mother, Hazel's track meet, or Hazel's report card. Hazel, the girl who'd just gotten her braces off, who wanted her tongue pierced but wasn't allowed, who spent all of the minutes on his family cell phone plan. Jodie knew more about this fourteen year-old girl than any other living person she'd not met. Maybe he didn't want to share those things with her anymore; maybe she'd never have to endure another word.

That realization wasn't as comforting as she imagined it would have been.

He cleared his throat – more a nervous sound than that he was trying to usher her out. But she was going anyway.

"Yeah, alright," she said, moving toward the open door. She tucked her glossy *Entertainment Weekly* under her arm. "I'll be going then." She waved her magazine in the air. "Thanks for this." She didn't turn to look at him again as she closed the door behind her.

Piper was halfway through her magazine when Jodie came back out. She had her hand full of Skittles, popping them one by one into her mouth as Jodie passed and said, "Come on, we're going now."

PIPER HAD ENOUGH OF HER OWN STUFF OVER AT TOM'S PLACE now that she didn't even need to stop home on those nights he picked her up from work. Jodie wondered if she would still need a ride home after she'd moved out. That would add at least another half hour to her commute, and though she was sure Piper hadn't even considered it yet, Jodie wasn't sure that she'd say no.

At home, Piper had most of her remaining things in boxes. Was it time for that already? It all seemed to be moving too fast. Here in the middle of the living room was a box labeled "photos", closed but without the flaps tucked in, and Jodie poked her hand inside it. She'd seen some of these before. Piper didn't keep her photos very organized, and she had too many of them, randomly stuffed into plastic quart-sized freezer bags.

Jodie put a bag of photos back down inside the box. "I thought you weren't supposed to be moving in with him until after the wedding?"

"Well, that's when I'll start living there officially," Piper said. "I'll have to move my stuff before then, silly."

"Yeah," Jodie said. "Of course."

The sight of all this reminded her of the time Amelia had broken up with Eric, how she went on about those photos Eric had taken. Jodie understood her brother though, the way he kept his albums so organized and specific – it would have killed him to divvy that up.

Amelia had spent so much time with them in those weeks. They amplified each other, Amelia with her knack for hosting parties, and Piper for entertaining. For that short time when they'd all been single together, it was almost like being in college again. Amelia would call almost every night after work, saying "Get the hell out here, you dried up, bitter old wench." And Jodie's lips would curl into the slightest of smiles. Amelia had no business cursing. Amelia cursed like a nine year-old girl trying something bad. She even giggled a little after she'd done it.

How fast those things could change – how could you count on any of it? How could you count on anyone but yourself?

Piper crouched behind the box of photos and shoved it toward the door with all her might.

"You're taking those now?"

"I might as well," she said, giving the box one last heave. "One less thing to take later."

She'd be over at Tom's place for the night. "This guy you set me up with – he could be a murderer," Jodie said. "He could be a rapist, or... I don't know. Nobody will be here to make sure I get home alive."

"I'll call to check in later," Piper said. "But he's not that weird. Tom knows him. And surely you won't be out past midnight, right?"

"Heh," Jodie chuckled. "I wouldn't count on it." She could count the times she'd been out on a date past midnight on one hand. Hell, she could count them on a couple fingers.

"You never know," Piper said, placing her tiny hand on Jodie's shoulder. "You might actually like him."

Jodie shrugged.

Piper saw Tom pull up then and she opened the door for him. He whipped up her box of photos on his shoulder and they left.

The apartment was quiet then. Jodie had a few hours left to kill before this date. Kill. What if he *was* a murderer? She wondered if any of them realized that most of the time, serial killers go unknown to even their closest friends and family. Didn't they know that? Jodie went upstairs to her bedroom and started looking at her clothes. They were all the same. Black pants or gray. Black shirts, or white, or gray. Her favorite one was silver, which she figured was just a fancy word for a sparkly shade of gray.

Her phone rang. There, she knew it. Whatever his name was, the serial killer date, he was calling to butter her up before the kill. She took the phone into her hand.

But it wasn't the date. It was Drew. She gulped hard, looking at his name on the caller ID, reading it over again. It wasn't that he called her infrequently, but any time he did, her heartbeat drummed in her throat for a few seconds. She had to steady herself.

"Hello," she said, casual as ever.

"You home?"

"Sure," she said.

"Mind if I pop by for a minute?"

"No, I don't mind, why would I mind?" She shook her head at herself and slapped her own forehead with her hand.

"Cool, see you in a bit," he said. Click, and the line went silent.

That was all he said.

And she had no shirt on.

She scurried to pull the silver top over her head. "Fuck," she said out loud. This was the same top she wore on her birthday, and

Drew had seen her in it. Did she really have no other clothes than this? No, of course she didn't.

She ruffled through her closet quickly, pulling out something black. She hardly looked at it before pulling it on. She went to the mirror, fluffing her heavy hair just to see it fall flat against her head again, pulling the scooped neckline straight across her cleavage. She pushed her breasts together haphazardly, finally glancing down at her white fleshy skin against the black top – so pale her veins really did show right through. She pulled the neckline back up a little higher.

She hurried downstairs, trying to find a casual arrangement to be in when he rang the doorbell. Would he think she was dressed up for him? No, he might have known she had a date tonight – it was possible, though not probable. She felt like a fool. So she tried to figure out which posture would make her appear the least flustered. Watching TV? Checking her email? No, that required too much attention. She grabbed her *Entertainment Weekly* and plopped down on the couch with it. She leafed through the pages, skimming over the pictures, the scarcely dressed celebrities, with their chiseled bodies and oiled skin. All of these men were her imaginary lovers. They were easier to deal with than real men. And the women with their perfectly put together outfits – Jodie would never admit she liked looking at the clothes, and she would never dare wear anything so bold. But mostly she loved reading about their breakups and divorces, which happened almost as soon as the relationships had even started. She would tell herself, *Do you see how hard this is? Not even perfect people can get it right.*

She wondered how close he was. What did he want? The possibilities flashed through her mind, from the mundane (Hey, you just forgot your jacket over at our place) to the wildest of her fantasies. (I'm leaving her, Jodie. I want to be with you.)

Jodie chided herself for even going there.

She flipped through the pages faster, bringing herself focus. She came to an advertisement for hair dye, three women with vivid shades of hair, scarlet, gold, mahogany, and Berges's handwriting all over the page: "Statistical estimate, how often does the carpet match the drapes? Best guess?"

"Ha!" He had read it, at least to page thirty-four. "Not very often," she spoke out loud to him, even though he wasn't there.

The doorbell rang. She went to answer it, forgetting to set down her magazine and finding it clutched in her palm. But as soon as she opened the door, all her panic stopped. It was just Drew. Drew with his coffee-brown eyes, his scarf wrapped around his neck, his fluffy, wind-blown hair, and his nose and ear tips that went red in the cold. He was her friend. He was love-starved for Amelia, and had always been. Jodie didn't know why she was making such a fuss.

"You're all dressed up," he said.

His eyes skimmed up and down the length of her. It flattered her that he would even notice. "I have a date," she said quickly. "You know, I figured someone should know in case he turns out to be an ax murderer or something."

"Jodie." He smiled, shaking his head at her. He placed his hand on her arm for half a second. "Give it a chance. I'm sure he'll be fine." Drew stepped inside so the storm door could close.

"Well, don't sound so surprised."

"I'm not surprised," he said. "I'm just happy for you."

Happy for her, and he meant every word of it.

He pulled a folded piece of paper out of his back pocket. "I wanted to bring this over," he said. "I was nearby anyway. Another girl for you to look at."

The roommate. She'd declined all of his previous suggestions. "Oh," she said. "Why didn't you just email them?"

"Why?" He laughed, shrugging his shoulders. "Because I wanted to tell you about her."

"Go on then," she said.

"This one, Barbie, but she has a cat."

"You know a girl named Barbie?"

"Ha, yeah, Barbara."

"That's all?"

He paused. "No," he said. "I wondered if you might know... why didn't your brother want to marry Amelia?"

"Well shit," Jodie said. "That's a sitting down kind of conversation, don't you think?"

"Sure," he said.

They went to the couch. She sat cross-legged, facing him. He slumped back into the cushions, seeming unsure of how comfortable to make himself.

"Well, he actually did want to marry her, for a while," Jodie said. "At least, that's what he told me. He proposed to her and everything."

"Yeah, she told me that. But then after, when they broke up, he was just okay with it?"

Jodie thought on this. "Yeah, I guess he was." Jodie remembered Amelia's face in Piper's sewing room, like Jodie had betrayed her herself. Had she told Drew about that? Jodie figured they probably told each other everything. She laughed. "Why are you gonna go fight for her honor or something?"

"Ha, no." His laugh was nervous, a small panic in his voice as if he were asking for her advice, but about what she didn't know.

Jodie thought of what Eric had told her, about why he was so okay with their break up. She had no idea when that started, how long her brother had been cheating on Amelia. She didn't know what Amelia had told Drew, or what Amelia understood herself. Jodie pursed her lips tight. None of these secrets were hers to share. "It doesn't matter, does it?"

"No, it doesn't matter," he said. He nodded once.

"Okay, then?"

She waited for him to respond, to confirm.

He smiled. "Yeah, of course."

There was a *Jerry Springer* episode on the TV. The woman on screen was wearing a sliced, cut-out shirt and six-inch red platform shoes – she'd been having an affair with her daughter's boyfriend, and was there in front of a viewing population of millions to tell the girl she was having his baby. Drew was staring at the TV too, but with so much concentration in his eyes that he couldn't have been paying attention to the show. She wondered how she looked, risking hazard to actually ask him, she tugged at the collar of her black wrap blouse.

He took the bait. "You look fine," he said.

"Ha," she laughed.

When she stopped laughing, he offered up a gentle smile. "No, really," he said.

His kindness made her heart fill, and at the same time want to poke her own eyes out. She wasn't used to it, and she didn't know how to take it. No one had ever been so kind to her – was he kind to her because he wanted to be? Was this as nice for him as it was for her?

"You're too much," she said. Her fingers felt flustered. She stopped moving them and crossed her arms instead. "So what are you guys doing tonight?" Drew and Amelia, Amelia and Drew. She asked about them as this solid and intertwined entity, which was exactly what they'd become.

"Oh, you know, just hanging out," he said, his attention occupied again. That was what he said when they were just staying in, the two of them, no one else invited. "Well I better let you get ready for your date then." He grinned, taunting her. She wanted to tell him to stay, that it was no bother, but he was already standing, handing her the folded-up page with the girl's name and email address on it. She hadn't needed him to find her any more girls after she'd declined the first bunch – it was too much – but if he wanted to, whatever he wanted to do, any little thing at all, she didn't want to stop him.

HER DATE'S NAME WAS COLIN. PIPER TOLD HER HE WOULD HAVE dark brown hair, be taller than average, and that he'd probably be wearing a sweater. Gaudy knitted patterns flashed to mind, but no, it wasn't a patterned sweater, just a black one, with a buttoned shirt underneath. He shook Jodie's hand. "Colin," he said.

"Yeah, she told me," Jodie said.

He was already sitting at the bar with a drink when she found him, so that was where they stayed. She tried to entertain his conversation. This place was odd without her friends. For their mismatched weirdness lately, it was even weirder here without the five of them. Jodie wished Piper had suggested somewhere else.

She sipped her martini. The voices were a cacophony, drumming in her chest. The sound was comfortable, but she could barely hear his voice, whatever it was he was talking about. That didn't concern her as much as it probably should have.

He drank too slow and she drank too fast.

"It's loud in here," he said to her. "You wanna go get something to eat?"

"Sure," she said. They slipped on their coats and left the bar together.

It was a Friday night and Main Street was lively for winter. Thanksgiving had passed, and the holiday decorating had begun, lights were wrapped around the trees and lampposts, and there were bell ringers in the distance. Couples walked arm in arm, close to keep warm. Jodie tried not to flail much in her two-inch pumps, as the heels slipped in between the cobblestone inlays of the sidewalk. She so rarely walked in heels, and to make things worse, Colin seemed to want to take her arm, as if she were inept at walking all together. She kept her space.

"Chilly at night this time of year," he said.

Something struck her hard about the way he said that – *chilly at night, this time of year* – she wasn't sure what though. "It's not that bad," she said. Oh god, they were talking about the weather, weren't they? It wasn't cold enough yet to warrant any of that. "So what do you do, Colin?"

"I'm a staff writer at the Detroit Free Press."

"Oh, right, my brother worked there, long time ago."

"Maybe I knew him."

"Oh, I doubt it."

"Really, what's his name?"

"Eric Larsen."

"Hmmm," Colin said, biting his lip. He had larger nostrils than average. She tried not to notice them, because once she had, she couldn't stop noticing how large they were, or how he had a couple of dark nose hairs peeking out from their edges. Jodie always hated this part of a first date, being forced to talk face-to-face, having to look at a person this close-up. No one wanted to look a person straight in the eyes for twenty solid minutes, so instead, you looked at the sun splotches on his cheeks, the pores on his nose, his smile lines and budding crow's feet. "I don't know him," Colin said.

"Right," Jodie said. She didn't think he would.

There was something about this night that stuck in Jodie's mind. Was it the time of year, maybe? Not too chilly to walk around, yet the distinct crispness of a dry fall night? This was maddening. And pointless. She didn't know which of them was more bored, but he had actually yawned at one point. "There's a blues bar on Eleven

Mile, live music. The Lighthouse Cafe if you want coffee. Or we could get popcorn."

Lighthouse? She turned to him, sharp and sudden. "The Lighthouse Cafe?"

"Sure," he said. "You like that place?"

"No," she said. That wasn't it. "Never heard of it."

That puzzled him, and he stared at her, perplexed. "Or we could get sushi."

How long had it been since she'd been on a date like this? She tried to remember, searching back through the months. If you didn't count Berges and that horrendous disaster of a wedding, then it had been about a year. The memory found her then, their tacky cocktail bar, with the pink neon lights twinkling through their drinks, a martini and a beer. Leaving that bar to wander these very streets with nothing to do. Drew with his bright smile and such undeserved kindness. The last time she'd been out with a guy, like this, was with Drew.

It had been early in the fall still, and Drew hadn't yet lost the tan on his forearms or the back of his neck. The bronze on his cheekbones glowed against his pale blue polo. It was early in the night still, and Jodie remembered wondering where Amelia had gone. Drew didn't say anything about her, but her absence hung between them, something heavy and ominous – it must have been, because they were so rarely apart, even then. Jodie had tried to forget her, and it seemed like he wanted to as well. They walked together, having nothing else to do, and he said, "I want to take the boat out. Do you like boats?"

Jodie had known *of* Drew more than she knew him personally back then. She knew him through Amelia, through snippets of the things Amelia said, or bumping into him at one party or another, the minor conversations they might have had about the weather or news headlines. "What, you want to take me out on your boat? Are you gonna murder me and dump me in the river or something?"

"Ha," he laughed. That smile. His teeth were not absolutely perfect, bright and lovely as they were, his front two teeth were inverted just so slightly, that miniscule kind of detail it took twenty minutes of having drinks with him to notice. "I won't murder you and dump you in the river. Scout's honor."

He raised his hand to shoulder-level, forming his fingers into the scout sign. Of course he'd been a boy scout in his youth. Normally she would have felt inclined to laugh at him, but no laughter came out. "Sure, why not?"

So they picked up a couple of six-packs and he drove them out to Lake St. Clair, where his boat was docked. "It's chilly out there at night this time of year," he told her, "Do you have a jacket?"

She shook her head.

"No problem," he said. "I have a sweatshirt in the car."

He took her along the lake shore, pointing out the lighthouses. The night was early enough that the horizon still glowed bright like the center of a flame, and deep, low clouds were the shade of fire.

He told her about his job. Most of the time he didn't get to captain the ship, unless it was a small charter job or someone was sick – he didn't have enough seniority – but he directed the tour instead, telling people stories about the lighthouses. She watched the light sweep across the sky, an arc too wide to follow, and she listened to the stories. He told her how old the lights were, who owned them now, and for the ones left unlit, when they'd been decommissioned. He told her about the people who had owned them before the Coast Guard had taken over the reins – the light keepers, the men who ran the lights and their families, all those children who grew up underneath night skies of sweeping light. He delivered his speech with enthusiasm and charm. How those old country club ladies must have loved him.

The boat made a sloshing thump every time the hull came down on the waves, a nauseating roll in her stomach. "Doesn't it make you sick?"

"No, why? Do you feel sick?" He asked it with such concern.

She shook her head.

"After you get used to it," he said. "It's relaxing. It gets into your bones and your blood. When you step on shore later, you'll feel like your whole body is still moving."

She wasn't sure if that was supposed to be a good thing or not.

He pointed to shore. "And this one is said to be haunted with the spirits of a shipwreck, just right under us here, from before the lights were commissioned."

Jodie leaned her head over the side, glancing down into the water, as if she could see through its blackness.

"People scuba dive it sometimes," he added.

"What, they just left them down there?"

He nodded. "Like a graveyard of dead ships."

The keeper's house had candles lit in each window – she couldn't make out the shape of the house much at all except the number of lit windows. "Why so many rooms for just a light keeper?" Jodie asked.

"It was highly favored that they had families – married, with children. They would often pick a family man over a single man. It even became a requirement in some stations."

"That's not fair." Jodie glared at him, as if he'd made this rule himself.

"It was for their own good," he said. "People aren't meant to live alone. The loneliness, the isolation – it drove men to madness."

She wanted to object – sure people could live alone. People did it all the time. But she didn't object; she wasn't sure she was right.

He navigated the darkened shoreline, tiny blips of light, one boat or two, flashes of green and red and white. The last blue of the sky had turned black, and she didn't ask how he knew his way, how he knew the coastline from the waves from the horizon. She leaned her head back to watch the stars, sipping her beer occasionally. He'd finished his speeches, stopped talking about the lighthouses and they just cut through the dark water silently, a world of weight in his thoughts. She didn't have much to say either, so she just let the wind blow her hair back. She held her hand out and let the icy spray catch her fingertips.

When they finally came back to shore, he docked the boat and they drank some more. It was warmer there. There were other people, on other boats in the marina. And as they sat there, drinking their beers into the night, as the waves rocked them in a steady lull that did in fact creep into her bones, the other people went home little by little. He picked the music and they talked. The white leather seating wrapped around the bow in a horseshoe shape. They sat on opposite sides, their feet stretching out toward each other in the center. There was still that heaviness, though he didn't mention anything specifically. She didn't ask him either.

Back then, it wasn't uncommon for them all to spend the night awake, at a bar or a party, with their friends, with Amelia. They did it all the time. But that night, it was just Jodie and Drew. It was nearly four in the morning by the time they'd drank all their beer and then sobered up drinking coffee he'd made in the cabin down below. The black sky had started to lighten again to that vivid electric blue, and on the horizon the first hints of color were starting to creep up, changing by the minute, warming to a golden glow where the water met the sky. For all the times she'd come home from a midnight delivery at this time of night, she could swear she'd never seen it quite like this, crystal clear and full of fading stars, a wide open expanse without the trees or buildings to block the way. The sky was bigger out here.

"It'll be sunrise soon," she said. Soon enough, but that would have been another hour at least, and it was another half-hour drive back to the west suburbs where they all lived.

"I'm spent," he said, already digging into his jacket pocket for his car keys. "We'll do sunrise another time."

She wanted to ask him, *Do you promise?* But she didn't. And he didn't try to kiss her, but he did engulf her, resting his face beside her head and wrapping his arms around her back. One of his hands slipped into her hair, buried there, fingertips at the base of her neck, holding her to his body. It stunned her. It was one of the strongest, warmest hugs she'd ever experienced. "Thanks for coming out with me tonight," he said near her ear. The hug lasted for hours, she could have sworn, though in reality it couldn't have lasted more than a minute. It was the longest fraction of a minute of her life.

Colin was still talking. He asked her, "Sushi?"

"Oh," Jodie said, inhaling deep and sighing it back out, the hard crash of reality against the most vivid memory she'd ever known. "Sushi," she said. She nodded, tried to smile but she was sure it didn't work. He placed his hand on her back and they started walking toward Eleven Mile again. She had to give the guy credit – he was either very ambitious, or very patient, or very polite, or just being very obtuse. It was nothing against him personally – he wasn't ugly, he wasn't rude or obnoxiously stupid, and his sweater wasn't even gaudy. But for whatever redeeming qualities this man possessed, Jodie just couldn't hear him.

She thought she was trying, but she couldn't bring herself to try because her head was a jumble of impossibilities. She didn't want to be here, with him. She wanted her life back the way it was. She wanted to flirt with Berges the way they used to before he got divorced, when it was still carefree and fun. She wanted to know how Hazel was doing – did she pass that algebra test she was having trouble with, would she be running with the track team again next fall? She wanted her brother back in town. She wanted her friends back, the five of them. She didn't want Piper to move out, and take her cushy pink pillows and ice cream. She wanted to rewind to the time before Amelia and Drew started sleeping with each other. She wanted Drew to hold her again the way he did that night, when there was nothing in his heart but kindness for her. She wanted to stay there. She wanted it all back.

"Oh, fuck it," she mumbled to herself.

"What?" Colin said.

"I think sushi is a bad idea."

"Oh, we could do popcorn."

"No, not popcorn. I can't." She shook her head, staring at him hard and wide-eyed.

"Did I say something?"

"No, you didn't say anything, or do anything. It's me."

"That's just something people say."

It wasn't a negotiation. She had to go. "Sorry," she said, already turning away from him. It probably wasn't a full-on run, but at the very least, she walked away quickly. This was a first even for Jodie, a date gone so wrong she had to run away from it. She found a bus stop and sat down on the bench, flickering pale yellow lights overhead and something that looked like used chewing gum near her hand.

She was fine, she told herself. She didn't need any damn knight in shining armor. She didn't need to be rescued, to be set up, to be paired with the most likely candidate. She didn't need to be completed, and she didn't need to be softened. She didn't need a husband, or a boyfriend, or a lover. She didn't *need* anything.

There was a newspaper on the other side of the bench, beside the gum. She was scared to even touch it for its filth, but she saw the print facing up, the singles ads. They were ridiculous, these people, desperate and searching, splaying themselves wide open in the pages of a discarded newspaper. She wasn't one of them, but she picked it up anyway. What would her ad say if she had one? Accomplished woman, good sense of humor, hates dating, likes cats?

Jodie was never the kind of woman to indulge in fantasy, yet when the drunken stupor wore off, that was all she'd been left with, impossibilities, the memory of a few shining moments and herself.

DECEMBER

3.1: secrets to keep

AMELIA HADN'T HOSTED A PARTY LIKE THIS IN A WHILE, but somehow everyone carried on just the same. Jodie couldn't understand how it didn't seem to sadden any of them, that their old friendships and acquaintances had become just a fond memory as all of their lives had grown so full and busy. Piper and Tom stood in their corner of the kitchen – Piper held a Sprite in her hand rather than a beer. She wasn't pregnant yet, as far as Jodie knew, but was hoping to be at the earliest moment possible.

Amelia came by with another snack tray and set it on the counter. She barely drank when she was hosting, keeping herself busy instead, filling drinks, making sure people were happy and well fed. Drew would try to steal her for just a moment, make her stop and enjoy her own party, slather her in kisses before she hurried off again to refill the pita chips and open another bottle of red wine.

The holidays were coming up quickly – Jodie hated the holidays. Eric had invited her to Christmas up in Lansing this year, in his new place with Ruth. She wondered how different it would be now that they were expecting. Would she feel like the tag-a-long to their little proper family? Ruth was eight weeks pregnant, and they'd just announced it officially.

Drew hovered near the kitchen table, keeping an eye on the six-packs. Jodie asked him, "Are you drunk?"

"No, not yet," he said. "We might need more beer soon though."

"Because you clearly drank most of it."

He laughed, tilting his beer bottle at her like pointing a finger. "And you clearly haven't had enough yet." He took another beer from the fridge and opened it for her.

The party was actually going really well. Everyone was getting along, maybe even too well. Drew had his eyes on Tom with Amelia. The tall sturdy man was losing himself in a wild air-guitar trying to impress her, which eventually earned him a heartfelt laugh.

"I don't think he's the one you need to watch out for," Jodie said, her eyes on Corbin who was charming the giggles out of Piper – how she held her fingers to her cheek and blushed at his strong, sculpted body, and his wise, soulful eyes. Jodie laughed. "Piper, that little tart. Man, I'm telling you, if that girl wasn't so religious, Tom would be in so much trouble." Piper could flirt all she wanted with Berges and Jodie knew nothing would come of it – Berges was all play, but not Corbin. Jodie had to admit she had been slightly curious about him herself. But she'd talked to him once, something about the malleability of time and space and that was where he lost her.

"Watch out for," Drew said. "For what?"

Jodie laughed. "Oh, you know about him, sex god or something." No, those hadn't been Amelia's exact words, but how they teased her about him when they found out. It was soon after she'd broken up with Eric, and she stopped over at their apartment one night, flushed and mortified. She couldn't believe what she'd just done. Amelia was so careful, so reserved. It wasn't like her at all. "Maybe it's something every girl needs to try once in her life,"

Amelia had bargained with them. "Reckless, wild, completely casual sex?"

Corbin had Drew's full attention then, a narrow sneer in his eyes, gripping his beer bottle like he probably wanted to grip Corbin's neck. It was a wonder Corbin couldn't feel that from across the room. "Really," Jodie said. "She wasn't even that into him."

Drew just stared, at Jodie, at Corbin, and back again, as if she were speaking some foreign language. Jodie wasn't sure if she was making it better or worse. It hadn't been her secret to tell, but it was out there now and she didn't know what to do with it. "My feet hurt," she said. "I've been standing all day." She elbowed him in the arm as she walked past, and the contact snapped him to attention.

The kitchen table was deserted, even though Amelia had laid out a lovely string of tea lights for ambiance. Jodie sat down first. She was surprised and pleased to see that Drew followed and took the other corner of the table.

"So how is it, being engaged?"

"Good," he said. "My mom's coming next week to throw us an engagement party. You're coming, aren't you?"

She might have mentioned out loud that she'd be there, but she hadn't ever filled out the RSVP card. *To celebrate the engagement of the future Mr. and Mrs. Weston.* "Yeah, I'll be there," Jodie said. "So she's taking your name then?"

"She said she would."

"That's surprising, I didn't think she would."

"Just because you wouldn't," he said, taking a sip of beer. Take any man's name, or take his name specifically? No, that wasn't what he meant. Her cheeks flushed at the thought. "It's not that surprising," he continued. "Plenty of women still do it."

"Kate never took Berges's name." Jodie was only half-aware

she'd said that out loud. "Ha, I don't blame her though. I wouldn't take his name either."

"So you've thought about marrying him then?"

"God, no! Not at all!" Jodie sliced a hand through the air, her beer bottle still in hand, and a few drops escaped the spout. She watched them splatter on the table.

"You *like* him," Drew teased.

"What are you, twelve?" she said. "I don't like him at all. Actually, I passionately *hate* him."

Drew's laugh echoed into the beer bottle at his lips. When he stopped laughing, he said quietly, "I'm glad she is though."

Jodie watched him, edging on telling her more. She waited.

"It just seems like a nice thing," he continued. "A family all with one name, where the kid looks a little like the mom and the dad."

"Hmmm," Jodie hummed. It was a nice idea. She never had that herself when she was growing up. "Are you guys staying here then?" She knew his parents didn't live here anymore, and it suddenly occurred to her that they might decide to leave.

"Yeah," he said. "I like it here. Somebody needs to take care of my uncle."

Only sometimes did Jodie care to hear much about her friends' families. It was hard to avoid Piper's multitude of sisters, even if she could never remember their names, and Berges never got very far without mentioning Hazel this or Hazel that. But Drew's uncle sounded like a bitter and disappointed man, like someone Jodie could get along with. She wished Drew would talk about him more.

Somehow the kitchen had cleared for a moment, and Drew hadn't seemed to notice that the two of them were alone. The living room was filled with voices, the music stopping and starting as someone shuffled through tracks. Drew stared off into space as he thought, and Jodie indulged in the opportunity to take him in, the depth in his eyes, the way the candles highlighted the tan left on his cheeks. She wanted to know what he was thinking about. She wanted more access to him than he ever allowed her. She wanted to know him – not just what he did for a living or what kind of beer he liked to drink, but where did he see his life going? Was he happy?

Jodie put her bottle to her lips, filling her mouth with a tiny gulp of beer and holding it there. Love. Who in their right mind waited until they were thirty years old to figure out what love was? She might have loved him, or maybe she loved him still. And she thought that, once, many months ago, he might have felt something too. Maybe they might have stood a chance. And before he ran off and married Amelia, Jodie needed to know. She swallowed the warm gulp of beer in her mouth. "Would you have dated me?"

It came out easily. Too easily. She didn't think she was very drunk, but in retrospect, she could feel the room spinning. She could feel the buzz. He didn't answer her, and she could almost imagine he hadn't heard it at all except for the look of impossible discomfort on his face.

He cleared his throat, stood, and went to take some beer bottles to the trash.

She needed to do something too. Anything. So she picked up a washcloth and started wiping the stove, never mind that there was nothing there but a few cracker crumbs. Amelia kept this place immaculate. Drew washed his hands. He did it too quickly, not scrubbing underneath his nails, or even in between his fingers; he wasn't a surgeon, after all. She scrubbed harder at the stove.

"You don't have to do that," he said.

But she did. Because she didn't know what else to do. She had all these secrets in her head, and this one was her own, to keep or to share. She might have loved him. It might have been real. And maybe it might have even mattered. And now he was engaged, his mother was coming to throw them an engagement party, and then he'd be married. Everything was changing so fast, and before it did, Jodie wanted him to know.

She took her hands from the stove and turned to him. He was already waiting for her to say something more, or even to just stop cleaning. "I thought you felt something once," Jodie said. "You probably didn't, but just humor me. Before you guys started dating or whatever, there was something?"

He looked ready to flee. He looked terrified. But it was more than just the possibility of being found out, of being caught – it looked like she'd actually hit on something true. She had expected him to deny it, but he didn't. "It wouldn't matter if I did," he said.

Her throat swelled with panic. "Wait," she said. "It could matter."

He stood back from her, stiffened. "What do you want me to say?"

"I know, you guys are all getting married and everything, you're gonna settle down and have a crapload of little redheaded babies." He winced at this. Too much venom. She always knew the exact moment she crossed the line with him – when it stopped being fun and started being vicious. "But if she'd have taken a little bit longer."

"She didn't take longer."

"But if you'd have given up on her."

"I didn't give up on her," he said. "I never would have."

"Never is a very long time," Jodie said.

She'd always wanted to kiss him. Right here, for just a second. She should have kissed him that night, a year ago, when he hugged her like he did, when his lips brushed her cheek under the almost sunrise, when he held her head in his hands. They never did do sunrise again like he said they would.

She reached out to his arms. He was motionless, eyes wide and confused as he pulled back from her. They each moved as if in slow motion.

"I'm sorry," he said, his hands on each of her arms, bracing her, holding her back – but holding her just the same. His palms were clammy, cold from the beer bottles, moist from nerves. Her hands were clammy too, but she didn't care.

There was apology in his eyes. "If I made you think that we... I didn't mean it like that."

He had felt something, and so had she – shouldn't this be talked about, before he went and got married, before it was too late? She continued to reach for him, feeling his fingers tense around her as she stumbled closer, finding his shoulders. He didn't seem to know if he should catch her or let her fall. She didn't know if she was reaching or stumbling. They were drunk. They'd lost track of their place in space and time – or at least she had. He was the first of them to look over, a shape and some movement in the doorway.

Amelia. And when he finally broke free from Jodie's hands and ran to her, it was faster and more sure than Jodie had ever seen anyone move. Jodie stumbled and braced herself on the counter. How long had Amelia been standing there? Jodie followed after them. She prepared herself to be yelled at, but Amelia didn't yell at her. Amelia didn't even look at her, only him. Amelia stepped backwards toward the living room. She whispered, "I was so stupid."

"It was nothing," he said. "What did you hear?"

She didn't answer that, just tilted her head sadly. "I actually thought this once, but then I didn't want to believe it was."

Jodie followed them as they backed into the other room, the voices of the party guests muffling their tense words.

"It isn't," he pleaded. "It's nothing." He tried to take hold of her, but Amelia only backed away and shielded her eyes with her hand. "It was never anything. It was never going to be anything."

"That's *not* the same as *nothing!*"

Amelia's shout had rang above the chatter of party guests, and she winced as the room full of people turned their eyes on her. She spoke to Drew in a low, crackled voice. "You tell these people to leave, and we can talk upstairs."

"Amelia," Jodie tried to call for her, but Amelia was already moving toward the stairs. "It wasn't his fault." Amelia didn't hear her. Amelia didn't see her, as if she was already dead, already non-existent. Jodie would beg Amelia to just yell at her. She could take it. But Jodie couldn't bear for Amelia to be mad at him. This wasn't his fault, it was a mistake. Partially a mistake. Jodie had been wrong. This wasn't just her secret to keep or to tell – it was his too.

Drew stood at the foot of the staircase with his back to the room, and Jodie watched them, all those eyes, glancing between the two of them, waiting for someone to speak. Drew turned quietly and began picking up beer bottles. "Party's over," he said in a voice more lifeless than Jodie had ever heard from him. He wedged beer bottles between his fingers, in the crook of his arm. Tom didn't say anything, but began to stack dirty plates.

Piper made her way over to Jodie. "What happened?"

Jodie hadn't moved. They should have all been gathering their coats and bags, but instead, they stared at her. They were waiting for an answer. They were staring, but Drew wouldn't look at her. Not even once. *Nothing,* he had said. The word echoed in her ears.

So she ran, swinging the front door wide open, hitting a wall of winter cold and breaking straight through it. She ran hard, until she hit pavement, and stopped. There was no space, just hard ground beneath her and city lights around her. Her head continued to spin, not helped by the swirling snowflakes falling from the sky, sweeping past her eyes in waves. She didn't need to look at the door. He wasn't coming. She wasn't coming. Jodie waited to hear them yelling, listening for muffled voices through the windowpanes. She should have gone, but at the same time, she wanted to hear it. But there was no yelling. Amelia's front door finally opened, but it was Piper who came outside, her bright yellow parka gleaming in the dark. "Silly Jodie," she said, a pitiful bend in her brow. "You're standing in the road."

Jodie looked down at her feet, standing firm on wet black pavement. Ahead of her, a red light held back traffic. Piper moved them across the street. The benches were cold and frozen, but they sat anyway. Jodie didn't feel the cold. She didn't feel much of anything but shock, the reality of the past twenty minutes hitting her hard.

She turned to Piper. "Did she break up with him?"

"Is that what you want to happen?"

"No," Jodie said. "I don't know."

Piper considered her carefully before speaking. "I don't think so," she said. "I think it just broke her heart. She was your friend."

Jodie turned her face to the sky, dark, filled with millions of snowflakes. "She's just my brother's ex-girlfriend."

"Do you really believe that?"

Jodie didn't answer. What were they really but her brother's ex-girlfriend and a guy she went on a date with for six hours? It was such a small fraction of time in the scope of their whole lives.

"It's easier to think that," Piper said.

She was right. It was easier. It made Jodie feel like less of a monster to say Amelia hadn't been her friend. She didn't feel the cold yet, but what she felt as the shock wore off was a numbness in her chest, a swirling in her stomach, nausea. "He hates me," Jodie said. "I thought maybe he was the only person alive who actually cared about me."

Piper pursed her small mouth and furrowed her eyebrows, more anger than Jodie had ever seen on her before. Jodie had to look away. "No," Piper said firmly. "He's *not* the only one. That's what you keep missing."

She started to feel the cold then, creeping into her fingers first, then up her arms, chilling her lips and her nose and her ears. Never in her life had she wanted the warmth of human contact more than she did right then. A hug? But she wasn't sure who would give it? She wished her brother was here.

"I miss Eric," Jodie said. "I'm gonna be an aunt, you know."

Piper sighed, let herself soften and a weak smile crept onto her face. "Really, a baby?"

"Heh," Jodie laughed. "Don't get too excited. It's a baby that lives a hundred miles away."

Across the street, Tom was waiting to cross. Green light, and the traffic poured across in streams. They both stood to wait for him.

"Can we take you home?" Piper asked. "It's on our way."

"No," Jodie said. She couldn't be stuck in a car with them for twenty-five minutes. Tom kept looking at her with dismay, like he only put up with her because of Piper. Now Jodie couldn't be sure he would even do that much. Would she be kicked out of the wedding party? She was scared to ask, because what if they'd confirmed it was true, that they didn't want her anymore? It made Jodie realize she actually *wanted* to be in Piper's wedding – she actually *wanted* to stand beside her best friend and wear that god-awful lavender dress after all.

The traffic cleared and Tom finally crossed. Piper held up one finger at him, and he nodded, walking toward the car instead. He started the engine and sat inside waiting for her.

"They're happy," Piper said. "Don't you want to see them happy?"

"Happy," Jodie laughed. Who was ever really happy anyway?

"Take one for the team," Piper said. "You might love him. You might even love him a lot. But you don't love him as much as she does."

Jodie shook her head. "I never said I loved him." The words were cold coming off her lips, and the numbness spread inside her. The way Piper looked at her, so sadly, with so much disappointment, Jodie couldn't breathe again until she turned away.

Piper climbed inside the car, placing her hand on the window, a wave goodnight. Then Tom pulled away, the exhaust sputtering out and leaving a heavy white cloud behind them. Jodie had her car keys in her pocket, and her dark, secluded, freezing cold car had never seemed more inviting. Her coat was inside Amelia's house still, where she had no intentions of going back to retrieve it. Jodie started to walk, reaching to her arms, trying to warm her cold skin with her own chilly hands.

3.2: pretty lies

THERE HAD BEEN A NIGHT LAST FALL WHEN AMELIA pulled Drew outside their favorite cocktail bar; she didn't want to fight with him in front of all their friends. Neon lights flashed out into the night every time the door swung open, strangers passing between them, coming and going. It was warm enough for the fall but Amelia ran her fingers over the goosebumps on her skin. She and Drew had been messing around for a few weeks at that point – neither of them knew what to call it besides "messing around." One minute they'd been friends, and the next they were sleeping together, and soon after that, he'd said it – he wanted to spend his life with her – and she'd never felt the world spin so fast.

"Fine." He laughed it off, moving her away from the door and all its traffic. "Pretend I didn't say it then."

"But you did say it."

"Then forget I said it. What do you want me to do?"

She didn't have an answer for him, and she wasn't sure she could forget it either. It was too much, too fast, too definite and heavy with expectations, and it felt ominously like the proposal she had gotten from Eric: *Marry me now or I'm moving on*. Drew might not have said that was what he meant, but it was – at least the future part. It only reminded her that everything was on a time limit, everything was clocked for speed and accuracy. If he didn't mean it now, he'd mean it in three months or two years or five.

There was rejection in his eyes. "Why don't you want to date me?"

"I didn't say that," she said. "I am dating you."

"No, you're with me sometimes. We're friends. We have sex. I'm not sure if you're really dating me. I'm not sure what we're doing." He had his thumbs in his pockets. There were people smoking cigarettes nearby, crushed butts littering the pavement – he seemed to be looking at them, or maybe he was just gazing into the space, composing a poem, something about angst and frustration.

"Okay," she said. "I love you – is that what you want?"

"I actually do know that," he said. "That's not the problem."

"What's the problem?"

He looked her in the eyes, sharp. "You're the last person I'd ever want a pity lay from," he said. "I can get myself laid, Amelia."

"I don't *pity* you," she said. People turned their heads as they passed and Amelia lowered her voice. "Don't even say that."

"I just don't know what you want," he said, slowly shaking his head, taking it back. "No, that's not even it. The thing is, I don't think *you* even know what you want."

It wasn't true. She'd always known what she wanted. It was simple: to be loved, not to be left, that was all. "It's growing on me," she said. "Why does it have to happen so fast?"

"We've been friends for two and a half years," he said. "That's not fast!"

"Or what?"

"Or maybe I can't deal with it anymore." He looked her in the eyes when he said it. "The back and forth all the time, not knowing what I'm allowed to say to you, never knowing if this is going to be something or if it's just a fluke."

She bit her lip to keep it from trembling. She had been right; she'd felt it coming all along. She wouldn't let him see her cry, so she turned, mumbling, "Fine, don't let me burden you then." She walked away from him quickly so that he couldn't stop her, though she wasn't sure if he was even going to try, and she didn't turn around to find out.

What Amelia saw was Jodie's lips parted, near her fiancé's lips but not yet touching, as if suspended in time – as if Drew had suspended Jodie there in time himself, holding her off but never cutting her free. It was his eyes Amelia noticed, how he considered Jodie's lips, how long he thought about them. Were they just coming together? Or had they already kissed and just began to part? Amelia stood there so long she could have counted the pounding heartbeats between the time she stepped into that doorway and then finally raised her hand to cover her gaping mouth, when he saw her there and let go of Jodie so that time could begin to tick again.

Amelia sat in their bedroom with the door closed, muffled sounds of people leaving, cars starting. And there on the floor were the details of their lives, tossed together in so much haste, the mismatched bedroom furniture, their mixed worn clothing, strewn and intertwined. Drew had pleaded with her to hear him, but all she could hear was a voice she thought she'd been free of for so many years, Lenny, and all she could feel was the foolishness she felt that night he sat her down on their ratty old couch, in that college apartment they shared. Lenny and his little girlfriend, they spent time together right under Amelia's nose. Amelia had even invited the woman to some of her parties. *She's just a friend, I promise*, he had said. *It's nothing, don't worry about it.* They had her fooled. They had her friends fooled too. How could a smart girl be so stupid?

Downstairs, the house had gone quiet. She heard Drew's footsteps moving through the house. She watched the door as if it might actually open on its own. She felt it pulling at her, the need to hear his excuses. They all had excuses, apologies, answers. She never could help handing out those second chances, some defect in her that needed to hear them out again and again. Didn't she know well enough already how this was going to end?

Lenny Hutchins was built like no young man should have been allowed to be built. Not just the body, the charm. He should have been an actor with how convincingly he played the part. All the girls liked him in high school, but he dated Amelia. They went steady, they wore each other's flowers for prom and passed notes to each other in the hallway. They took each other's virginity one winter afternoon while her parents were out of the house. He lay on top of her, the two of them under covers with her bra still on. *I love you*, he said. *It'll be okay if we're careful.* They were perfectly careful – every single time for six years – but whether it ended up okay would depend on the definition of "okay". *I don't know how it happened,* he finally told her, but his eyes said he did know, that it hadn't been a mistake, and that he wasn't even sorry. Like a record stuck on a loop, having forgiven him one time, then two, having taken him back again and again. He promised her, and she believed him. Before she knew it, he was sitting next to her in their old college living room with all those lies in his eyes, and he said, *I think I might be in love with her.*

Amelia tucked her legs underneath herself on the bed, still wearing her shoes, the covers twisted and clenched between her fingers. She was too shocked to cry, her eyes wide and burning, her limbs trembling. If she tried to stand, would her body even hold her? She'd been so careful this time. She'd been so sure. She took all the precautions, she waited so long. And now she saw it happening all over again – the phone calls, the inside jokes, the stolen moments, the drinks, the favors, checking up on each other – and Amelia just stood back and watched it all unfold like a goddamn fool.

A soft thud, his palm or his forehead pressed to the wood. "Melie." Drew's voice was muffled from behind the bedroom door. It wasn't locked, she would have said if she could speak, but she couldn't. He tried the handle. "Please let me explain." Drew approached her with his hands out, like offering his submission to a scared animal. There was panic in his eyes. The voices mingled in her head, the things Drew said, the things Lenny said. *It's not like that. It's nothing like what we have.*

"Melie, please listen to me. She got the wrong idea, that's all."

"Did you kiss her?"

"No," he said.

She turned her face to the floor. "The way she was touching you."

"She's never done that before. Not like that."

"Like what then?"

He was confused by the question. He didn't answer it.

"Do you love her?"

"No."

"Does she love you?"

He hesitated. "I don't know. I don't think she really understands what she feels."

From what Amelia saw, it had looked like she understood quite well. "What did she say to you?"

"She said..." He stalled and Amelia couldn't tell if he was drawing a blank or protecting Jodie's secrets, trying to think up a lie or deciding not to tell one. "She wanted to know if I felt something for her."

"And you said?"

"No. I said 'no'. I never felt anything for her. I mean, not in the way she thought."

"Why would she think you did?"

"I don't know."

Jodie didn't flirt for no reason. She wasn't boy-crazy, and she didn't crush on people. It didn't compute. "Why would she get the wrong idea?" Amelia wanted so badly for this to not be true. She wanted to believe, the way a girl might want to believe in the tooth fairy or in ghosts, or the way a hiding child might close her eyes and really believe that she can't be seen.

But with the way he looked at her, full of so much apology, it could only be true.

"Okay," he said. "There's something I never told you."

"Oh God," she whispered. Here it was. Her heart exploded, a thousand splinters of glass slicing her ribcage. She couldn't breathe. He waited, as if to ask, did she want to know? No, she didn't. She didn't want to know. She wished for a lie instead, a pretty one, something she could believe in. Something they might laugh about until it all blew over because surely this was all just a mistake. A misunderstanding. This could not be happening to her again. She shook her head, *no, no, no,* but he started anyway.

"I didn't think anything of it, I swear," he said. "But a long time ago, we – Jodie and I – we went out. She might have thought it was a date."

Amelia had so many questions, but she couldn't ask any of them.

"It was last fall," he added.

"We were already together last fall."

"I know." He looked like he might cry himself. What right did he have? "But we were fighting, and I..."

"Was it or wasn't it? A date?"

"Melie, I don't know. We didn't do anything. I took her out on the boat. We talked. What do you call that?"

She wanted to know what he called it. She breathed in, held it, letting the air out slowly from between her lips. "Just the two of you," she repeated, saying his words over again as if she could make sense of them. "On a boat for hours. How many hours?"

"I can't remember. A lot of hours."

All night into the next morning. She remembered exactly which night that was. They'd had a fight, and he told her he slept over at his uncle's place. It had been a lie. How much else had been a lie?

He reached out to her but his hands were no comfort. He surrounded her in his arms but she couldn't move. She couldn't distinguish the voices because they all said the same things. "She's my friend, that's all," he said, gripping her arms with his hands, trying to make her look in his eyes but she couldn't. "But I don't care about her like I love you. It's not like that. We're just friends."

She heard him, but what he was telling her she'd heard so many times before. It sounded like an echo, a repeating curse. *She's just a friend, I promise. It's nothing like what we have.* A choke swelled in her throat and she shouted, "It's bullshit!" She broke free of him, pushing him away. "I won't let you *tell me* she's your friend. She is *not* your friend."

She squeezed her eyes shut to hold back the tears. When she opened them again, she saw him stunned silent. She began to breathe again and went for their bathroom, not bothering to turn on the light.

In the dark, she turned on the faucet and splashed her face with cold water, gasping for breath in between splashes, then she folded her hands into a cup and pooled water to drink, the chill opening up the swell in her throat. She wasn't going to cry. No, she gulped that down hard as the cold water. When she opened her eyes again, she found his reflection in the bathroom mirror. He stood with his back to the door jamb, not inside the bathroom, not outside either, his thumbs in his pockets and his face turned down to the floor.

She held herself up on the sink. She twisted the ring he'd given her around her wet, slippery finger. It felt like it might just slip right off, like it was that impermanent. It might just fly off her finger, be rinsed down the drain like something she'd decided to wear for a time but then decided wasn't the right fit after all. It had grown on her, the idea of this. She wanted so badly for this one to stick. More than any other time before, she wanted just once to really believe.

She studied him for a moment, his familiar shape, the way he stood when he was feeling attacked, the way his hair curled behind his ears and neck, the way he bit the tip of his thumb as he thought. She thought they knew each other so fully. She trusted him more than anyone in the world. Did she even know him at all?

"She was your backup plan," Amelia said, taking a sharp, deep breath, watching his reflection in the mirror. "You were just holding on to her in case this didn't work out."

"That's not what I was doing," he said.

"Do you love her?"

"No."

He answered too fast. He didn't even consider it.

"A year ago," she said. "You were thinking about dating her at the same time we started dating. Why me then? Why not just date her?"

"You know why," he said. "It wasn't like that. It just crossed my mind." He exhaled then, looking away from her eyes. "I waited a long time for you to figure out if you wanted to be with me or not. Yes, it crossed my mind that you never would."

He flipped on the bathroom light switch and the brightness singed her eyes. She squeezed them shut, peeking at him, all that apology on his face. He hadn't been crying after all. She wondered if it looked like she had. He came closer, reaching out to make contact but stopping before he did. "I don't want to be with her," he said. "How can I prove it to you? What do you want me to do?"

Here it was, the entire contents of their relationship, built on fallacies, taken out from the shadows to prove itself in the light. Couldn't they see it now, all those fault lines and fractures, the pieces so precariously stacked, how so slight a tremor would send them crumbling? Couldn't they see how they were always meant to break apart and topple? Wasn't it clear now exactly where they'd fall? Every time either of them spoke, it only got worse. One more lie came out, one more mistruth or twisted reality, one less thing left to believe in.

"I want you to go downstairs," she said. "I don't have anything else to say right now."

She looked at the floor until he began to move. She closed the door, starting the shower and letting the room fill up with steam. The water was hot, and she could have stood forever in it. Her body felt like sobbing, but with the shower spray in her face, she couldn't tell if she was or not. She brushed her teeth, brushed the curls in her hair flat and pulled them into a tight ponytail – too tight. She felt a headache coming on.

When she came out of the bathroom, his pillow was gone and the linen closet had been ransacked for blankets. Somehow, even though she'd told him to leave her alone, that disappointed her even more.

She crawled into bed. She never fell asleep completely, drifting in and out of dreams, hearing him come upstairs, peeking his face inside the door. "Melie, do you want some water? Are you hungry?" He came upstairs one last time to say goodnight, but he didn't come to bed with her. He didn't offer any more apologies or excuses. He just stood inside the doorway for a moment and she kept her eyes closed so he'd think she was sleeping. She didn't hear from him again after that.

He wasn't even thinking about this. She knew him, and she knew he wanted to forget it was ever said, to gloss over it and carry on. She couldn't do that. So she thought about it for both of them. There were so many lies and mistruths that she didn't even know where to begin deciphering them. Which should she try to make sense of first? That he'd lied to her? That he'd actually dated Jodie in some capacity? That it had happened while they were already together – and was that cheating? Did it matter whether it was cheating or not? Or that Jodie couldn't have actually been a real friend after all, because if she had, she never would have needed to ask him what he felt? Amelia wasn't sure which betrayal hurt more.

She thought about it all to exhaustion and eventually she fell into a restless sleep. Then the restless sleep turned into morning, the kind of morning that glowed golden on the windowsill, the sky flashing from darkness to light within minutes. She watched the morning light creep across the room, filling it, the brightness building.

There was no sound from him anywhere in the house. She got out of bed.

She went to the front door, pulling the blinds aside. His Jeep was gone. He'd left, just like that, no word of where he was going, when he'd come back, or even *if* he'd come back. She went to the kitchen, picking up shopping receipts, looking for a scribble of his handwriting, some note, anything. All she found were fragments of poems she couldn't decipher. There was nothing else. In the three months they'd been living together, and for so long before, she'd never left him in the morning without a kiss goodbye. Was he leaving her? Did she want him to?

She ran back to bed and buried herself under the covers, fighting the dull throb of tears trying to escape. She reached out to the place where his pillow was still missing. His half of the bed was cold. It hadn't been the bad dream she hoped it was.

3.3: painkillers

AMELIA SAT IN HER MOTHER'S OFFICE AT THE LOTUS. It was Tuesday night; she had to shadow Mindy in an hour and a pounding migraine began to fill up her skull. She closed her eyes to the world. The TV was off, and there was no music playing, but her eyes still felt singed, though the lights in this room weren't even very bright. Her brain wound around itself, wrapping its tendrils around her skull like a hand. Every sound was torture, the click of her mother's keyboard, two teenage girls through the window and their incessant chatter, a truck backing up out on the street, *beep, beep, beep, beep*. She reached into her mother's desk drawer for a bottle of Motrin, took two pills out, hesitated only shortly before picking out a third and washed them down with strong coffee.

Her mother picked at her keyboard, emails to clients, order forms for suppliers, or answering phone calls about the day spa packages. Her efficiency was something to revere, effortlessly splitting her attention in seven directions without a single missed keystroke. She couldn't tell her mother what had happened. Her mother, who had been with her father since they were fourteen, perfectly married for twenty-nine years. How could she tell her mother that she was flaking out of her third major relationship? How could she admit that she wasn't cut out to be loved forever, to get married, to have a family, or that those grandbabies her mother so desperately wanted would be coming from the sperm bank after all? Amelia gripped her forehead and took tight breaths. The headache only persisted; she wanted to throw up.

Without looking away from the computer screen, Claire asked her, "Did you have a bad day at work?"

A bad day at work? Well, yes, because of everything else. Her mother had never had a bad day at work. Her mother was a robot. "I just have a headache," Amelia said.

Her mother glanced over to her finally, at the cup of coffee in Amelia's hands, and she shook her head. "You drink far too much coffee. It wouldn't hurt you to cut back a bit." Then she turned back to her email, *clickity-clickity-click.*

Amelia just sipped her coffee, which she hadn't had too much of. She needed much, much more, in fact, because she had hardly slept at all in the past couple of days, and her mother bought the best coffee – rich and woody, strong. Not to mention organic and fair trade. Her mother did everything right.

Claire reached out to touch Amelia's forearm, a gesture both tender and condescending all at once. "You have class soon, don't you, sweetie?"

Amelia exhaled heavily. "Yes," she said. And she rose to head out to the studio.

The previous class had just ended. Corbin was still there on the floor, talking to his yoga friend, the earthy brunette with that dreamy smile. It seemed like the most engaging conversation anyone had ever had. When he caught sight of Amelia, he squeezed the girl's arm, whispered something to her and leapt up from the floor. He moved so fast it made Amelia's head swirl. "So how are... things?"

She had told Corbin she didn't need him to look out for her – part of her usually liked that he did anyway, but now it only made her stiffen. He'd been there that night at the party. He'd been standing there in the living room with everyone else when she and Drew pushed through the bodies and up the stairs to yell at each other. She wasn't in a position to ask Drew these things, how long did everyone stay, what did they hear, did they all see it too? Was it really what she thought it was? "Oh, that," she said. "Things have been better."

Amelia couldn't remember ever feeling so terrible in her life. All the emotional drain exhausted her, while the corresponding worries kept her from sleep. Her mind was the unmoving pieces of a broken machine, the stuck cogs and data errors. Nothing made sense. No thought process brought her anywhere at all except back to where she started – how she knew Drew, how she thought they knew each other inside and out. For three years, they'd been so close. Could she really be so naïve? It only reminded her that she should have known better. She'd been lied to for much longer than that before.

She grimaced. "How much did you guys hear?"

"Enough," he said.

"Don't tell my mom." It came out more desperate than she'd meant it and made a wave of concern wash over his face – never any judgment, just concern.

"Really? I wouldn't. But you haven't told her?"

Amelia shook her head, but there was this pinch between his eyebrows that only grew tighter with worry. She straightened her shoulders. "I just don't want to bother her, you know? She has enough to worry about, with my dad and all."

"Huh," he muttered. The concern on his face didn't soften.

It wasn't that she needed his opinion. Why should she need anyone's opinion? She'd like to think she could handle these kinds of decisions on her own – she should be able to – but she didn't have much faith in her own instincts anymore. "So what do you think?"

"About?"

"About... things?"

He hesitated. "It's not my job to like your fiancé."

"So you don't?"

"I didn't say that either." Corbin stood solid with his hands on his hips – he didn't lie, but she knew when he wasn't telling the whole truth either.

"What then?"

He only shook his head. "I know a few things, Amelia, but this isn't one of them. You can trust me on that." He picked up her hand, holding her ring up in front of her. "But you're still engaged. So what does your gut say?"

He said it like it was really that simple. Was it really that simple? That lovely ring on her finger, too pretty to be true. No, she hadn't decided to give it back, though she hadn't really decided anything at all. It had only been three days and she was still in shock. It seemed so easy to make things worse. It seemed to be the only way to go. With something held up so impossibly high, the only way to go was down.

After the first night, she hadn't asked Drew to sleep on the couch again – she hadn't really had the guts the first night either, but he went so easily. The second night, he'd fallen asleep first in bed, and she climbed in next to him. She hadn't forgiven him, and she wanted him to know that – but for what? All those ambiguous offenses that blended in her mind, one collective lie. She wrapped herself tightly under the covers next to him, no arm or leg touching his – without his warmth, she was grateful to be wrapped so tight. He fell asleep quickly as he always did and she listened to his breath, rhythmic and calm. She resented him for that, for not being angry. She tossed long into the night and slept badly when it finally came.

She was standing in the studio with Corbin when Drew came

in. Drew froze at the sight of them together. Corbin also went silent at the sight of Drew; even Amelia had never seen so much contempt in Drew's eyes. And Amelia knew her mother was waiting there in her office, listening to everything, just ready to spill out every last opinion she had about Amelia's problems. It wasn't a conversation Amelia was prepared to have. She went to Drew at the door and pulled him into the lobby.

The lobby was a small room, a glorified hallway with a desk that they couldn't afford to have anyone attend full time, posters of palms, fit bodies doing yoga on beaches in front of a vivid sunrise. The same soothing reed flutes filled the air, only they sounded closed off and tinny between the enclosed walls.

If he wanted an answer on her part, she didn't have one. She hadn't decided to give the ring back – she hadn't let the conflict materialize that far, but it occurred to her then that he might ask for it. That he could take back the ring, take back his intentions, his feelings, everything he'd ever said to her. Men could do that – they could love so hard, so fully, so sure, and then they could take it all away. Maybe she didn't know him like she thought she did. She imagined she could see the thought processes behind his eyes, that he might be deciding if all this work was worth it. Should he just cut his losses and let her go? She could hear it already – those echoes, all those same voices. She braced herself for it. *I'm sorry, you were right. I think I might love her.*

He held up his hand, raising the braided hemp strap that kept her favorite yoga mat rolled, 'the only mat she'd ever found plush enough to keep her bones from digging into the floor in Boat Pose. "You forgot your mat," he said.

She felt so relieved she could laugh, but she held it back because he wasn't laughing.

"Though I'm sure your yoga buddy could have lent you his," Drew added. "Looks like he helps out with a lot of things around here." Drew pointed into the studio like it was a scandalous place. Inside, Corbin stood with his friend again, holding a strand of her hair in his hand. "And if you think *anything* Jodie and I ever did, or didn't do, was *anything* like that, then you don't know me at all. Now it's my turn to ask a question. What *is* the big deal with Corbin?"

"There's no big deal."

"You're hiding something."

Her face flushed. "I'm not hiding anything," she said. She hated lies. "I just never said it. It never came up, 'Oh, by the way, me and Corbin, we had sex a couple years ago.' It was nothing. We were only together once. Or, well, twice, if you count the..." She stopped.

"So it's true? You actually fucked him?"

"It's different," she said. "I was single, he was single."

"When was the last time?"

"I don't know, maybe about three years ago, just after Eric and I broke up."

"When you said you didn't want to date anyone?"

She would hardly call what she and Corbin had done "dating". But she didn't say that out loud. "I didn't want to date anyone, and I didn't date him."

"But how is this different? You actually slept with that hulk, and I'm not supposed to think about that? You're still friends with him – you want me to be friends with him. And all that time I was waiting for you to figure out if you even wanted to date me at all, you were screwing around with him? And he's still hanging around, 'helping'." Drew made quotes with his fingers. "And now you want me to think about Jodie and something that might or might not have been a date, while you're still friends with *him* who you *fucked*?"

His finger pointed at Corbin like a dart, and she'd never seen him so angry. Her body willed itself to cry, but she held that back. Her voice was void of power. "I never didn't want to date you."

He'd been the one caught with his hands wrapped around one of her best friends, and here he was angry with her? She exhaled a shallow breath. "The difference is I don't want to be with him. And I never wanted to be with him romantically. And neither did he. At all. And that's just one of his girlfriends – he's not like that with me."

"Sure he isn't." Drew shoved the yoga mat into her hands. "Have a good fucking class."

He swung the front doors open hard and passed through, letting them sway. He kicked a short potted bonsai outside on the sidewalk, sending the pot rolling heavy on its circumference and a tremor through the plant's branches. Amelia watched it, waiting for the thing to decide whether it would finally tip over or come to a rest. Drew was still walking. He had nearly cleared the corner, and then he was gone. The plant didn't tip, but eventually came to the ground again, having sprinkled some of its potting soil out onto the pavement.

In a rush of voices, a group of pregnant women came into the lobby for their evening class. Amelia backed up against the wall, pressing herself against it to let them pass, tinny reed flutes echoing against the closed walls, then spilling out into the larger room as the doors opened. A whole group of them poured into the lobby at once, but there was only one person trying to exit. It was Corbin's friend. "Oh, sorry." Her voice was nearly swallowed by the crowd of chattering pregnant women, and she pressed herself back against the wall where Amelia stood to let the others pass through. "Busy night," she said.

It was Amelia she was speaking to. It caught her off guard, though the girl had never looked over to make eye contact. They'd never been formally introduced before. Amelia didn't even know her name. "Mmm-hmm," Amelia agreed softly.

Was this one of his girlfriends? The word nagged at her – Corbin hadn't ever called her that himself. Amelia had been telling Drew the truth, that Corbin wasn't ever like that with her, so connected, so starry-eyed. And truthfully, he wasn't usually much like *that* with any other women but this one. Amelia hadn't taken the time to notice that difference. This girl, when he was with her, he was more attentive than with the others. When he spoke to this girl, it was like they were the only two people alive on the planet. Amelia didn't know anything about who she was. She wore modest yoga wear, nothing showy, nothing scant or seductive. He didn't talk about her with the casual freedom he would some of his other flings. He really didn't talk about her at all.

The girl held her head down as the people passed, her mat strap slung over her left shoulder, her left hand holding it in place near her chin. A thin strip of gold sparked the light, so much more plain than the ring Amelia wore on her own finger, but there just the same. A wedding band. She was married?

Amelia's heart started to pound. She was married. Corbin was seeing a married woman? And where was his honesty now? What would her parents think if they knew? Had he been lying to them all, or was this just another one of those truths he didn't say out loud? How many things could a person keep hidden, never saying them out loud so they never had to lie, though the truth was there the whole time? And wasn't that a form of lying in itself?

"Excuse me," the girl said as the last person cleared the lobby, and she passed out into the cold evening, her head still tucked down.

Amelia stood still in the lobby, empty after everyone had left it, before she entered the studio where Mindy was waiting to greet their class. The faces swirled around her, gentle smiles, friendly dispositions. She put on a smile of her own. She tried to unwind, let her mind and body float to some place better than where she was. It was impossible. She couldn't focus. It was all too much. She didn't know what in this world was true anymore.

Standing in front of all those women, the thought of Downward Dog and all that blood rushing to her head made her stomach churn. She couldn't do it. She must have had a terrible pain on her face because Mindy was staring at her with a swaggering grin. Amelia didn't want to admit failure, to give up, to let everyone see that this one little thing, a fight, a man, could destroy her so wholly. She didn't want to, but it was what it was – a failure.

"You know, you were right," she said to Mindy. "I don't have a center."

The grin on her face morphed into confusion. "What are you talking about?"

"I mean, don't worry about my shadows. I'm never going to be a teacher, and you don't have to bother doing any more of my shadows. I quit."

"Oh, Amelia" her mother said from the side of the room, shaking her head in disapproval. But Amelia brushed past her in the hallway. She could still hear her saying, "Aren't you overreacting just a bit? You really can't put people on the spot like that."

Amelia wasn't listening anymore. She closed herself in the dark room at the end of the hallway, their massage room. She let her back slide down the wall to sit on the cold floor. She felt woozy, and breathed long and slowly, fighting the urge to throw up. She had no answer or excuse for her mother. There was no potent sandalwood here, but soft oils and aromatherapy candles instead. Behind her eyelids, the darkness throbbed with her pulse, the heavy swells and lulls. She kept breathing, finding comfort in the darkness, nearly black, with only the spill of light coming underneath the heavy curtains in the doorway.

Corbin's footsteps were quiet for as large a man as he was. "You could lie down here if you want. I don't have any appointments." She opened her eyes. He held the curtain aside, standing in the doorway and the glow from the other room surrounded him like an aura, if she were to believe in such a thing. His would be a clear and serene color, sage green. "When you get home," he added, crouching down beside her. "There's a spot, here." He reached out to the base of her skull with light pressure. It felt like heaven. "It'll help the headaches."

But then she thought of Drew, of his anger. *He's not like that with me*, she'd told him. But wasn't he? She didn't know. She pushed Corbin's hand away in more haste than she intended. He took a step back from her. He was only trying to help – always trying to help. He was such a pleasure to have around. Always so kind and generous and honest. That was what her father always said about him – *You don't find honesty like that very often*. He spoke to their customers, who all knew and trusted him; he charmed them. That was his game, the charm. When is charm ever true? In Amelia's experience, charm was exactly the opposite of truth. The whole world seemed to spin and pulse with the veins in her head, a million tiny vessels. She just wanted to disappear.

Amelia stabilized herself on the wall and rose to stand on her wavering legs. "She's married, that girl you talk to," she said. She wasn't asking him a question, just putting the truth out there in the open.

Corbin didn't ask who. He knew exactly who she meant. "I'm not sleeping with her," he said. "She's a good friend. And yes, she is married."

Just friends – it never meant what they wanted it to mean. There was always more to the story. And what Amelia had suspected of him was right; his response only confirmed it. "Like her being married would stop you."

The only light in the room was a slit in the curtains where he'd left them open, but it was enough to see the life had fallen dead from his face. "Is that really what you think of me?"

"But you would," Amelia said.

"I never claimed to be a perfect man, but I'm not the monster you think I am." He stepped away from her, back into the hallway, stopping at the lockers where they all kept their things. His paper bag of clothing and a couple books. She moved to stand near the doorway, squinting into the light. He stopped then, looking her hard in the eyes. "You know, you're right. If she would, I would. Go ahead and judge me for that."

He started to walk again.

"That's not what I'm doing," Amelia said, shouting after him. But if he heard her, he didn't show it. And anyway, he was right.

3.4: the gaps

JODIE HAD TAKEN ON A PROJECT AT THE CLINIC TO KEEP herself busy. Busy was a good thing to be. When she'd managed to send her entire social life into chaos, she figured she should focus on her professional life instead. They had a store room full of birth control samples from drug companies, advertisement posters that were no longer relevant, samples from formula companies, breast pumps, nipple creams, and newborn-sized diapers that parents could only use for three days, if at all. Sometimes she got the feeling she hadn't made the best impression on the other doctors and nurses there, so she offered to clean out their store room to make space for a birthing class they wanted to offer. Jodie wanted to prove to them that she could be agreeable – or at least useful. If nothing else, Jodie had always been an achiever.

And Jodie *could* be agreeable sometimes. Some of the things she found in the store room were still good, and Jodie had a pregnant sister-in-law. She would send some of it for Ruth and the baby. Jodie was still getting used to the idea of all this new family. For as long as she'd known, it had been just her and Eric.

Though she was never the type to crave social time, so she'd intended to send the package by mail. "Why don't you just bring it over yourself and pay us a visit?" her brother had said. "You are coming for Christmas, aren't you?"

"Sure I am."

"You can bring someone," he offered. "Are you seeing anyone?"

Her brother didn't have a clue what was going on here. No, she wasn't seeing anyone. Never was, and never would be for all she cared. It was better that way. Jodie always did better on her own. She always thrived on her own. People only stood in her way.

But when Jodie saw the line at the post office, she considered changing her mind about that visit. It was December. She should have known better than to brave the post office before Christmas rush, the impossibly long waits, the stress in everyone's eyes, the bell-ringer standing outside in road salt and cigarette butts whistling, "Up On the Rooftop." She'd probably be in that line longer than it would take her to drive the ninety minutes up to Lansing herself.

She turned around and headed for the main doors. Outside there was the sound of Christmas carols, chipper and bright, sung to the beat of an incessantly clanging bell. That was when she lifted her face and saw them, two heads of red hair. Amelia and her mother, in their bright belted coats, Amelia in turquoise, her mother in red, bursting vividly against the cool winter gray of the city sidewalks and sky and salted roads. Jodie stopped, hard, gripping her package in one arm and pressing the other hand to the glass door, bracing her body from running face into it.

Then an impact, bodies colliding, smashing into Jodie's back and knocking the wind from her lungs. "Ugh," a girl grunted behind her, wearing too much perfume and holding a Blackberry in her hands. "Learn how to walk or something."

People scattered around them both. The girl started to walk again, stepping past.

"Fuck you too," Jodie said, though her voice came out squeaky. The girl only continued on, swinging the doors open to the cold.

Jodie retreated back into the post office, trying to look inconspicuous near the rows of cushioned mailers, patterns for birthdays or Christmas or generic floral prints. She watched Amelia and her mother as they walked down the street. Somber faces on both of them, though Amelia's mother always had a somber face. Jodie couldn't make out much through the glass, and from this distance – they moved their lips slightly in a casual conversation. When they came to the intersection, Amelia's mother placed two fingers on her daughter's back, lightly guiding, as if she were a child who couldn't be trusted to cross the street on her own. Jodie couldn't remember the last time her own mother had touched her like that, or at all.

When they'd gone, Jodie stood there at the window so long that some of the post office staff were staring at her, probably ready to alert the police to a terrorist threat on her behalf. She took her package and went back home.

JODIE'S APARTMENT WAS EMPTY AND DARK INSIDE ON THESE early winter evenings. She flicked on some lights, turned on the news, recorded voices filling the emptiness, Beck Johnston Chevrolet, *you won't find a better deal in Detroit, guaranteed...* an anti-depressant commercial, *some patients experienced death in testing, but this has not been linked to the product...* Chuck E Cheese, in a goofy and lilted voice, *Thursday nights, half off admission on parties of 8 or greater.*

Jodie wasn't on call for deliveries. Her brother was seventy-five miles up north. She didn't even have any liquor in the house. Only the silence, and the yellow notepad of names that still sat on Jodie's kitchen table. In her email, there was another list from Drew. No matter if they'd been too pretty, or hadn't had stable enough a job, or were too chipper or cheesy, it didn't matter anymore. Jodie couldn't call these girls. Not after what she'd done.

Jodie turned her head to the sound of keys in the lock, and the front door popped open. It was Piper. Piper wouldn't hold a grudge, but Jodie could feel the disappointment in her eyes. She never thought she could do wrong enough to disappoint Piper.

Piper came over to sit next to her on the couch, a tiny bright sigh, looking at her with so much pity. Jodie didn't need to be pitied.

Piper had mentioned that she made plans with Amelia for that afternoon, and Jodie wondered how it went. She knew she had no right to ask, for all the mess she'd caused. It wasn't her business to know, but she wanted to know anyway. She asked it cautiously. "So are they... okay? Did they sort things out?"

"They're having a rough time," Piper said. "What did you think would happen?"

Jodie didn't know what she'd expected to happen.

Piper shook her head. She checked in on Jodie more often in those days following the party, like she was waiting for Jodie to combust. Piper reached over to stroke Jodie's flat hair. "Oh Jodie, what are you going to do?"

Do? What was there to do? Jodie stared flatly at the television – she didn't even know what was on. "I'm not going to do anything." There was nothing to do. There was nothing to say. What she'd done couldn't be taken back now.

Piper still had Jodie's hair in her hand.

"Aren't you staying with Tom tonight?"

"No, silly, not tonight. I thought we could hang out."

It's not true, Jodie. She could hear Piper's lecture in her head still.

Piper, she meant something to Jodie. She was the only one Jodie would claim.

LATER THAT WEEK, DESPITE HER BEST EFFORTS TO TRY THE POST office again, Jodie found herself driving I-96 out to Lansing to see her brother and his wife.

Ruth came to greet her at the door and Jodie inhaled the warm smell of something baking. Jodie had the package in her hands. "I'm glad you decided to visit," Ruth said.

Jodie shrugged. "Yeah, well, the lines at the post office this time of year." Ruth guided her into the living room.

"Well thank you then," she said. "Eric's just out picking up dinner. You know, I'm not much use in the kitchen these days." She eased herself onto the couch, sighing heavily and arranging her shirt around her plump belly. "So how's your friend?"

"Friend?" Many names flashed though Jodie's mind then, friends betrayed, friends upset, friends who might or might not have actually been friends.

"Gary, was it?"

"Oh, Berges. I mean, Gary, yeah." Jodie was surprised to know her sister-in-law actually remembered him. She didn't know if they were friends anymore. And that wasn't like Piper said about the others, some ploy to make it feel easier. She and Berges had certainly been friends once. Jodie knew they had.

Ruth turned up the corner of a smile. "Well I remember you two looking pretty friendly. That's too bad. He seemed nice."

"Ha, nice?" Jodie's voice drifted into a lazy chuckle. "Nah, you don't know him then."

"Well make yourself comfortable," Ruth said. "Can I get you some tea, coffee, wine? I can't drink any of it right now, so you might as well have one for the both of us."

Ruth winked and Jodie was stunned. Was that a joke? A barely-funny one, maybe, but a joke all the same. Maybe she did have a sense of humor after all. She must have, to have married Eric. Jodie finally began to laugh. "Wine, sure," she said. "But you don't have to get up."

Ruth waved her off and went into the kitchen anyway. The living room had all of Eric's stuff hidden and disguised by things that must have belonged to Ruth. Jodie didn't blame her – she knew her brother had terrible taste in home decor, with his plastic magazine racks and La-Z-Boy chairs. Jodie spoke loudly toward the kitchen. "You tossed that hideous old La-Z-Boy?"

Jodie could hear her in the kitchen, the clang of glassware, the pop of a wine bottle. "No, I let him keep it in the bedroom," Ruth said.

The television was on, but the sound turned down so low it was inaudible. Jodie watched the moving lips. She wandered around the room, picking out the things Ruth had let Eric keep. A throw blanket over her armchair, his *National Geographic* and *Time* magazines that were mixed with her *Reader's Digest* in a lovely wooden magazine rack – the rack was hers. There was one of his college photos on the bookshelf, which held one single corner for his travel photography books. The end tables, simple mahogany and not too scratched up – those had been his. A small reminder of his once bachelor life, mixed into this new life she made for them together.

At home, Jodie felt the opposite. Her life with Piper, the things that had grown to be theirs together, were being split up and taken apart. Piper made her claims and took her things away to start her new life with Tom. It only left gaps.

Jodie touched the spines of books on a bookshelf. In between sections of books, she scanned the framed photos in the spaces, a wedding portrait, Ruth's family, and one of Jodie with Eric as children. She couldn't even remember being that tiny.

On the bottom shelf were Eric's perfectly kept photo albums. Jodie didn't keep any photos of them herself, and any time she found one, she'd hand it off to Eric – he was better at it. He kept them in albums, dated by years, and painfully lined up in rows, dating back before Jodie was even born. He was a journalist – he documented things.

Jodie ran her finger along the volumes of family history. 1983, 1982, 1980. 1977, the year she was born. Jodie picked it up. Her birth, documented. She was a grayish baby with tiny eyes and too much hair on her head. She reminded herself of a Troll doll. The pictures went on. Her parents took her home, recorded first smiles, first side rolls – she was a log-roller, from one side of the room to another. Her first time sitting up, five months, an adept child even then. Six months, first food, pureed butternut squash. Seven months, and then there was nothing. The pictures had stopped, a gap, a complete time warp. The next photo, she was twelve months old, standing in the middle of the room, a fat leg reaching ahead of her to take a wobbly step.

In those lost months, the divorce had happened. Her first tooth, her first word, the first time her hair had been long enough for a ponytail – they'd all been too distraught and occupied to document it. So it didn't happen, it was skipped over, as if she'd fallen into a fold in the fabric of time. Did she break the marriage? Was she such an awful child that they couldn't bear the union for one moment longer?

Jodie closed the album and slid it back to its place. Ruth would be back in seconds, back to her white and powder-blue living room with doilies and ruffled slipcovers on the chairs. And Eric's photo albums. Jodie scooted back from the space, rubbing out her knee marks on the carpet as if she hadn't been there at all. She had returned to the armchair again by the time Ruth hobbled into the living room with a glass of wine in one hand and a chocolate milk in the other.

"It's hormone-free, don't worry," Ruth said. She rubbed her round belly. "Only the best for your niece, I promise." Ruth looked up, smiling.

Jodie waited for something to sink in. "Oh, a niece," Jodie said out loud.

Ruth nodded. "It's a girl."

"Well how about that," Jodie said, trying to imagine how her awkward brother's genetics would look on a girl. "Well, I hope she gets more of your looks than his then."

Ruth smiled, a genuine gesture. "Thanks, Jodie."

Eric came home then, and Jodie stood to greet him. Eric kissed his wife and then hugged his sister. How ordinary they looked, like a regular family. Did he escape the curse, or was he only putting on an organized front? Underneath all of this, the wedding, the family, wasn't he just the same as she was? He could pretend all he wanted, but wasn't he just as much a wreck?

Eric took their take-out into the kitchen. "We're cursed you know," she told Ruth. "Me and him." She told it as a joke, though in her heart, she believed every word of it.

Ruth looked up at her, not sharply, but stern. She shook her head. "It's not true, Jodie." In her eyes, it wasn't defensive or even trying to plead her case. It was as if she were simply speaking the truth.

"Well, just me then." Jodie looked down to her lap, pressed her hands to the place where the photo album had been.

"No, not you either," Ruth said.

3.5: one truth

JODIE WAS ALONE AT THE OFFICE. IT WAS 9:30 AT NIGHT, and their last appointment had been at 4:30, but Jodie was still working on clearing out the store room. One of the nurses had offered to stay and help for a bit, but even she had family to go home to eventually. She'd salvaged what was usable for Ruth already, and the rest she stuffed into black trash bags. She ran a damp cloth over the shelves as she went, and her eyes were rimmed red from all the dust. She hated that it looked like she was crying. Because she wasn't. And she wasn't sorry either. It overwhelmed her how not sorry she was. Because if she admitted she was sorry, it would mean she was wrong. And she wasn't wrong either.

There were no windows in the store room, but she could hear the icy sleet on the windows of other rooms. The sky had been pissing mixed ice and rain all day. She would need to head home soon as the night grew colder, dipping below freezing, leaving all that sleet to harden into ice on her windshield. She didn't want to have to scrape that off later.

It wasn't her turn to be on-call for deliveries that week, but it would have made things easier for her, those phone calls ripping her out of the bed she wasn't even sleeping in at three in the morning. There would always be babies to be delivered, to be welcomed into this dreaded world kicking and screaming. That was appropriate, she always thought. They should be terrified.

She took down one more unlabeled box from the top shelf. She lost hold of it, the box toppling from her grip and crashing to the floor, scattering expired birth control samples over the floor, throwing dust up into the air.

"Dammit," she said. "Why doesn't anybody throw this shit away?"

She had to leave this allergy pit and do something else. She went to the bathroom and splashed her eyes with cool water, looking up at her sallow face. Her eyelids were the color of strawberries and starting to swell. This was a bad idea. She was full of bad ideas, it seemed.

She went to her own office in search of a Claritin. She raked through her desk drawer and found nothing, just pens and paper clips and sticky notes. She went to her office window. The icy cold rain drenched the small parking lot. There were three cars out there, but she didn't recognize whom the others belonged to. One of the lawyers working late, or the cleaning crew? Jodie leaned forward slowly until her forehead touched the window, realizing then that she could press her eyes against the icy glass. The cold felt good on her swollen skin. With her eyes closed, hands on the window sill and face pressed to the glass, she remembered Piper's voice that night, sitting on that cold bench in the snow: *It's easier to think that.*

But it wasn't easier. Not in the end. She never said she loved Drew, but that didn't mean she didn't. And she told herself again and again that Amelia was just her brother's ex-girlfriend, but that didn't change the truth. So instead, Jodie told herself she wasn't sorry, that she didn't take back telling Drew how she felt. She couldn't. Because she didn't know if she'd ever loved a man before she loved Drew, and she couldn't be sorry for telling him that.

How could loving someone be so wrong?

Jodie pulled her face from the window. Her eyes had cleared a little, though her breath had fogged up the glass, which was starting to form ice on the outside screen. Raindrops glistened in the streetlights. Her car sat in her parking spot, the best spot in the whole lot, and this time of year it didn't even matter. There were no leaves on the trees and there was no sap. Any of those parking spaces were just as good as the next, but that didn't matter. She didn't know if she and Berges were friends now, but if Jodie could tell herself one truth tonight, it would be that she never wanted Berges to resent her over some stupid parking space. And at a time when she could count all the friends she had left on one hand, she wanted to make sure he was one of them.

Jodie ran back to the storeroom looking for a tool box of some kind, finding only medical equipment, sterilized vaginal speculums, tubes of ultrasound jelly, boxes of medical gloves. The fluorescent lights over her head flickered and buzzed. She tried to think. She went to the office kitchen instead. She pulled utensils out of a drawer, a measuring cup, chip clips, a wine screw. Who the hell drank wine in an obstetrician's office?

A butter knife. She grabbed it and burst quickly out of the office, down the stairs to the parking lot. To her parking spot.

It was freezing cold, the rain hovering in between water and ice, finding the warmth of her skin and melting there. Her fingers were freezing, and she didn't even have a proper screwdriver, but with the flat edge of the butter knife, she turned the screws holding the name plate on her parking space. If it hadn't been a brand new parking lot, with brand new signs and screws, she would have been out of luck. It wouldn't have worked. But these screws were new, shining gold in the yellowed parking lot lights, even though they were made of aluminum. She took the metal name plate off her pole, took the metal name plate off his pole, and she switched them, standing on a file room box to reach, screwing the screws back in with her butter knife, torquing on the handle tightly. It slipped, slashing her palm on the sharp edge of the name plate. The cut burned, but she didn't have time to care. There was a stack of fast food restaurant napkins in the glove box, and she wrapped her hand in them, and she drove.

Berges lived in town, not too far from the medical complex where they both worked. He had one of those stylish, newly built loft apartments they'd just put up near Main Street – the ones that only men like him could afford to live in, nearing middle-age, highly successful, and divorced.

Jodie buzzed his apartment number.

A girl answered back through the speaker. "Who is it?"

"Oh," Jodie said softly, half unsure she even had the right number. "I was looking for Berges– I mean, Gary."

"Alright," the girl said. The front door buzzed.

Jodie reached to grab it quickly before it locked again. Then she remembered her hand. It hadn't bled through the stack of napkins yet, but only because she'd been clenching it so hard.

She took the stairs up to the third floor where he lived. When she knocked, it was that same girl who answered the door. It was only when Jodie saw her that she realized who it was – a girl she'd never met before except in the pictures hanging in his office, yet Jodie knew more about this little girl than any other living girl on the planet.

Hazel.

And Jodie knew it because despite being tom-boyishly pretty, the girl somehow managed to look just like her dad. Jodie had helped select so many birthday cards and Christmas presents, all those details, a March twenty-seventh birthday, clothing size three in juniors, her favorite color was aqua. Jodie had picked out outfits, songs for iPods, and even suggested how many minutes to add to her cell phone plan. She'd listened to endless hours about Hazel's grades, and Hazel's track meets, and Hazel's bitch mother. Now there she was in actual physical form, barefoot in pink Hello Kitty pajamas, a little taller than Jodie had imagined she would be.

"Uh," Jodie stammered. "Is your dad home?"

Hazel just stared at her blankly, then shouted, "Dad. For you." Then she vanished into the apartment.

Jodie heard his voice from inside. "Hazel, you shouldn't answer the door this time of night." Jodie hadn't even thought about the time. She noticed a clock hanging on his wall, reading already past eleven. He stood there considering something, whether to invite her in or not, whether to shout at her, whether to call the cops? But then he saw her fist clenched around the napkins. "What did you do to your hand?"

"Oh, it's nothing," she said, but he'd already taken her hand into his, moving the paper towels aside to see what was underneath.

"You can have your damn spot," she said. "I don't want it anymore."

He didn't understand what she meant, only watching her curiously. "You need to get that disinfected," he said, pulling her inside.

He sat her at the kitchen table and opened up a medical bag. He disinfected the hand with a towelette. His hands were warm and so perfectly precise, though the alcohol stung worse than the gash itself.

"Don't think you're getting anywhere near me with that needle," she said.

"I'm very good at what I do," he said, a gloating pride in his smile.

"No, just slap some Band-Aids on it."

He took out three butterfly strips and patched together the two-inch gash. "This shouldn't scar anyway," he said, not like the arrogant prick he usually was, but with tenderness, like he actually cared that her hand might scar.

"You have Hazel?" Jodie asked, though it was obvious from the girl's presence that he had her.

"I have her Wednesdays now too," he said. "I pick her up from school and take her back Thursday morning."

"I didn't know."

"Because I didn't tell you."

There was a time he would have told her. He would bitch about having to deal with Kate's lawyer and how he'd have to close his office three hours early one day every week, but with that gleam in his eye that said he really wanted to have Hazel there all along. If nothing else, they had been friends. Good friends even. They'd been friends for years.

"What are you doing here, Jodie?" He pointed at her hand. "Besides whatever you were..." His voice trailed off, carrying an edge of annoyance, and something like disappointment.

"You can have the spot," she said. "That's all I wanted to say."

She might have had tears in her eyes, or maybe it was just the sting of allergies. Maybe it was the nothingness, the numbness in her chest that kept growing wider until her whole body felt the chill. That night, when she blew through her entire circle of friends in a single moment, neither of them would look at her – not Amelia, and especially not Drew. Not even once, like she hadn't even been there. *Nothing*, he had said. She was nothing to him at all.

Jodie stood up quickly. "I should go," she said, already headed for the door. She turned back for just a moment – she wasn't finished here, not yet. "People just do things sometimes," she said to him. "We don't mean it – we're just selfish. We need to do what we need to do and sometimes other people get hurt. We try to make it right. Sometimes we can, and sometimes we can't."

He was too shocked to be bitter, and too cynical to be accepting. She understood that well. She didn't need anything else from him.

Jodie swallowed hard and took a breath. "I'm sorry Kate divorced you."

His face softened with more graciousness than she'd expected. "It wasn't your fault," he said.

"I *know*," she said. "But still."

Her eyes filled fast with tears, and she let her hair fall forward to cover them. Then she felt his hands, taking hold of her arms, rubbing the chill from her skin. She leaned her head to his chest, her face close, her lips almost touching his skin, but she stopped. There. Just an inch of space before contact.

"Jodie," he said. "Where's your coat?"

She'd left it in the office. She hadn't considered how freezing it was outside when she'd been in that parking lot with a butter knife in her hand and adrenaline coursing through her veins. "It's not here," she said.

"Wait a minute," he said.

He went to a closet next to the door, rustling around inside briefly. He came back with a coat, heavy black leather. She loved that coat on him. It made him look harder than he really was; it made him look good. He helped her into it, sliding the sleeves over her arms, hanging the weight of it on her shoulders. His hand lingered there on the collar, folding it down, pulling the fabric together across her chest. "Bring it to work with you tomorrow?"

She nodded. "Okay."

"And be careful driving out there. It looks shitty."

"I will."

"And Jodie?"

"Huh?"

"You were right about Kate," he said. "I got in touch with her lawyer a few weeks ago. We talked about it. That's why I have Hazel on Wednesdays now too."

She nodded. Her own eyes must have grown wider than her whole head because his eyes said "thank you," even though she knew he wasn't going to say it out loud. He didn't have to. He said she was right, and that was even better.

He let go of her shoulders so she could step away, and he watched her from his doorway as she went. Hazel had the TV on too loud, some reality drama as she talked with a friend on the phone, her shrill teenage laughter filled the quiet gaps. He had Hazel every Wednesday now, and Jodie was glad. She was happy for him.

Outside, the mixed ice had finally changed over to fluffy snow that melted on the warmer pavement as it touched. The coat smelled like him, like clean linens and surgical soap. She pulled it tighter, his warmth still hidden inside, wrapped around her skin.

It felt like a hug.

3.6: the beauty of bar lights

HE HAD IT UNDER CONTROL. AS FAR AS WHAT IT WAS OR wasn't, on his end, he had things under control. But he'd made a mistake. He thought Jodie would have understood where the feelings started and stopped. But she didn't. On top of that, Amelia certainly didn't understand, and Drew was beginning to doubt that he did either.

So he walked around their house, surrounded by her, all the earth-toned wall art, the bamboo in clay pots, the bookcases that held more framed photos and trinkets than books. She'd given him one room for his books and a desk, and his stacks of literary journals he could never read fast enough and a cork board for his mother's postcards. Amelia had been spending more time at her mother's house that week; she wasn't even here and yet she was everywhere.

She'd left some of his mail on the desk, "Change of Address" labels slapped across the fronts of them. Even the US Postal Service validated his new place in this home with their bright yellow redirect stickers. A cell phone bill, his car payment, another poetry rejection, credit card spam. Amelia insisted those credit card offers needed to be shredded, at the risk of someone trying to steal his identity, but he just added them to an endless pile in a shoebox under his desk. Who wanted to do that much shredding?

Drew looked closer at the poetry rejection. They usually came in his own self-addressed envelopes – which he thought this was at first glance, until he noticed the label, written out to his old apartment address with a yellow redirect sticker over top of it, was not written in his own handwriting.

He opened the letter.

Mr. Weston,

Thank you kindly for your prompt attention to this matter. We tried to reach you some time ago about a poem you submitted, "The Beauty of Bar Lights," in which we included our congratulations and a publication contract. Our work on the issue is drawing to a close and we require your response. Please contact us within ten days of this letter, or else we will have to consider your publication forfeited.

Sincerely,

Molly Horowitz, Poetry Editor, Moon River Review

"What the hell," Drew said. He had never received any acceptance letter or contract, and he was pretty sure he'd notice one if he had. He opened up his email and searched for "Moon River Review". No results found. He opened his paper files and sifted through them, dozens of them. He scanned the letterheads and signatures, spreading them out on the floor, so many rejections, all that failure spanning back through his whole writing career. It was shocking how many they amounted to, but none of them were from Moon River Review.

He shuffled stacks of books. He sorted through his pile of credit card spam, glossy envelopes shouting *"0% Interest for 12 Months"* across their fronts. Nothing. He turned out his recycling bin on the floor, more junk mail, paper drafts of poems with his own red pen scribbled in the margins, a misplaced banana peel turned black. Nothing. He opened the closets where he kept his old college textbooks, he dug through drawers of pencils and erasers and pens bleeding ink, and he jabbed his finger on a stray staple. Nothing.

He kicked the chair in the corner.

A pile of clothes began to slide, collapsing and unfolding slowly, falling from its resting place to the floor, the crew jacket and shirts he'd never gotten around to washing. Inside the folded jacket was a stack of mail. "Goddamn," he said. He went to it, turning the envelopes in his hands, pizza delivery menus, credit card spam, two opened poetry rejections and three more unopened self-addressed envelopes. He opened them.

The first: "We enjoyed this, but regret that we cannot use it at this time..." The second: "This was lovely, but not quite right for us. We encourage you to send more of your work in the future..." The third:

Dear Mr. Weston,

Thank you for submitting your poem, "The Beauty of Bar Lights."

There's such frustration coupled with a strong command of metaphor. We especially enjoyed the theme of shipwrecks, and quiet sensuality in your use of the water. We'd love to include this in our spring issue, and we'd be happy to offer $50 and two contributor's copies. You'll find a publication agreement enclosed; please return it as soon as possible. And congratulations!

Molly Horowitz, Poetry Editor, Moon River Review

Congratulations. He read it over again to make sure it said what he thought it said. He couldn't even remember what the poem was about, but they wanted to publish it? He knew of the journal too. No, it wasn't *The New Yorker*, it wasn't *The Atlantic*. But it also wasn't some nameless zine printed on copy-paper and stapled down the middle. It was a well-respected university-run publication, and they wanted to pay him money! His mouth hung open as he read the title back, trying to remember the poem he'd sent. He opened his laptop and searched through the files, finding it dated almost a year ago. He clicked open the poem. He couldn't even blink as he scanned over the words.

He remembered now.

It had been just over a year since he wrote it, since he sent it off in the mail to sit in a slush pile somewhere. A year ago, a night when he thought he'd had enough of Amelia pushing him away, when all he wanted to do was love her, but she wouldn't let him. He thought he'd had enough of it then. He thought he was giving up. They'd had a fight in the parking lot of the bar that night, and she left. But he stayed, and Jodie was still there. He'd found her interesting for that short time – she wasn't nearly as plain as she thought she was, her sharp features only matched by her sharp tongue and piercing blue eyes. They had drinks, playful banter, conversation, a whole night together. And at the end of the night, instead of going home with her, he went home alone and he wrote this poem. He told her he would. It was one of the very first conversations they had, in that bar with neon lights in her spiteful eyes, the flirting, the anger, the fascination. *I'm going to write a poem about you.*

He forgot that he actually did it.

He forgot that he'd actually *sent* it in the space of those four fickle days when he was sure he and Amelia would never work things out.

He skimmed over the lines again, the piercing eyes, the silky darkness between her legs – "quiet sensuality" be damned, this poem was dirty! Drew slammed his laptop shut. "God-fucking-dammit." He'd had a poem accepted by a real, paying literary journal. But of all poems, why this one? Amelia couldn't see this one. Not ever. She would know exactly what it was about. Who it was about. It was the indisputable, physical proof of exactly what had been between him and Jodie. This poem could never be published.

But he had ten days to decide.

No, no, this poem couldn't be published. There was too much truth in it. There *had* been feelings, even if he thought they both understood where those feelings belonged. Not here, and not in the future, but back then in that one single night on the boat, under the stars. He thought they had an understanding. But he was wrong.

He got his keys, got in his car and started to drive.

They hadn't heard from Jodie at all in the five days since that night. All this time had passed and the mess she'd left them with was still raging. It was eating them alive, and what did she have to say for any of it? He needed to hear from her, but even by the time he pulled into the parking lot in front of her building, he had no idea what he had to say himself. He sat in his car, watching snowflakes melt on the warmed glass. He loved the first snow flurries of the year, that moment when winter remained on edge, kicking up a dusting of snowflakes and then taking them back, like it couldn't quite decide if it wanted to be winter or not. Light flurries had been falling on and off all week, but nothing stuck.

He didn't know how Jodie could do this to them. That's what he would ask her. How? Why? He thought they knew each other better than that. But then, how well did they really know each other? Were they really friends, or was this the leftovers of some ill-fated romance that got aborted before it even began? He had so many acquaintances and knew so many people, but he didn't know how many of them were really friends. They were names and phone numbers and a growing collection of faces on his Facebook page. He knew them on such a superficial level. But who did he really know? Who really knew him in return?

Amelia. She knew it. She asked him, when she saw what she saw, and he lied. He said it was nothing, but it wasn't nothing. Whatever it was, it wasn't nothing.

Drew got out of the car and walked up to the door. He knocked and Piper answered. He knew Piper too, in that superficial way he knew any of them. She smiled sweetly. "Drew, how are you?" She didn't wait for him to answer. "Jodie's not here." Her voice was weighted with curiosity. He wondered what Jodie had been saying about him. He couldn't even imagine it – she'd never been the type to gossip.

"Oh," he said. "Alright then."

"She's working," Piper said. "Worker bee, that one. You want me to tell her you were here?"

"No, actually, don't."

She looked at him doubtfully, and somehow he knew she was going to tell Jodie he'd been there anyway. He stepped a full pace back. He shouldn't have been there. "No, don't mention it," he said again.

HE DROVE FOR A WHILE WITH THE MUSIC UP LOUD. HE ENDED UP at his uncle's place, where he took out the garbage, replaced the batteries in a beeping smoke alarm, and fixed an error message on the cable box. By the time he got back home, Amelia was there with her mother. He hadn't realized what time it was – she must have just finished work. He heard their voices chatting in the kitchen, the sputter and hiss of the coffee machine. Amelia called to him, her voice sounding strangely chipper compared to the past few days. "Drew, honey, is that you? We're in the kitchen."

"Yeah," he called back.

"My mom's here."

There, the chipper, that was why.

Then he remembered the letter. He'd left it open on his desk. How long had she been home? And what had she seen already? He knew he needed to show his face in the kitchen, but he needed to get rid of that letter first. He jogged up the stairs, finding the door still ajar and his computer screen gone to its screensaver. When he touched the mouse, the screen flashed on and there was his poem, front and center. How could he have been so stupid?

He quickly closed the file on his laptop, shutting the lid and stacking some books on top. It was ridiculous – like that would stop her from gaining access if she wanted to. He folded the letter, stuffed it back into its envelope, and tucked it in between the pages of a poetry compilation. Amelia wouldn't read that one. She didn't read any poetry except for the ones he wrote – all the ones he wrote.

"Drew," Amelia called up the stairs. Drew turned to the sound of her voice, ears perked, waiting for the sound of her footsteps.

"Hang on, I'm coming," he said, closing up the room before she had a chance to come find him.

In the kitchen, Claire sat at the table. Amelia stood at the counter getting their coffee ready. Drew greeted them both, standing quietly in the doorway, not wanting to intrude on whatever mother-daughter time they were enjoying. Drew found Claire to be a stern and unapproachable woman. Both like Amelia and different in so many ways. When they first met, Claire had said to him, *A poet, how charming*. He felt how she scoffed at the idealism, though he hadn't wanted to be so rude to argue with her about it then. And he would have loved to tell her about this poem, his first publication, to prove that it was a worthwhile "hobby" after all. Of course that was impossible now.

"I just wanted to say, Drew," she started. "Amelia tells me your parents are going to be in town. I'd love to meet them."

"Sure," he said. "Of course. We'll have to arrange something."

It was then he noticed Amelia, as she turned from the counter with two saucers in her hands, two cups of coffee in matching cups, one perfect dollop of whipped cream rising from the middle of each one, a painted calm on her face, a beaming smile. "Mom," she said, holding out a cup to her.

Her mother didn't know. He would have no plans of telling his own family, but that wasn't the same. Amelia and her mother told each other everything, he thought. But with the casual smile painted on her lips, the straightened back, how her head was held so high. Couldn't her mother see the heartbreak in her eyes? Because there was no disguising that.

Drew caught Amelia's attention, asking with his eyes, *Really?*

She raised her eyebrows at him, a silent plea, *Just let it go.*

Drew left them to talk and finish their coffee.

After Claire left, Amelia came to join him in the living room. He had a golf game on TV; it made him miss the summertime. She sat opposite him on the couch, as if she couldn't get farther away. Her whole physical being changed with her mother gone. She stretched her neck, eyes closed, kneading it with her hand. She shivered and pulled her knees to her chest, her arms wrapped around, her whole body folding into a tight ball. "She needs me, you know. She's all alone."

Drew shook his head. "I didn't say anything."

"Well you had that look."

"What look?"

"Your annoyed one," she said. "Your 'I don't like your mother' look."

"Melie," he said. "I like your mother just fine."

It wasn't true. He couldn't stand her mother.

"It's not fair," Amelia said. "I love your mother. Couldn't you stand to tolerate mine?"

Tolerating her mother was exactly what he did – was he supposed to tolerate her happily? They were running out of things to fight about, yet had resolved absolutely nothing. "You haven't told your mom, have you? About..." What did you call this? A fight? A disaster?

"It's not the kind of thing I'm proud to announce, you know."

"I just thought you would have."

"Do you think I should tell her? Do you think I want to?"

"No," he said. "Of course I don't want her to know."

Amelia glanced over then, her sad eyes were worn red and tired. "Why don't *you* want her to know? Because it's true?"

"No, I mean, I told you everything."

"But she wants to be with you," Amelia said. "And you knew it?"

"I guess, yeah, I kind of knew it."

"You think I'm being silly? You think I'm overreacting? You think you should carry on having your little crush, and she'll carry on trying to win you over, and I should just be fine with that?"

"I didn't say that."

"What are you saying then?"

"Nothing."

She hesitated. "So, have you heard anything from her? Jodie?"

"No," he said quickly. And though it was the truth – he hadn't heard a single word from Jodie since that night, five whole days now – he couldn't help but feel like a liar. For knowing Jodie had a crush on him, for the poem he had hidden in his office upstairs, for lying straight to Amelia's face when the only thing she asked of him was the truth. He'd been at Jodie's apartment only hours ago. He'd gone there with the intentions of speaking to her, even if it hadn't worked. What if Jodie had been home? What would she have said? What would he have said back? Could Amelia see the lies on his face? She watched him, waiting for him to say more. He shook his head, as if to shake the thoughts out of his mind. "No, I haven't. Nothing at all."

Amelia turned back toward the golf game, staring through it, exhaling slowly. "It's probably a good thing. I don't think she's good for you."

Somehow that never occurred to him, that Amelia wouldn't want him to talk to her again. Maybe ever. "Oh," he said. "Are you really gonna go there? It's not like I'm telling you to stop seeing Corbin."

"That's not the same," she said, squinting at him. "He doesn't like me like that, at all. We were never like that. We were cheap and meaningless. We were nothing. How can you say this is the same? I didn't even know him when we were together. He's friends with my parents. He works for them."

"How many times?"

"What?"

"How many times did you sleep with him?"

"Two," she said.

"Two times? Hell, what didn't you figure out the first time?"

She was offended. "What are you accusing me of?"

"I'm not," he said. "I just don't like it. You go over there. He comes over here. Even once he's gone, our house still smells like his damn hippie massage oil."

"Well at least he's in love with someone else. He's not trying to break up our relationship like she is. It's not the same. She's *toxic* for you."

He was silent.

"Just because we slept together doesn't mean I liked it. It doesn't mean we were good, because we weren't. We didn't work like that, and I'm kind of glad to know it."

"Well I'm not."

"You should be."

He exhaled hard. "This isn't about Corbin."

"What's it about then?"

She waited for his answer, her red eyes wide and scared and tired from all the coffee and sleepless nights. He didn't have an answer for her. She clutched her knees to her chest so tight her fingers had turned white.

3.7: shards of color

THE STORE SMELLED OF PET FOOD, URINE, AND AMMONIA. Amelia's headache had mostly gone, but with her head surrounded by a chorus of scuffles, barks, meows, tweets, and turning hamster wheels, the buried twinges of pain threatened to reignite without notice. She breathed through her mouth but still managed to receive the scents anyway. Her mother had wandered off for a moment, and Amelia stood in front of a row of cages holding dogs of all sizes. They ranged in age from puppies to full-grown. Her mother had insisted on an adopted dog. "It's the right thing to do," she said. "There are so many poor, unloved animals in this world."

Amelia understood these dejected, cast-off, unwanted animals. She crouched down in front of a skinny white terrier, mindful not to touch the floor with her fingers. She wanted to stroke its head but didn't dare stick her fingers through the bars. She tilted her head and cooed at him, "Who didn't want you?"

A voice asked, "Do you want to hold him?"

"Oh no," Amelia said, rising up from the floor. "He's for my mom." Then remembering the public service announcements, Amelia added, "She knows about it, I mean. She's here somewhere. I do know you're not supposed to give dogs for Christmas gifts and how people end up abandoning them again – it's not that."

The woman laughed as if it had been a joke. "It's okay, it's no problem," she said.

Before Amelia could argue otherwise, the woman had unlocked the kennel and eased the small dog into Amelia's hands. She didn't know what to do with it, holding it out in front of her, then vaguely to her chest, no better than she'd know how to hold a baby. She rarely held her cousins' babies – not because she didn't want to, but because she'd never been close to her cousins in the way they were close to each other, her deficiency in relationships emerging early and strong.

The little dog reached up to lick her face with its eager, adoring tongue. Amelia wasn't sure if she was being kissed or about to be mauled. She worried briefly about the germs, but then surrendered to it, basking in the unconditional affection, the innate need to love and be loved.

Amelia heard her mother's careful footsteps on the linoleum before she spoke. "Oh, Amelia," Claire said, stepping beside her, looking at the dog and making a face. "It's so *small*."

Amelia handed the dog back to its caretaker.

Claire looked at a few other dogs, larger and louder ones. They walked between the kennels, not speaking much. Except to mention, "Mindy is closing up the spa this afternoon for me. All that time she put in for your workshop application, it's such a shame to see that go to waste. The poor girl." Amelia clenched her teeth. Of course her mother wouldn't mention the yoga class outright, only *the poor girl* – as if saying, *And that's your fault, of course*, with her pointed chin high. Amelia could wait for her mother to say more, but she knew it wouldn't come. Just that little pin jabbed in her side, left to sit there, sting, and throb.

Claire stopped in front of a tan-colored Labrador, nearly identical to the one she'd just lost. "Now doesn't this look like a good puppy?"

Amelia felt like she was seeing a ghost. "But doesn't she look just like Lady?"

"She's just the same breed, that's all." Claire stroked the dog's head and it looked at her with large, affectionate eyes. "Her eyes are all different."

Claire filled out the paperwork and they had the dog to take home that afternoon. Amelia followed her mother out to the parking lot, walking the dog ahead of them on a leash. "You're just so highly strung today, Amelia. Help me get this dog home and I'll fix you something warm to drink." Claire slowed for a moment to reach out to Amelia's hair, stroking it away from her face. Then continued on.

Amelia stalled, for just a moment, watching her mother go on. The veins in her temples filled, and she took in a deep breath of cold air.

Claire turned around. "Well, come on then."

Amelia started to walk.

They let the dog climb into the back seat and they both sat up front. She was a girl and Claire hadn't given her a name yet. The dog peeked its head up between the seats, panting at them with hot breath. It wouldn't remedy her father being gone, but somehow the family did feel more in balance with a dog. They'd gotten the last dog when they moved here fourteen years ago, after Amelia's father had been deployed that last time. Amelia had only lived in that house for four years before she went to college. It was the longest she'd lived anywhere in her whole life. Home, when Amelia thought about it, had always meant people more than it meant places. Home was her mother, and their dog, and sometimes her father too. Even since she'd been grown, the houses she slept in came and went so quickly, a college dormitory, a rented apartment with one boyfriend, a rented condo with another, a crash-pad with friends, and finally her own home which she'd been in for three years. All those moves, resting for a time before she had to disassemble it all and move on, and sometimes she caught herself doubting that the house she shared with Drew would be hers to keep for long.

Her mother's house was a small, two-bedroom ranch with white shutters on the windows and a mailbox out front in the shape of a barn. It was just the two of them when they first moved in, and they hadn't needed much space. It had taken Amelia a few years to truly settle in there and trust that after all their relocation, that one single place would finally become a real home – and stay that way. Amelia stayed nearby for college and came home for weekends and breaks. It took her time to believe that the new friends she made would not be friends she had to leave behind, or that boyfriends would not be boyfriends she had to break up with. Of all the homes she'd slept in through her childhood, it still amazed her that this one remained, and her mother hadn't even moved many of her childhood things from her room. Where were the others, she sometimes wondered? What children were sleeping in those rooms now?

But it wasn't the worst trauma she would ever go through – she did well for a military brat. She made new friends easily and always kept ahead of her school work. But when she was fourteen, they moved here, back *home*, to the place where her parents had both grown up and met and fell in love, where two of her four grandparents were still alive. It would be best for her, her mother told her. She'd go to the same high school for four years, spend time with her extended family, and be allowed to settle for a bit.

Maybe that was the first mistake, because then came Lenny.

They stood in the kitchen, watching the dog enter the mud room leading out to the back yard and she sniffed Lady's bed, considering it carefully before finally lowering herself to rest in it.

Claire smiled at the dog. "She took right to it, didn't she?"

Amelia couldn't stop looking at a picture on the wall of the breakfast nook, their family including Lady, everyone was all smiles and this new dog looked just like the old dog, like one life swapped for another. Amelia went to her mother's coffee maker and pulled out the used, wet grounds, plopping them into the trash. She started a fresh pot.

They settled down at the table, beside windows looking out onto the street. Her mother lived near enough to the center of the town that had it been warmer, there would be people walking by. But this time of year, everyone drove. Amelia swirled a spoon around her coffee cup, watching the steam rise up from it.

"Where's Drew?" her mother asked.

"Home, I guess," she said.

"And how is your friend's wedding coming along? Which one is it getting married again?"

"Piper," Amelia said.

Claire nodded. "Ah, that's right. She'll make a lovely bride."

For some reason, Piper's wedding only brought Jodie to mind. How were they going to manage to share this wedding together? When the coffee maker beeped, Amelia poured two cups, bringing them back to the table. She rested her elbows on the table and kneaded her temples.

"You feeling alright, sweetie?"

"My head hurts," Amelia said.

"It's the coffee. You know I told you about that coffee."

"It's not the coffee," she said. "I always drink this much coffee. It's just been a rough week." Amelia sat back in her chair, hands gripping her coffee cup on the table, just a little too warm for her skin but it felt comforting.

Claire tilted her head then, a look of disappointment on her face that Amelia couldn't understand. "You're fighting with Drew already, aren't you? You've been sulking for days. I know you'd never spend so much time over here otherwise."

"I haven't been *sulking*." Amelia's eyes started to glass over, but she wouldn't cry. Not in front of her mother. There was so much her mother didn't know, that she couldn't know, not without Amelia admitting what a complete failure she'd been. She didn't have the heart to admit it all out loud. She pulled the coffee cup to her lips, sipping and swallowing the hot liquid. "You have no idea how lucky you and Dad are. I wish it were as easy as just getting married and having a baby and living happily ever after."

When Amelia picked up her head, her mother's lips were pressed tight. "You know your grandmother divorced at a time when it wasn't very normal for women to get divorced," Claire said. "Think about having to grow up the girl of divorced parents back then."

"I know," Amelia said. Claire never spoke very kindly of Amelia's grandmother, but Amelia had loved her. And Amelia knew that her second husband had been an amazing man that she'd lived her golden years with until the day she died. Amelia didn't know what the right answers were.

"Do you know?" Claire's voice was tense. "You try making something work for thirty-three years. You try that and *then* you can give up. Then you've earned it."

"Give up on who? I'm not giving up on anyone. You and Dad are different. You guys are childhood sweethearts."

There was a pause before Claire continued. "Yes, well that's very romantic, isn't it?" she said. "But a lifetime is a long time to spend with someone. You might find out if you didn't run off at the first sign of trouble."

Amelia couldn't breathe for a moment. "Is that what you think I'm doing?"

"You don't have to glare," Claire said. "You know, sweetie, sometimes I'm not sure you want it. You don't seem like you want it very badly. Eric was a fine boy – he wanted to marry you. He even came to ask your father. And you and Lenny were always breaking up and getting back together again."

Amelia had no words. Lenny? Her mother had no idea what really happened with Lenny. Her mother didn't know anything about how hard Amelia had tried, or how pointless it was, or how she should have left him a lot sooner than she did. And in the end, it was still him who left first – it would always be him who left first, no matter how many times she rehashed it in her mind, no matter how she dissected it. He left her. How much longer would she have taken it?

Veins swelled under her skin, throbbing at her temples. Amelia put her hands to her head, pulling at the roots of her hair. "You have *no* idea what I want."

"Hmmm," her mother hummed, pushing herself back from the table as the nameless dog came over to nuzzle her hand. "You're mad at me now, aren't you? There are things you don't know, things you couldn't understand."

"How do you even know what I understand?"

The look on her mother's face then was one Amelia had never seen before. Or at least one she hadn't seen for a very long time. She still held the nameless dog's face in her hand, but she looked at Amelia with such surrender. Amelia's mother never surrendered to anything. She was a military wife; it was her job to be a rock. "Listen, Amelia," she said. "This isn't easy for me to tell you. Your father and I..." Claire paused for a deep, steady breath. "You know we love each other very much, right?"

"Yes, I know," Amelia said.

"What's happening now – your father being away, I'm afraid it's more complicated than just his work. It's more than that. It has been for some time."

"What is it?"

"All those years, all those deployments – it takes a toll. When we moved here, when you were fourteen, that wasn't a mutual decision. It wasn't quite how we told you. It was – well, more like a trial separation."

"But you never divorced. That was years ago. Whatever it was, you've worked it out now, right? All those stories? You seem so in love."

"The stories," Claire said. "What I remember was a very long time ago, and we were very different people then. Amelia, we haven't always been perfectly happy. We didn't tell you at the time. We thought you were too young to understand. But I think maybe we haven't done you any favors by not telling you."

Amelia bit her bottom lip, like waiting for a car crash she could already see coming.

"Before we came here, the summer you were twelve," Claire started. "Just after your father was deployed, we were having a really rough time. He didn't want to give up his work. And I didn't think I could stand it any longer. So he chose to stay in, in the end – that was his decision. And then he was deployed again. And I was angry, I was *so* very angry. You don't know what I've given up for you and your father, following after him for all these years while he chose his work again and again. All the other lives I could have had."

Claire's eyes were desperate. "I wanted a home, Amelia. I wanted to stay in one place. I wanted my family. It was hard. It's still hard. It's lonely, and it's starting over and over, again and again. And it takes a toll. I have to say, I've done things I wasn't proud of."

Claire didn't have to say what. Amelia felt the ground drop out from under her. She swallowed hard. There must be more, some clarification, some excuse. Behind where they sat, their family photos smiled down on them, posed and smiling for the cameras, the perfect family. They were high school sweethearts. All those stories – the engagement, the bonfire, *I can't do this without you. Marry me, Claire*. It didn't make any sense – where had it gone so wrong? "Why?" Amelia asked. "How could you do that? Does Dad know?"

"Yes, he knows," Claire said. "He's known for some time now."

"But don't you love him?"

"Of course I do," Claire said. "But we were having a rough patch, and there was this friend."

"That's all it took? That's all?" Amelia's voice pitched high and she had to look away, shaking her head at the room.

"It was more complicated than just that," Claire said, a severe pinch in her brow. "The circumstances. You just don't understand. You wouldn't understand. The way you drop these boys at the slightest hint of trouble."

"No, I don't. I don't understand. How could you do that to him?" Amelia recounted all the times she'd been lied to, betrayed. And her own mother, the foundation of everything she'd ever known, had once inflicted all that hurt on someone. She'd done it, and she was accepting it, like it was just an ordinary mistake? Just a standard pothole in the course of an ordinary marriage. Hadn't she read the reports, the statistics, forty percent, fifty percent, sixty percent, affairs and divorces and endings to things that were promised to last forever? No, there couldn't be any truth left in this world. She should have known better. How could she be so naïve?

"Amelia," her mother pleaded. Amelia wouldn't look her in the eyes. "I need to tell you this. I need you to hear me."

Amelia shook her head slowly. "I don't want to know." The strange dog had sat in the middle of the room to watch them, back and forth. Claire didn't say anything, but just rose from the table and took their cups to the sink. She started the dishwater. Amelia had never felt so alone. This home had never felt so false. She had to go. She didn't know how to look at her mother anymore. She took her phone from her pocket and under the table, she texted Drew:

At Mom's, come get me.

It was about four minutes before there was a knock at the door then. Claire went to answer it, opening and letting the cold wind in. It was Drew. Amelia didn't even need to turn around, she recognized the weight of his footsteps on the floor, the black boots he wore, the scent of him – clean clothes and fresh air – brought in on the cold wind. She turned to face him finally.

His eyes were full of concern. "Hey, what's up?"

Claire spoke over them, "Do you want some coffee, Drew?"

Drew didn't answer, but finally saw the dog and said, "Oh." He staggered back from her, bafflement on his face. He looked to Amelia for answers, though Amelia had none to give. She had nothing.

She stood up. "Actually, I think we'll go," Amelia said. "I just have a headache. I need some pills."

Her mother's lips were pressed thin. "Suit yourself," she said. Her mother went to the coat rack first, took Amelia's coat in her hand and held it out to her. She had to have the last word, didn't she? "We'll talk more about it later."

Amelia didn't agree or disagree, but just took her coat, sliding her arms into it, wrapping the belt around her waist. She stepped outside the front door where Drew waited. They got in his car, and he started to drive.

He turned the radio down low. "Tell me I'm not crazy, but that dog – it looks just like the old one, right?"

She nodded lightly, staring out the window. He didn't try to hold her hand, and she hadn't offered it. He spoke words she couldn't quite focus on. She saw him glance to her at stop signs, watching her carefully. She nodded again. His form felt familiar, his deep voice, so full of poetry and song, even if she couldn't process the words. Nothing in the whole world felt true, but here he was.

They stopped at a red light, and she looked over at him. Her lips trembled and he looked at her with terror, a panic on his face that said, *This is it.*

But she wasn't going to break up with him. That wasn't it.

"What's wrong?" His nervous voice barely reached her. There was all this distance between them – not just the seatbelts and gear shift – but he was still angry. She could see he was still angry, but despite the anger, he was here. He had come back for her. He hadn't left her, and when everyone else she knew had lied to her, there was nowhere else to turn. She wanted to recount everything to him, all those lies, all those careful mistruths, exaggerated memories, and wrong ideas. They all jumbled up in her throat and swelled there. Her eyes burned. "My mom," Amelia started. "It's all lies." But that was all she could get out before she started to cry.

The light turned green, and he had to drive. "What's lies, Melie?"

He pulled into a parking lot. It was a Saturday morning, and dozens of people walked by with Christmas shopping in hand, on their way to their brunches and holiday sales, with their friends and smiles and laughter. She wiped at her eyes furiously, trying to hide the tears behind her hands. It was no use – the deep, heaving sobs fell out of her, her nose running in the cold. He took off his seat belt, reaching for her cautiously, as if she might have batted him away, but she didn't. She let him hold her. Right then, despite all the doubts and disbelief, she needed him. Right then, she welcomed his arms around her. She clung to him, breathed and cried into his scarf and hung her weight around his shoulders. She needed that safe place in him that she used to have. She needed it back. Just for that one desperate moment, when she didn't know what in her life was true anymore, she needed one thing to believe in.

When she'd settled enough that he could drive again, he held on to her knee with one hand, steering with the other, never losing touch. The car heater blew out cold air, the car not having had enough time to warm up yet, and Amelia shivered. Their breath started to fog the windows. He pulled up in front of their house. She could feel the swell in her eyes still, though the tears and sniffling had stopped. They both had their seatbelts on still, a peppy chorus piped through the radio, *"Repeat the sounding joy, repeat the sounding joy..."* The holiday cheer was inescapable.

"Tell me why people do this to each other?" she asked him. "Because I don't get it."

"I don't know," he said. "I didn't do it."

She turned to him sharply. "But you could. Don't you get that? It's terrifying. Any time you want, even if you love me, even if you think you never could, you could do it. Something could be wrong, or off, and you'll meet someone, like Jodie, and you can just hop right into bed with her. Whenever you want. You could just stop loving me. You can! You could!"

"But I won't," he said.

"How do I know that? I can't know that."

"Maybe you can't. But you can trust me."

That was too scary. Trust was not something Amelia doled out so easily, and considering how easily he fell for Jodie, he would do well to follow her lead. "Maybe you should learn to trust people a little bit less," she said. "Because people are mostly disappointing."

She let herself out of the car. He followed after her. She fumbled for her keys to unlock the door, her fingers still trembling and unsteady. She stepped inside the house, leaving the door open for him.

Then she saw it, stopping in the middle of her dark living room. Lights and bright bulbs sparkled through the glassy haze in front of her eyes, like broken shards of color, a kaleidoscope. "We have a Christmas tree?"

"I was going to ask you," he said. "But you wouldn't answer your phone. Are you mad that I put it up?"

She shook her head. "No," she said. "It's nice."

His hand found her back, running along the belt of her coat. She almost started to smile but held it back. She turned to him finally. "I'm so tired," she said. Her voice shook and she tried to contain it, though she failed. "I need some more coffee, do you want some coffee? I think I should go make some coffee."

"No." He shook his head, taking her shuddering shoulders in his hands, holding her still. "We don't need any more coffee."

3.8: poem about a freckle

SHE TOLD HIM SHE WANTED COFFEE, BUT WHAT SHE ACTUALLY needed was sleep. So she slept, and he lay down with her, stroking her hair, keeping her warm. He read books and magazines, resting beside her, sometimes reaching for a notebook on the nightstand to write something down, some line of poetry, something inspired by all this chaos. Was this it then, one of life's great tragedies? Was it even close, or was there more yet to come?

Sixteen hours later she finally woke for real. "I could sleep for a week," she told him. "I feel like I've been hit by a train." He had his arm around her already – she had never pushed him away, never rolled him off, or wrapped herself in covers like she'd gotten in the habit of doing those past few days. He leaned down to kiss her neck – first she moaned lightly, but then she stopped herself, eyebrows pinching together. This wasn't over yet.

"I love you," he told her.

"I know," she said, rolling on her side to face him, peering at him from those sad eyes, all that disappointment. She kissed him hesitantly, as if at any moment she might decide to stop kissing and walk away from it all. He kept kissing her until she closed her eyes. He kissed her until she let herself feel something, until she touched him back, even if he knew it was only physical desire and pent-up sexual frustration. It had to be better than her detachment, so lonely she might as well have not been there at all. He couldn't take it.

Friday turned into Saturday, and then Saturday turned into Sunday, one fluid expanse of time divided only by sunrise and sunset and sunrise again. It had been a long week. They tossed between the sheets, letting their eyes open slowly. They spent the morning waking up, rolling from one side to the next, never losing hold of each other for a minute.

He told her once, pointing to a freckle on her cheek, the same honey brown as her eyes, *I'm going to write a poem about this freckle.* He had begun that poem in one of his notebooks, but it sat there still unfinished. He couldn't find the words. The idea was beautiful in theory, but like she was, even bigger and more important than his words could describe.

In the morning, she reached up to touch his face before she'd opened her eyes, running her fingertips over the stubble. He hadn't shaved in three days. "What day is it?"

"Sunday," he said.

"Sunday? What happened to Saturday?"

He kissed her forehead. "I think we were kissing."

They were supposed to be picking up his mother from the airport later that afternoon.

For three days now, in her waking moments, Amelia had been talking about her parents. And what that meant was that she asked him every imaginable question about his parents instead, breaking down the pieces of her world and putting them into place. She wanted to know everything – why didn't his mother marry his birth father? How did she meet him? How did they break up? Did they fight? Did they cheat? Did they throw things? She seemed to need this, to analyze her own world in parallels to another, and the closest available world she could find was his.

But the problem was, he didn't know most of those answers himself. He gave her what she needed to know, but he didn't want to linger on his parents' mistakes. He didn't want to stir up all those old questions he didn't have the answers to.

Amelia took her hand from his face and grinned at him, rising slowly from the bed to prop herself on one arm and face him. "Are you going to shave for her?"

"I probably should."

"What's your dad like? I mean, your step-dad? What do you call him?"

"Just Richard."

"Is Fenton coming?"

"No," he said. "He couldn't get away just yet. Maybe closer to Christmas."

"Did you call him?"

"No, why?"

"I was just wondering. Why don't you call him more?"

"I hate phones."

"But he's your brother. I wish I had a brother to call."

"Fine, have mine then." Drew's laugh was more stiff than he'd meant it to be. He had been too young to remember most of this. Very young, and Richard came along soon after, and that was all he remembered. The only dad he'd ever known was Richard – his brother's dad, his mother's husband – the man who raised him, who attended his graduations and "liked" his Facebook statuses, but said very little of anything else.

But Amelia was intuitive, more than she realized, more than he hoped, asking just the exact questions he was so reluctant to talk about. "Melie," he said, taking her hand, holding it still. She asked too many questions, so he swept one arm under her and rolled her onto her back in one swift motion. She giggled as he sat over her hips, pinning her to the bed. They needed to be talking a little less and kissing a little more, so that was what he did. More kissing and much less clothing. Much more skin, and much closer. He slid his hand up underneath a thin purple nightgown, indulging in her soft curves, her warmth. He kissed her until she stopped trying to ask questions, until she kissed him back, until she wrapped her legs around his back and pulled his shirt up over his head.

If he was angry with her, he didn't want to be. All he wanted was to put things back the way they were. They were so happy. This bed was their cocoon, their sanctuary, before everything else made it all so complicated. All he wanted now was her warm legs wrapped around him, her fingers clutching his shoulders, her soft breath in his ear. He wanted that perfect dreamy bliss in her eyes as he satisfied her, when she locked her fingers behind his neck and pulled him down to kiss her as she came, as he came with her. He didn't want to be angry at her. Because when they weren't angry, when they could both set their worries aside, they loved each other madly. There was nowhere more perfect than being in this bed, wrapped up in her.

They made love slowly, and when they were finished, he let himself collapse onto her chest, his face tucked into the mess they'd made of her hair. When the bliss had settled and spread and worn off, she began to think again, her eyes gazing off across the room, her fingers making tender, lazy strokes at his back, all that quiet worry mixed with the desperate need to make sense of things.

"Did your mom want to move to Chicago, when she got married to Richard?"

"I think so," Drew said, rolling off her chest onto his side. "I never asked her."

She watched her own finger tracing shapes on his skin, her eyelashes blinking open and closed as she processed it all. "And what about you, did you want to move to Chicago?"

"I was six. What difference would it make?"

She shrugged. "And how come he didn't adopt you then?"

"He did, legally."

"But your name, they didn't change it? I mean, don't step-parents usually do that?"

Drew had never thought so much about any of this until she started picking at it, digging it up. And now that he did think about it, the feelings coming up were not happy ones. "Damn, Amelia, I don't know."

Her eyes went stunned wide, already brimming with tears. She was the type to cry a little when she made love, but this was different, and one drop finally broke the barrier to roll slowly down her cheek. She scrambled out of the sheets twisted around her legs, trying to break free of the bed.

"I'm sorry," he said, reaching out to touch her arm, but she flinched away. "I didn't mean to yell."

He never meant to be mad at her. He didn't want to be, but he was. He was mad about all the questions, and he was mad at his mother for never telling him the answers. He was mad about the mistrust, when he hadn't done anything wrong. He was mad that she'd fucked Corbin, and that he hadn't fucked Jodie, and that the two things were still somehow very different. He was mad at Jodie for having opened it all up. He was mad at Amelia. He was. It was just a mistake; it was a year ago. Everyone else got so many chances with her, and it wasn't his fault they all destroyed her. It wasn't fair – the hell he was going through to make this right again, and she still wouldn't forgive him?

"I'm sorry," he said. "Goddammit, I'm sorry. I'm sorry for everything. What do you want me to do?"

She kept moving, picking up random pieces of clothing from the floor, making her way for the bathroom. "I need to get dressed," she said.

"Are you still coming with me to pick up my mom?"

"Yes," she said, inside the bathroom then.

"I'm not forcing you."

"She'll be expecting me there." She was already closing the door, her voice being muffled by it. "So I'll be there." The door shut, latched with a click. The shower started.

He found his own underwear in the mess of sheets and put them back on.

THEY SAT ON A ROW OF BENCHES NEAR THE INTERNATIONAL arrivals gate. People came and went around them, juggling bags and cups of coffee and still had their passports in hand. Amelia kept glancing over to the arrivals screen and saying, "It's on time." She'd said it twice already because he figured she didn't actually want to talk to him for real. She wasn't asking questions of him anymore. She'd probably never ask him another question in her life, but that was not what he'd intended.

But it meant a lot to him that she was there with him. He understood that she didn't have to be. He'd made his mistakes too, and he knew she was angry. He was sorry for shouting at her. He knew she was trying hard, but he also felt her prepping for disaster. "When did she say she was planning this party?

"Next weekend," he said. Why, did she want to call it off? There was no point going through the trouble of throwing an engagement party for an engagement they weren't sure was going to stick. He waited for her to say more, but she only accepted his answer and nodded her head.

The flight was still on time, and estimating another twenty or thirty minutes to make it through customs lines and pick up their bags.

She asked him, "Do they know we were fighting?"

Were, she said – past tense. Maybe he read more into that than she'd meant. "No," I didn't tell them.

"That's okay," she said, nodding softly and she looked him in the eyes when she said it, a soft, sad smile on her lips. He hadn't seen her smile since that morning, before they had yet another fight. He wished they were back in bed again, making up. They'd do it right this time, with no fights afterward.

Another rush of arrivals came streaming through the gate, and they both stood to scan their faces. He saw Richard first, tall and sturdy, carrying their bigger suitcase, and then Moira at his side with the smaller one. "Okay," he said, placing a hand on Amelia's knee. "That's them. She saw us. There's no turning back now."

"Oh, my baby," Moira squealed from yards away, passing her small bag to Richard and trotting over. She took Drew into her arms, squeezing him tightly. Richard stood by quietly as Moira went on. "The flight was long, much less accommodating than I'd hoped, and that was after we'd just been to visit your brother before the holidays – you called your brother, didn't you honey?" Drew nodded, but his mother had stopped, almost mid-sentence, and she turned to Amelia. "And Amelia," she said, taking Amelia by the shoulders in her hands, holding her out in front of her. "You look lovely as ever, darling." She looked to Drew. "Oh, isn't she just divine?"

Amelia stiffened, but smiled politely.

"She is," Drew said. It was the first sure thing anyone had said all day.

"Nice to see you again, Mrs. Dyer," Amelia said.

"Oh, dear," Moira said, shaking her head, still holding Amelia by the arms. "That just won't do, now. If you won't call me 'Mom,' then at least call me 'Moira.' What do you say?"

She waited for an answer and Amelia blushed, nodding, "Okay, Moira," she said.

In the short breath of calm, Drew managed to greet his step-father before Moira began again. "We have so much to catch up on

– but there's plenty of time. We're staying for a couple of weeks, you know. Longer possibly, if it suits us. And we'll have plenty of time to get ready for the party next weekend. Your cousins are coming! Your brother said he would try, but he has exams – he's not sure he'll even make it for Christmas. It breaks my heart, but he said he'd try. But now I'm just positively exhausted. We have lots of time though."

Moira had already cued Richard to grab their bags, and Drew went over to help him. He worried about leaving Amelia alone with his mother, even if it was just long enough to get the bags into the car. Amelia just smiled the way she did, polite and lovely as his mother accosted her hand to see the engagement ring. His mother turned to him for a moment and she nodded her approval, mouthing the words, "Yes, lovely."

THEY DROPPED HIS PARENTS OFF AT HIS UNCLE'S PLACE AND LEFT them to get some rest. As much time as he and Amelia had spent in bed that week, Drew felt like he could have spent another week there, sleeping, making love, making things right.

He watched Amelia from across their bedroom as she stripped off her layers, high-heeled shoes, earrings, sweater, she let her hair down, shook it out and pulled it over her shoulder. She stood in front of the mirror that hung over her dresser but she didn't look at herself in it. Her eyes were anxious. Maybe she could tell whatever secret he was holding onto wasn't a good one.

It was on the tip of his tongue. She hated lies. She hated secrets. But she wasn't ready for this. And in his heart, he knew it didn't matter. It was just a poem, a moment that had been captured a long time ago and had long since passed. Jodie started this, but this wasn't about Jodie anymore, and it was never about Corbin either. It wasn't about how much her mother hated him, and it wasn't about the details his own mother never told him. It wasn't about which furniture he couldn't replace or which walls he couldn't paint. It was about him and about her, about their relationship and how skittish and fragile it was, how very hard it was to hold on to. It was about how they'd been falling apart since before they'd even begun. Wasn't it enough that they loved each other so madly? Shouldn't that be enough?

In the mirror's reflection, she glanced up to him. "Sometimes I think I can feel you giving up on me."

She said it like she hadn't yet decided that wasn't what was actually happening.

There was a time he almost gave up on her, a time he let her go for one whole night, and he tried on the idea of Jodie. They shared drinks and conversation and friendship that night, and he did consider what it would be like to just cut his ties with Amelia and try to date someone else. If he was ever going to give up on her, it would have been then. Not now. It would have been that night when they were stretched as far as he thought they could go, when they were breaking and he felt them breaking. It would have been that time he reached out the next best thing, a girl so much unlike Amelia but interesting and funny and bold in her own way. And he tried it with her. He indulged in her conversation, and he enjoyed her wit, and laughed at her banter, and he admired her sharp features and the way her shiny dark hair caught the moonlight. There was that night he wondered what it might be like to love someone else. There was a time he almost gave up on Amelia, but that time wasn't now. "That's not what I'm doing," he said.

"It would be easier if you did, but I'm glad that you don't."

He crossed the room to her. He leaned to kiss her bare shoulder, leaving his lips there on her skin. She inhaled, exhaled, heavy and shuddering breaths. She closed her eyes and he watched her face in the mirror without taking his lips away. He wished she would reach up to touch him, but that she wasn't pushing him away was something. He pulled her back to bed.

When they made love this time, she was a fraction less sad than the last time, which was a fraction less sad than the time before that. Maybe that was how people got over things, progressing in fractions that were too small to register until they looked back and couldn't remember having moved so far. It felt like the poem he'd meant to write about her freckle. The one he had wanted to be powerful and poignant, to reflect that stubborn hopefulness he saw in her sometimes, but that instead couldn't be written at all. He could never find enough words. All he had were these tiny fragments, a kiss, a touch, a promise, a moment of not giving up.

WHEN SHE SLEPT THAT NIGHT, STIRRING LIGHTLY WITH HIS movements, he got up to use the bathroom. But he didn't come back right away. In his office, there was a poem, and if he let it be published, she would find it one way or another. The scenarios went through his mind – would it be sooner or later? It would be his first publication and it would be out there forever, sketched into the universe, the concrete proof all laid out in words of exactly what had been between him and Jodie. He could try to keep it a secret. And maybe many years later, when they were healed, when they'd been married for forty happy years, maybe then he could mention it. But not now. Now it would only destroy them.

But that choice – sooner or later – wasn't his, and the risk of what could happen wasn't a risk he wanted to take.

He went to his office and found the acceptance letter, with the contract still inside, unsigned. He flipped open his laptop and searched his files for the poem, hardly remembering what he'd called it, but he remembered the date, September last year. Delete. He cleared his computer's recycle bin. Are you sure you want to permanently delete these items? Yes.

He picked up the publication contract.

Outside the door, there were only the sounds of a quiet house. He listened for her footsteps, but he didn't hear any. He took a pair of scissors – he couldn't use the paper shredder because of its noise – and he cut the letter into thread-fine strips, watching as they fell into the basket, strings toppling through the air until the whole document was in shambles, beyond hope it might ever be patched up or pieced back together again.

When it was done, he reached inside the basket, hearing the paper crinkle. He turned the strips between his fingers, holding them loosely in his palm so that he might remember their weight.

3.9: the earthy brunette

AMELIA WALKED THROUGH THE SMALL, PRIVATE COLLEGE campus where Corbin taught, carrying a loaf of banana bread in her hands. They had his office – if you could call it that – on the fifth floor, where he said they stuck all of the adjunct professors. It was a tiny closet of a room, under a stairwell, where he couldn't even stand fully in a portion of the room. Corbin wasn't the chattiest of men. She didn't know what she needed to say to him, but that she was sorry was probably one of those things.

His door was open when she arrived, but she tapped her fingernails on the glass panes to let him know she was there. "Amelia," he said, not in surprise, but like he should have expected it.

"Are you busy?"

"No," he said, closing his laptop, rising carefully from behind his small desk, bending his head down to avoid hitting the ceiling. She helped herself to a hard wooden chair that looked like it had been through several lifetimes. Beside her was a small rusted window and a folding card table that looked ready to snap under the weight of all his books. The room was painfully basic. He didn't hang posters or lay rugs. There were no pictures of family or friends, no clutter lining his shelves, no souvenirs from the many travels he'd had. He didn't even have a radio. He just had books, and an electric tea kettle.

"Tea?" he offered.

"Sure," she said.

On the other side of the small room, his kettle sat on a metal cafeteria cart, with tea bags, sugar, paper insulated cups and a jug of filtered water. Near his desk was the same paper shopping bag she saw him bring into the spa, which likely held his workout clothes and possibly a few more books. Amelia knew he could afford an actual duffel bag – she'd seen how much her mother paid him, and while it wasn't much, it was enough for a duffel bag. Maybe she'd buy him one for his birthday.

He glanced over to where she was sitting. "So you never told me what you said you wanted to tell me."

"Oh," she said, she laughed lightly. "Drew might hate you a little."

"Did I do something to him?"

"No... to me, actually." Amelia breathed through her teeth. He had no idea what she meant – she had hoped, at one point, that he'd forgotten it entirely, but now she felt offended at the idea of being so entirely forgettable in bed. "Us, two years ago, at a wedding? And a time after that?"

"Oh that?" He raised his gaze from the tea kettle to the wall, a blank space, a thought, and she blushed at the idea of him trying to remember, or trying not to remember, or whatever it was he was doing. "That doesn't count," he said. His voice drifted off, half amused, and she hoped he wasn't trying to remember what she looked like naked. This must have seemed so silly to him, as many people as he'd been with. Like two nights out of his whole lifetime would have been so memorable or cherished.

"Your mom invited me to Christmas," Corbin said. "She's wondering if you're still coming to Christmas. And she wants you to call her back."

"Oh geeze," Amelia said. "That's going to be some Christmas."

"So does that mean Drew's invited to Christmas again?"

She began to smile. The thought of Drew, his touches, his kisses, the last several days they'd spent in bed – making love to avoid fighting, making love as a proxy for making up. Maybe it was close enough. But part of her wondered if they'd lost something, broken something that couldn't be fixed. She hoped not. "Yeah, he is," she said.

He had nothing to add to that, only turning to point to five boxes of tea. "What are you having?"

She couldn't read their labels from here. "Not black," she said. "Green, if you have it. Or herbal. The caffeine, I'm trying to cut down on it. One sugar – one-and-a-half, if you can, but not if it'll waste. You don't have honey, do you?"

"No," he said, chuckling silently at her. He handed her a steaming, insulated paper cup. *100% post-consumer materials,* the cup proclaimed on its side. He didn't go back to his desk, but instead leaned precariously against one of the card tables, his cup of tea held secure in one hand. "I didn't think the two of you would fight for long."

"What do you know? You don't even do relationships."

He shook his head. "You assume too much."

"That girl? The earthy brunette? So is that a relationship then?"

His eyes flashed to life with both delight and sadness at the same time. "She is earthy, isn't she? That wasn't who I meant though."

"Who then? Oh God, not Mindy."

"Mindy?" He looked confused, offended, and shocked too. "No, not Mindy."

Amelia laughed. "Is she even out of high school?"

"She's actually twenty-four."

"That makes me feel old." Amelia frowned. He still hadn't told her when he'd had a relationship, or with whom, but she found herself more interested in knowing about his yoga friend.

But he answered first. "Christa," he said. "She was an English teacher in Japan. We dated for four years."

"And let me guess, you two broke up amicably when you went your separate ways, in perfect peace and harmony?"

He smiled cautiously. "Actually, yes. We did."

Amelia laughed hard, falling into the back of her chair, careful not to spill her tea. Her laugh felt fractured, but good. "Do you realize that you don't live in this universe?" He didn't respond to that, but just sipped his own tea and watched her.

"So am I allowed to talk to you? Can I talk to your mom?"

"Just be careful, my mom might try to sleep with you." Amelia laughed again, a hearty but splintered sound. Corbin wasn't amused. She held her cup between both hands in her lap. "I was just kidding. I don't think you'd sleep with my mom." She knew it on his behalf, though she couldn't vouch for her mother anymore. She always assumed, if nothing else, her parents would always be certain. Corbin was right, she assumed far too much most of the time.

"Amelia," he said. "That's not nice. Your mother is a fine woman. You can't judge a person's whole integrity on one moment of weakness."

She nodded first, at its truth, then she stopped. Because he knew it. She felt the blood rush from her face, felt it flush clean. "Wait, you know what I'm talking about? How do you know what I'm talking about?"

His eyes were nervous, and she wondered if they were talking about the same thing. Let there be some hope that they weren't talking about the same thing, but she didn't have faith or hope anymore. "Your father told me about it once," Corbin said.

She stopped staring blankly at him, and instead stared blankly off into the room. "They told you, before they told me?"

"It's not an easy thing to tell," he said. "Especially not to you. They know you look up to them." Corbin waited for her to say something, but she had no words. "And your dad talks a lot," he added.

It was true, he did. "I miss my daddy. I don't trust women. At least with men, you know what they want or don't want – no games about it. Every woman I ever got close to either lied to me or tried to stab me in the back. And my mom? They just always seemed so happy. More than just happy." She didn't want to say the word, perfect.

"To be honest," Corbin said. "I always thought they seemed very sad."

She felt inclined to take offense on their behalf. His truths were always so harsh, but in the end, they were always very true. "Go on," she said. "Because I know you want to. Don't you have some metaphysical speech for me about how life and love are separate and undefined, and you can't possess love?"

"I wouldn't take my advice on that subject if I were you. I clearly don't know what I'm talking about in that department."

"But wait," she said. "Maybe there was something to it? You can't possess love, can you?"

"No," he said.

"It can only be shared. And maybe you can't help where it goes?"

"Maybe," he said.

"And maybe it's okay, because if Drew did have some kind of feelings for Jodie, then he couldn't help them? He can only help what he does with those feelings?"

Corbin looked at her with something like sympathy, but she also wondered if it might have been pity.

"Maybe he didn't mean it?"

"He probably didn't," Corbin said. "You and Drew aren't like your parents. You don't seem sad together."

"Drew doesn't like you," Amelia said. "Why do you vouch for him?"

"He doesn't dislike me, he's just insecure."

"He's not insecure."

"Amelia," Corbin said. "Of course he is. He just found out. It's completely normal."

She smiled at him suspiciously. But he seemed somber then, retreating for a moment into his own memories, the way he often did. He didn't do relationships, but maybe it wasn't because he didn't want to. Amelia imagined he was thinking of his friend right then.

"I know the difference now," he said. "Between caring about someone and being in love." He blushed a bit at the word love, and she wasn't surprised. She knew exactly what he was talking about. *I care about you*, he always told them. He had said that to Amelia once, so long ago she could hardly remember the context. He said it still sometimes, but back then, before she'd known him for long, before she knew how ethereal he was about everything she took so seriously, she thought it meant something else. Something more than just exactly what he said.

"So you love her then, your married woman? Have you ever said that before? I mean, not in a vague and metaphysical way?"

"I didn't say it," he said. He stopped, wringing his knuckles out. "I think I was supposed to, but I didn't."

A small bit of anger sparked inside her. "Why didn't you say it, if it's true?" She felt silly, but if it really was love, and he really felt it, and he thought she felt it too, why would that be so hard to say?

But then, wasn't that just what Jodie did? Amelia didn't know what was right or wrong anymore. "So who is she then?"

Amelia wasn't sure if she was more dying to hear about the woman, or if he'd been dying to talk about her, but it came spilling out of him, this one woman out of so many. "Her name is Leila," he told her. "She's very smart, though she never went to college. She comes to my office sometimes to pick through my bookshelf – history and science are her favorites. She has library cards in five different counties." He laughed lightly at the idea of it. "Sometimes, you can stumble across something you desperately need, that you didn't even know you were lacking. That's how she feels to me. But she's been married for ten years now. She was eighteen when it happened. They have two kids, a girl, four, and a boy, seven months. One looks like her, and the other looks like him – I mean, I've never met her husband. I can only figure." He stopped for a moment. "And I have no idea what I'm doing."

The silence his story left was enormous, as if there was nothing in the world big enough to follow. Amelia clenched her hands in her lap. "She seems to like you too," she offered.

He nodded, steadily, his head slowing to a stop. "I hadn't intended that."

"Let me guess, you'd take it back if you could?"

"No." He gasped for air, as if there wasn't enough air in the whole room to breathe. "I wouldn't. I could never."

Amelia waited for him to say something more. He was the one with the answers. He was the one with the truth, and the only truths she knew she had to dig out herself. He really hadn't disappointed her so much as she let on sometimes. And it wasn't her place to say, but she would say it anyway. "You're not a bad guy, Corbin."

The corner of his mouth turned, not quite a smile, but almost. "I try not to be."

He started to think then, pacing on his feet. She hadn't ever seen him teach, but she imagined this was how he looked in front of his lecture halls. How it must wear him out. "It's just so rare a thing," he said, gesturing with his hands. "All these people, all these connections, and how many of them really matter? And then you find this one, *only* one – maybe you don't believe in soul mates, then you can call it a really good match. But something goes wrong. Anything can go wrong, a mistake, a misjudgment. Maybe someone got married too soon – maybe it was a mistake, or maybe not. But in a blink, it's snuffed right out. There's so many ways it can end." He stopped pacing to look her in the eyes. "Maybe what you have with Drew is something more than what your parents had. And look how far they've made it. He makes you happy. I've known you a long time, and I haven't seen you so happy as you are with him. It's so rare a thing. You know that, right? You have to believe that."

It was all too much to take in. She took a deep breath, and he waited, as if asking her if she believed it? Did she? She could feel the sadness in her own eyes, and how he had hoped that wouldn't be her answer. "We're okay," she said. "You don't need to worry about me."

"Hmmm," he said, drawing it out long, and she couldn't remember having ever seen so much doubt on his face. It made her laugh. "Well, he'd better take good care of you then," he said.

"He will."

Somehow she doubted that he would stop checking up on her. She didn't believe in karma, but if it was true, then he must have had a lot of good energy coming his way. Maybe one day it would just hit him all at once. "You'll be okay too, you know."

He folded his hands over his chest and bowed lightly. "Namaste, Amelia."

She bowed too. "Namaste," she said.

3.10: all these things

AMELIA AND DREW SPENT A LOT OF TIME AT HIS UNCLE'S place that week. She imagined they would, with his parents in town, but what surprised her was that it was fine. The two of them had developed a sort of quiet truce between them. Plans for the engagement party went forward, without any official apologies. Neither of them put a stop to it.

Mitch had given Amelia a key to the small study where he kept all of his bank books and files. Drew told her she was meant to let herself in whenever she needed to. That was why he gave her the key. It was against her sensibilities to just walk straight in like that, but Drew told her he'd only be irritated if she asked every time. She came to sort through his bills and balance his checkbook twice a month. She brought him stamps and talked with his stock broker. The man had a ridiculous amount of money. Drew hadn't ever told her that outright, or maybe he just hadn't thought of it being a ridiculous amount of money, being raised around it like he was. It was much more than Amelia ever saw in either of her own parents' bank accounts.

Amelia enjoyed Uncle Mitch. He knew about disappointment in a way Drew couldn't understand, but unlike her mother, he wasn't cynical, or unfathomably lucky like Drew's mother. He was just there, steadfast and dependable. Amelia appreciated that, though she was never sure how he felt about her marrying Drew, since he was not an emotionally open man like his nephew was.

As the rest of them talked in the living room, Amelia touched Drew's knee and excused herself to take a few minutes to tend to Uncle Mitch's bank books. Bills didn't stop for family visits, and she wasn't much interested in Richard's line of work, operations management, though she was sure it was a necessary job to be done. The study was just as dark as the rest of the house, though for being a tiny room, the one single window bathed the room in just enough light. An orange and red Tiffany lamp sat on the desk and cast the shadows with a warm glow.

After a half an hour, Mitch hobbled into the doorway behind her. "Is it all still there?"

The money, he meant. He asked her every time she visited. "Yes, sir, every last dollar. And a bit more. Your portfolio is doing well this quarter."

She had finished her work, so she closed the books and took up a few envelopes to post in the mail.

"What do you think of this house? Be honest, now."

The question was weighted, and she wasn't sure how to answer it. The house was large, too dark, and a little musty in places. The decorating style was something out of a 1960's hunting and fishing magazine, mixed with a mismatched vintage charm. "It's big," she said. "It's really nice."

"You're lying," he said, and her cheeks burned hot. "My girls always said I should have remarried. They say it needed a woman's touch."

Amelia exhaled. He didn't seem to be angry at her for the lie. She'd had good intentions.

"What would you do, if it was your house?"

"Oh, wow. I don't know." It was so big and so many of the rooms were unused. It was hard to say what would work without imagining who might live in it.

"Well, don't make me ask again, child."

"Okay, I suppose a lighter coat of paint to start, in the hallways. I think it would open up the space. A pale blue or... yellow. Definitely yellow."

She started with generic improvements, the obvious ones, and he nodded, listening, expecting more. It was fun, imagining what she would do with no worry of who wouldn't like it or how much it would cost. He had her by the arm, and he led her from room to room – or rather, she led him. They talked in hushed voices compared to the elaborate story Moira told in the living room. They walked past the others, the living room bright with light from the patio doors. Moira paused her story to see them each time they passed, unsure what they were doing. It must have looked like Amelia was taking him for a stroll.

She went on, and they hobbled down the hallways together. "The kitchen is nice," she said. "There's lots of space and storage, but the curtains are too heavy, they don't let any light in, because those windows are really not that small. And you know, I really don't prefer granite counters over wood."

"Really?" he said. "I spent a lot of money on those counters."

She grinned. "Wood is harder to take care of, but I much prefer them for cooking. Granite is just so cold."

She spent a few more minutes in the kitchen. It must have been clear that that would be her favorite room. As they passed the living room, she said, "I'd put a piano in here."

"Do you play?"

"No, not at all," she laughed. "But somebody should. And a skylight too."

"And this room?" he said, leading her past his den, with its battleships and books.

"I wouldn't touch a thing, of course."

His eyes gleamed. They'd come back around to the study again, back where they started. Moira's voice carried on down the hallway, but the two of them were alone. "Would you do that for me, dear?"

"What do you mean?"

"Take as much money as you need, hire all the help you need. All of it – everything you just said – if you don't mind helping an old man out. I don't think I could see to all of that on my own."

"All of it?" Amelia closed her gaping mouth. "But that would cost a fortune."

"Well, you know I'm not broke, don't you?"

"Yes, of course, but..." She knew he had the money for it, and from what she knew of decorating her own little condo, it would hardly make a dent in his savings. But it was so sudden.

But he didn't retract his order, so she pulled a notebook out of her purse and began to make notes. "The paint, and you liked yellow?" He nodded. "And the kitchen? The wood counters too?" Yes, he nodded at all of it. She stalled again. "But... are you putting it up for sale?"

"No, this house isn't for sale."

"Oh," she said. She went through the list with him again, the paint, the skylight. "The piano too?"

"Well, let's find someone who wants to play it first, eh?"

She smiled. "That's a good idea." She went back to her list, itemizing by room, numbering by priority. She estimated the cost for each task, and tallied the total which made her fingers tremble just to write it. She showed it to him. Approximately $85,000, and that was just a ballpark. He glanced at it. "Very good then," he said.

Amelia took the list and the outgoing mail in one hand and he took her other arm as they started back to the living room. Still in the hallway, she asked him, "But why me?"

They stopped walking. "Well, I suppose that's a secret," he said. "And the secrets of a man's estate are a very confidential thing." He paused, patting her hand as it rested on his arm. "But seeing as how I trust you with my bank accounts..." His smile was a playful smirk, a challenge.

She nodded. "Yes, sir. Of course."

"I hear you want to marry that boy over there." He glanced toward the living room where they could just make out the tops of their heads over the couch, Drew sitting next to his mother. "And that boy has always been as special to me as my own children. More so, in some ways. I'm not going to be around forever – I hope I'm not around forever. But I've accumulated all of these things, and all of this money I'm not using. They're just things, you see, but they represent my life. And they're all going to be his someday. So I suppose I'd better hope that you'd like to live here as well."

Amelia had no words to say, but she nodded with enthusiasm.

"You see, Drew is good at fixing things," he added. "Light bulbs, door handles, lawnmowers. He's a good boy. He takes care of things, and he means well."

She didn't think he could have known that they'd been fighting, but Amelia saw that he meant for her to know that. And she also understood that all of this was meant to be kept a secret until the time came. She hadn't known him for long at all, but the thought of it made her want to cry. "Well, I hope you're around for a long time still."

Uncle Mitch laughed, a deep, echoing roar. "Don't curse me, child."

They began to walk through the rooms again, but this time with a clear idea of who was meant to live here. They picked out imaginary furniture, colors and piles for the floor rugs, mirrors to amplify the light, and the kind of house plants that could thrive in all those dim rooms.

3.11: enough

THE ENGAGEMENT PARTY WAS SMALL, BUT MAGNIFICENT. Because it was the dead of winter, it had to be an evening party, as the sun set before it was even five o'clock. It had been Amelia's idea to make use of the low lighting, lining up hundreds of colored tea lights on the tables and white Christmas lights strung in a canopy across the ceilings, a magical ambiance that seemed to put everyone in good spirits. Or maybe that was the wine. Amelia kept trying to refill empty wine glasses before Moira had to say, "Won't you just sit down, dear? We've hired someone to do that!"

Having nothing to do with her hands but show off her engagement ring and raise her glass to be refilled by the waiter, Amelia actually settled in to drink the wine. It calmed her nerves, but gave her giggles and the hiccups instead. Drew imagined she must be thinking about the last party they'd had, when she didn't drink anything at all, but was sober as she watched it all go so wrong. She was on her third glass tonight, and he hadn't had more than a few sips yet.

"That wine came highly recommended," Uncle Mitch added. "Ninety-four points, the shopkeeper said, and I paid thirty dollars a bottle." Drew imagined his uncle counting up the empty bottles, trying to figure out how much it had cost him. But Mitch didn't seem to regret it – he glowed from the side of the room as everyone mingled and came together again around him, no matter what the cost.

Drew had managed to find a new housekeeper just in time, and the rooms were all dusted, the linens fresh, and the house was lit up and full, breathing and living again. Anna and Leslie had come home with their husbands and children. A few neighbors and old family friends were invited. Drew stepped aside to dodge a renegade game of hallway tag the children were playing, and he glanced over to see if his uncle would shout at them, but there was no shouting. Only smiles and laughter, voices bouncing off the walls, and a bed waiting for each of them to sleep in.

Piper and Tom arrived with a brightly wrapped gift and a bottle of champagne. Piper glanced up at the lights and twirled in a circle. "Oooh, they're so pretty!" She didn't mention Jodie, or that Jodie was sorry she couldn't make it, or that Jodie had said anything at all. When Piper stopped twirling, she took Amelia and Drew, one hand in each of her own. She must have been talking to Jodie, because the way she tilted her head and said, "You guys, I'm so happy for you. I'm so happy you did this. This is *magical*." It was like she'd witnessed a miracle that this party was still happening at all.

Amelia and Piper were talking when Richard walked over to them. "How's your writing, kid? Any luck yet?" He was the only one who ever acknowledged that Drew was a poet. As Drew exhaled, his whole body deflated. He couldn't tell them. Even if Amelia hadn't been standing right next to him, it would have been too great a risk. "No, nothing yet," he said.

His mother came to join them next, a glass of champagne perched between her fingers. "But no need to give up your poems, darling," his mother said. "It might happen someday." Drew chuckled lightly at that, but her smile twisted to a frown of mild disapproval. "Don't you boys shave anymore?"

Drew had meant to shave. He really had. In between everything else, it had completely slipped his mind.

"But you should see your brother now," she added. "A full face of hair. You would think he was raised in the mountains. Does he send you pictures? I wish you boys would send each other pictures more."

Then Richard spoke up, from his quiet and steady place beside Moira. "Sometimes the mind doesn't know what it's capable of until the time is right."

Drew could only assume he was still talking about the poetry thing, though it was anyone's best guess.

"Well, yes," Mitch said, raising his wine glass to that, a vague appreciation on his face that he hadn't understood that comment either. The others did the same. Glasses clinked, cheers were given.

After the night wound down, Drew followed his mother into the kitchen to see that the help was paid and set for the night. The caterer wrapped leftovers in foil as the two waiters rounded up glassware and swept up cocktail sticks. They were positively spoiled, it was true. In the kitchen, Drew asked his mother, "Do you think my life has lacked tragedy?"

His mother considered him with a look of such complete bafflement it bordered on horror. "Drew, honestly, what a ridiculous thing to be disappointed in."

He laughed and made himself busy holding the door open. "No, I'm kidding." He wasn't, really, but he didn't know how to explain that to his mother. She was still shaking her head at him.

The catering team had cleared out their equipment and Drew closed the door behind them. The remaining voices in the living room had softened, only close family and friends left, and the children had gone up to bed.

Moira edged cautiously around the kitchen, watching him with concern. Drew poured himself a glass of wine, as the night had finally proven that it wasn't going to end in the chaos their last party did. He took a sip and let the strong flavor slip down his throat and ring in his head. His mother was still watching him.

"If that was supposed to be a joke, darling, I'm sorry, I just didn't get it."

"No, mom," Drew said, still chuckling to himself. "It's nothing."

"Well aren't you having a good time? Your uncle spent a lot of money on this party."

"It's not that at all. We're having a great time. This is all great."

Drew raised his wine glass and smiled giddily until his mother stopped trying to decipher his secrets.

"I didn't see Amelia just now."

"Oh, maybe she stepped outside for some fresh air?"

"She doesn't smoke, does she, dear?" Her prim brow had furrowed.

"No, she doesn't."

"Well, that's good then. It does terrible things to the skin you know." She shook her head, holding her hand over her heart. "Your brother smokes now, did he tell you that? You should call him. You should have a talk with him about it, dear. I think he'd listen to you."

Drew grinned – Fenton had made it seven years before their mom found out he smoked. But there was enough worry in her eyes to pain the world. "Of course, mom. Sure. I'll call him tomorrow."

Moira sighed. "I worry about you boys."

"What's to worry about?"

"Oh, it's silly maybe, but I worry you two don't like each other very much, and I just don't know why."

"I don't know, Mom. We're fine. I like him fine."

She watched him, and he stopped smiling. "It's just that I love you both so much," she said. "And you're talking about tragedy or something, and I hope you don't think we've given him any more than we've given you. I know things were rough in the beginning, but we've come out okay, haven't we?"

He knew if he didn't hug her she would probably start to cry, so he set down his wine, and he hugged her. But Fenton had one thing Drew didn't have. Drew didn't resent his brother for that, and Richard had never been unkind or unwelcoming to him. He asked her, "But why didn't I get Richard's name when he adopted me? What was the point of us all being so different?"

"Don't you know what that meant to your uncle and me?" She broke their hug and held him out in front of her. She waited for him to respond, but he was missing something. "Your cousins," she said. "Anna and Leslie – their mother changed their names when she took them, and well, now they've both got their husbands' names. You're the only Weston left, dear."

"Oh," Drew said. It was so simple, yet so obvious. She smiled at him and squeezed his arm before passing through to the living room, leaving him there with all that responsibility and pride.

Drew followed after her, holding the last sips of his wine in hand, but by the time they'd rejoined the rest, only Richard and his uncle Mitch were there. Drew looked at each of them, considering them both, wondering what god-awful thing his uncle might have said to send Amelia running. "Amelia's just stepped outside for some air," his uncle said. He pointed to the glass of wine in Drew's hand. "Sometimes I forget you're old enough for that, son."

"I'm twenty-eight," Drew said.

"I'll always remember you like you were five," Mitch said. "Tearing up those hallways with the girls." His uncle had a comfortable look of nostalgia on his face. Drew nodded. He swore he'd never torn up anything in his life, but those hallways when he was five, he really did.

Drew grabbed his own jacket then and found Amelia out on the back patio. The colonial estate sat on a decent patch of land, and his uncle kept a once-landscaped patio behind the house that he didn't pay much mind to anymore. Large boulders surrounded an emptied fountain, and it was impossible to tell if the plants had all shriveled up for the winter, or if it had already happened before the cold.

It wasn't snowing anymore. It wasn't even trying. The heavy dark snow clouds had moved out and left the sky cold and crystal clear. Amelia walked along a wall of ivy and reached out to touch the leaves. Wilted plants were laced in between, and she inspected each shriveled bud as her hand passed over. When Drew was a boy, he used to climb that ivied trellis to catch a glint of Lake St. Clair in the sunshine. Or on clear nights like tonight, he would have barely been able to make out a tiny blip of light at the mouth of the Detroit River, the Belle Haven light signaling ships safely through the narrow passage.

"I just wanted some air," she said.

"They're too much, aren't they?" His parents had only been in town for a week and already he felt ready to escape. He loved his family dearly, but all in one room together, they were too intense.

"No, it's not them," she said.

"Did my uncle say anything to you?"

"No, why? What would he have said?"

Drew sighed. "Good. Never mind."

"They're great," she said.

He laughed out loud. "You don't have to say that."

"They are, really," she insisted. "Don't you know that?"

She actually waited for an answer from him, which filled him with so much shame he could only muddle a laugh. "I guess they are," he said. "I know they are." He reached to her waist, slipping his hands around, their bodies coming together slowly.

He caught her eyes for a moment, sad and somber. He pulled her body closer, and she rested her chin on his shoulder. She shivered lightly, and he rubbed her back until she stopped. There were no more arguments to be had, no more complaints, just the dull throb of the damage done and the hope that they weren't too broken to heal. Last fall, they'd had what they thought was the biggest fight they could possibly have. They didn't speak to each other for four days. He'd been prepared to let go of it all, but then she showed up at his apartment, and she hadn't even been able to speak before she started to cry. It had taken all the faith she had just to show her face there that day, and then she crumbled, an unspoken surrender, and he gathered her up in his arms, promising so many things – that they would never fight again, that they would never hurt each other again. He'd had the best intentions, but he knew now that it had been a lie. "Never" was an impossible promise. They would hurt each other. There would be mistakes. No one could be that perfect.

There were no crickets, no sound at all but the muffled noise of cars in the distance, and a soft breeze between the tall trees. It was almost indistinguishable from the sound of waves washing up on the shore just a few blocks away.

"I'd like a garden like this someday," she spoke into his shoulder. "We could put some white honeysuckle with the ivy, and maybe my mom could help us with a koi pond. What do you think, could we?"

There wouldn't be room for all of that in her tiny yard, but he didn't tell her so, because when she finally glanced up at him, waiting for his answer, there was a glow in her eyes like she could see the future again, their shared yard and all the plants and rocks and bubbling fountains she could think of, and here she was asking him to take part in this imagined garden with her.

"Sure," he said. "Anything you want."

When they'd been missing for several minutes, the patio door slid open. Drew's mother came outside. "Oh, there you kids are." She wasn't wearing her coat, having just picked up a throw blanket to wrap around her shoulders like a shawl. Richard followed, taking his place beside her in his quiet and steady way. A dozen curious faces stood behind them waiting. "We were all just wondering, because I don't think you told anyone – haven't the two of you set a wedding date yet?"

Panic spread through Drew's body; after everything, he was barely sure they were still getting married at all. But then he turned to find Amelia's smile, somber but full of that stubborn hopefulness he had always loved so much. "We're just waiting for my dad to come back," she said.

She reached out to his hand, placing her own small hand tentatively into his palm, giving just that little bit so he could take hold. It was enough.

MARCH

4.1: martini friends

A S SOON AS THE SNOW HAD MELTED, THE FIRST WEEK OF March, Piper moved out. Her wedding wasn't until May, but she dropped the whole charade of not living with Tom. She'd spent most of the winter slowly moving her things, piece by piece, so all she had left to do now was hand Jodie her keys and the rent money she was always late for. Jodie had never needed Piper's money anyway.

Jodie had called one of the girls from the lists. It was Amelia's list. Emmy, the actress, who promised on the phone that she was indeed working. She was thirty-one, had no kids and lots of boyfriends. Jodie wasn't even sure if it was ethical or not to call someone from Amelia's list, considering everything that had happened since. She tried to soothe her conscience by telling herself that these women must have actually wanted a roommate. It would have been a terrible thing to put somebody out over technical difficulties. She also tried to gauge how close Emmy had been to Amelia when she called, and since Emmy had only known her from a few classes in college, years and years ago, Jodie wagered that it would be fine.

Any time Piper stopped back, even though it had only been days since she moved out her last pieces of furniture, Jodie's heart filled.

"Like I wouldn't come back to visit," Piper said, swamping Jodie in an eager hug, which Jodie didn't fight.

"How do you like living in your house?" Jodie asked.

"Oh, Jodie, it's stupendous! It's everything we ever wanted."

Jodie smiled.

"When does your new roommate move in?"

"Next week."

"Do you like her?"

"Only as much as I like anybody," Jodie said.

Piper's face went serious then. "Amelia came in today."

"Amelia always comes in to get coffee, doesn't she?"

"Well, yeah. Except she didn't get coffee, she got a smoothie. And she asked about you."

Jodie's heart rose in her throat. "What did you tell her?"

"I said you were fine. Working. I told her you got a cat."

Jodie scrunched up her face. "*Why* did you tell her I had a cat?"

"Because," Piper emphasized, gesturing with her hands. "I didn't want to say you hadn't chosen one of her roommates, but then, I didn't want to tell her you did either." Piper shrugged. "So I told her you had a cat. You want one anyway though, right? It'll be like an imaginary cat. To see if you like the idea of it."

Piper waited for some kind of response from her.

"What kind of cat do I have?"

"An orange one," Piper said. "With lighter stripes. He's fat. It's a *he*, by the way. You have a boy cat."

Jodie considered the idea of a boy cat. It wasn't the worst fantasy she'd ever indulged in.

She would be fine, because this was what people did. People moved on and moved forward. It was the natural progression of things. People grew up and paired off and moved in together, and then they had babies together, raising those babies to become new people. Jodie never wanted to have children. If she never got married, she would be fine with it. If her roommate didn't work out and she ended up alone, she would enjoy her own space. If she decided to get an animal, it would probably be a cat.

JODIE AND BERGES HAD FALLEN BACK INTO THEIR OLD HABITS of having lunch together when they ended up at the hospital at the same time. She didn't know why she thought that was a good idea, since he ate the most disgusting things for lunch. Pork rinds? Beef jerky? Turkey jerky? Sardines? Barbecue ribs?

"Have the shrimp," she told him, and then emphasized, "Please."

"What am I gonna do with some little frou frou shrimp?"

"Fine, then chicken," she said. "Have the grilled chicken salad. Caesar if you want."

"Living on the edge," he said.

She smirked at him.

Then he stepped forward to block her way in the lunch line. "But wait a minute, that's not fair. You let Piper eat cheese steak in front of you all the time. I've seen her do it."

But I don't kiss Piper on the mouth, Jodie thought, and then she felt her cheeks flush hot. She didn't routinely kiss Berges on the mouth either – only once, in fact, or well, several hundreds of times in one night – but she couldn't say she'd be opposed to doing it again.

He finally picked up the chicken salad and they paid for their food. She sighed hard as she sat down at a Formica cafeteria table. "I don't have anyone to get martinis with anymore."

She said it before she realized how much it sounded like a confession. He sat staring at her with salad dressing on his lip, waiting for a story, eager eyes like he expected fireworks and a car chase and possibly a bank robbery too. "What did you do?"

There were so many feelings involved it made her feel itchy.

"Nothing," Jodie said, the word festering in her gut. "You know, just people getting hitched and stuff. Moving on."

Her story failed to enthrall. He turned back to his salad while checking his iPhone.

"So I have a new roommate now," Jodie offered. "She's an actress, happily single, pretty, has a lot of boyfriends. I think she does porno."

His eyes lit up and he put down the phone. "Really?"

"No, not really," Jodie said. The point being, she only needed a new roommate because Piper had moved out, and Piper had moved out because she was getting married. And now Jodie needed another date, to yet another wedding. "I mean, Piper has this wedding coming up..."

"Oh, yeah?" he said. "Are you asking me or telling me?"

"What's the difference?" She laughed at her own joke.

He smiled.

"And you should come get a martini with me some time."

"Can I have a beer?"

"Sure," she said. And when he wasn't looking, she added. "Because I pissed off all my martini friends."

"Doesn't surprise me, Sunshine."

The whole story wasn't his kind of story, and she wasn't sure she wanted to tell it all anyway. She'd said it for herself, and somehow it felt soothing to say it out loud. It was her fault, not theirs, and she wanted to put everything back the way it was, though she didn't think that was possible anymore. The damage had been done.

She cleared her throat. "And then next Saturday, my brother's having this dinner party. Asking, not telling."

He took a fat bite of his chicken salad. "Sure," he said. "What time?"

4.2: the center

HER MOTHER SAID, "AMELIA, SOMETIMES I DON'T THINK you make decisions so much as fall into them." In ten weeks, Amelia had managed to come to speaking terms with her mother again. They'd managed to have Christmas together, and New Year's Day, they'd gone together to return gifts and purchase new ones. Amelia had grown accustomed to the new dog, who looked just like the old one but treated her like a stranger still. And she'd stopped taking her birth control pills, finding herself the only way she'd ever resembled her cousins in the least – remarkably fertile.

Amelia couldn't even imagine how her mother had decided to do something as spontaneous as having an affair, being there on the precipice of such a decision, maybe considering something for herself, with that much immediacy, for the first time in her life. To do it, or not to do it, and then finally plunging forward.

Her mother was wrong. Amelia's decisions were made in the quiet in-betweens of her life – every worry, every internal debate – so that by the time the actual decision presented itself, she'd already deliberated over it a thousand times. There was little need for planning. There was no use in asking herself what she wanted yet again. The decisions were made when she wasn't even paying attention. She made decisions all the time.

"But it's actually a great time," Amelia said. "I've got enough time in at work that maternity leave won't be a problem, and the baby will be born in the fall when Drew comes off-season again, and by then Dad will be getting back, hopefully, so I can get back into shape after a few months and we can have the wedding next spring."

Her mother only shook her head. "I just don't understand it. You're engaged to be married and you decide to have the baby before the wedding? What sense does that make?"

"Dad's not home yet," Amelia said. "We're waiting for him to come home before we have the wedding. And if we waited, by then I'd be... thirty-two..." She lost steam. There was more she wanted to say, that they actually wanted time to have two children, and that she knew she wasn't getting any younger. Five gray hairs were now tucked underneath her part line – even they were breeding before she was. She had it all sorted out in her head, but her mother had that unbelievable ability to make her feel like a child. She was a grown woman with her own home and a stable job, deciding to have a baby with the man she loved – what was so wrong about that?

Her mother only pursed her lips, muttering a "Hmmm."

Amelia stood. "Mom," she spoke firmly. "It's not your choice to make."

She unclenched her fists, finding that she'd dug her fingernails into her palms, a line of half-moons printed on her skin.

"Well..." Claire whispered, her eyes wide, looking at Amelia painfully, then as if staring too long at the sun, she glanced away.

Amelia felt instantly bad about shouting, but she didn't take it back. She grabbed her purse from the floor. "I have to go," she said. Her mother nodded, but didn't turn in her direction.

IT WAS TAX SEASON, AND THEY WERE TAKING APPOINTMENTS twelve hours a day, each of them taking a long two-hour lunch in turns, and being bribed with donuts and cake to stay as long as they could. Amelia had not found donuts or cake appealing since she was a child, but at nine weeks pregnant, her stomach churned at the idea of her usual lunches of turkey and hummus on rye, or tuna salad with celery. But donuts she could eat – she couldn't stop eating, whether they were covered in cinnamon and sugar, or drizzled with chocolate, or plumped full of Bavarian cream. She was certain this child must have been all Drew.

Amelia was walking to meet Drew for lunch, and as she caught sight of him a few blocks down, that was when she saw Jodie. You recognize a friend's car when you see it, even if it's just an ordinary, black, four-door sedan like any number of cars like it. She and Jodie had the same model, because Amelia had recommended it. Jodie bought black, and Amelia had it in beige. You don't then forget the car just because you happen to not be friends with that person anymore. Amelia still remembered. It went by, and the sight of it still stopped her a little. She wondered if it always would.

Jodie used to talk about turning into one of those bitter old cat ladies, but she wouldn't – she was too strong for that. She was too fearless. She wouldn't be bitter. If Jodie ever ended up alone with a house full of cats, it would be because she wanted it that way. Amelia could make out the back of Jodie's head, the sleek black hair, hands gripping the steering wheel, the aggressive posture she kept even while driving. Jodie didn't turn her head, she didn't glance up to the rear view mirror. No icy cold eyes in the reflection. Nothing. The light turned green and she went.

Drew caught up with her and asked, "What are you looking at?"

Amelia didn't know if she should say. But before she could decide, the answer fell out of her. "That was Jodie's car."

He looked too, but Jodie was long gone.

Jodie wasn't the problem; she never was. Amelia knew how the bitterness started. It was the fear. The fear of being broken, one time, then two, again and again, until the fractures became too much. And then she couldn't have even helped it, because the fractures would become the very thing that poisoned her from the start – an impossible life filled with poison. She would replace the fear with detachment. She would fill the loneliness with bitterness. She would let the poison destroy her. And not only her, but she would let it destroy the one person who actually wanted to help her heal.

Amelia didn't see the poison as it crept into her own life. She didn't see it until it began eating him alive as well, and that was when she saw it happening, and that was what really terrified her.

Amelia took his hand. "Your baby wants lunch."

They waited for a table, the smells making her early pregnancy stomach both ravenous and nauseous.

"Have you told Piper about the baby yet?"

"No, not yet," Amelia said. "I was about to."

Drew held the restaurant buzzer in his hands, passing it from one to the other like a hot potato. "I told my brother," he said. "I mean, I emailed him."

Amelia grinned.

"Do you think Piper would tell Jodie?"

"She might," Amelia said. Perhaps it was the reason she hadn't told Piper yet, knowing the two of them shared everything.

She had wondered what he thought of it all, but she'd been too scared to ask – after so much trouble, after almost losing each other, it hadn't been the time then. But it was just the two of them now, and their brand new little family. There was no place for poison or resentment here. If he was ready, then there was one more thing Amelia had left to say. "I'm not going to say you can't be friends with Jodie," Amelia said. She searched his eyes – she hadn't anticipated what he might think of that. But all that responsibility, she couldn't hold it anymore. She hadn't expected him to look so surprised, conflicted, afraid – he seemed to wish she would make that decision for them. But she couldn't. She touched his cheek, rough with stubble. "It's up to you what you want to make of that."

Amelia and Drew had sandwiches and fries for lunch and still had an hour left of Amelia's lunch break. They walked down Main Street looking in shop windows, a comic book shop, an antique store, a wine shop that she had no use for anymore. It would rain soon, the sky heavy with it, the air thick with moisture. For now, everything was cold and gray and dry. A jewelry store, the poster in the shop window advertised emeralds shaped into a four-leaf clover pendant. "Who wears that kind of stuff?"

"Damn," Drew whispered, a smirk on his face. "I'll have to take back your St. Patty's Day present then."

Amelia laughed. "You'd only have to walk around with me wearing the thing." Through the store window, she could barely make out a birthstone display. She tugged his arm pulling him into the store. "I don't want anything, I just want to see something."

The baby was due on the cusp of Libra and Scorpio – opal or topaz. She'd lied about not wanting anything. She wanted one of those Mother's Day pendants with the birthstones of her children laid out in a row. Maybe more than just two. Maybe three. She wasn't *that* old yet. She still had time.

"Whose name is the baby going to have?"

The heaviness of his question surprised her. She hadn't noticed how worried he looked as she'd been daydreaming about silly birthstone jewelry. "Yours," she said. "We all will eventually, right? It doesn't matter if we're not married when the baby is born. I mean, I don't care about what's traditional or not. I don't care if the baby comes before the wedding. It doesn't mean anything one way or another."

"No, I know it doesn't matter."

He wasn't convincing.

"I do want to take your name," she said. "I really, honestly do. But I can't until we're married. Legally, I can't."

"I know," he said. "I know. Don't worry about it."

When they decided to start trying for a baby sooner rather than later, he seemed to be fully on board with the decision. She didn't know if maybe he hadn't expected it to happen so quickly, but she always felt that he was worried about something. She hadn't expected it all so quickly either, but she was happy now. She was excited about it.

He started to laugh.

"What? Tell me," she said.

"It's silly," he said.

She grinned. "You're just marrying me for my health insurance, aren't you?"

"Ha, you got me." He laughed, letting a hand drift to her belly, swiping across the surface like he was saying 'hello'. "It's just... I always wanted a family all with one name."

"Is that all?" She touched his cheek. This wasn't for her mother, or to prove to prove her mother wrong. This was for him, because it mattered to him, and then she knew just what they could do. She wrapped her arms around his waist. "We could go get married."

"We are getting married," he said, confused. "I thought."

"I mean, yes," she said. "But that's our wedding. What I mean is, we could get married. Now. And have our wedding later. Nobody would even have to know." She let out the deep breath she'd been holding, the release of all those decisions and worries. It felt so impossibly simple yet perfect. Like the moment they laid in bed at his old apartment, just the two of them and the simple choice, yes or no. Like the moment they first kissed, the night they first became a couple, all those sudden bursts forward that could only happen after so much consideration.

She pulled him over to the wedding band displays, and they looked at the rings, simple bands, some etched, some with stones embedded in them.

"Is that what you want? I'm fine, really, you don't have to do this for me."

This was what she wanted. She hadn't known it until it burst out of her mouth. "Yes, it is."

They picked two wedding bands, bought them and left the store.

It was raining then, the sky having finally broken. She pulled a hood up over her head and they darted in between umbrellas and lampposts. They took a number at the counter and sat down to wait, with wedding rings in her purse and a clipboard to fill out. "Do we need a witness?"

"Let me guess, you could call Corbin?"

Amelia frowned at him. "You don't need to hate him. Whatever you're worried about – we were never like that, we never will be."

Drew sighed. "I don't hate him."

"Really? If you just give him a chance – true, he's a little boring sometimes – but maybe you guys could be friends some day."

Drew scrunched his eyebrows.

Amelia's eyes lit up. "You should take him golfing! I don't think he's ever played before."

"Heh," Drew chuckled. "No. That might be pushing it."

"I'll call Piper. She's just a couple blocks away, and she'd love to be here." Amelia picked up her phone and sent a text, laughing lightly. "She's going to burst, just watch."

"What did you always imagine your wedding would be like?"

She wasn't sure how to admit this, certain it probably made her defective as a woman. "Actually, I don't think I ever imagined it at all."

"Really? Why not?"

She shrugged, searching back in her memories for something, a favorite color, a dress style, a scene – the way little girls design their wedding with some faceless groom they haven't even met. But there was nothing. Maybe she never believed it would actually happen for her. "It's not that I didn't see myself married – I did – I just never really thought about the wedding, not that specifically."

He looked sad, though he smiled, glancing down at her khaki pants, with their stretchy pregnancy waistband. He laughed lightly. "I imagined you in a dress, that's all."

"Do you want to stop? We can wait, if you want."

He shook his head. "No." He reached over to her lap and laced his fingers through hers. "I imagined a lot of things happening differently, but I like the way things turned out."

Amelia's phone beeped, a text from Piper saying that she'd be right over.

The registrar called their number just five minutes after Piper showed up at the courthouse, still wearing her Beaners apron and smelling like cappuccino, tears in her eyes and a bouquet of white roses in her hands. They filed their paperwork, signed their names, and paid their fee. The vows went quickly. Amelia knew she wouldn't remember them later, and Drew mentioned wishing he would have written something. It didn't matter. The words they had were plenty.

Amelia headed back over to her mother's place that evening after work. Claire was washing a few dishes in the kitchen when she stepped inside. Living alone, she'd taken to washing the dishes just as soon as she used them, almost immediately. Every dish in this home was instantly clean. Amelia wished her mother would find a few new hobbies.

"You're here," Claire said. "I'm surprised to actually see you. So you've been spending time with your new mother-in-law? Is she perfect, everything you hoped for in a mother? You're ready to forget about your old mom then?"

Amelia sighed. "Oh God, Mom, don't do that."

Moira and Richard had stayed for four weeks, and she and Drew weren't fighting anymore. With tax season and then the pregnancy, maybe she had been a little absent. Amelia did love Moira, with her glamor and adventure, all those wild stories she told when she'd had a little too much champagne. She was easy to love, but she wasn't her mom.

Claire raised her eyebrows and shook her head, as if she didn't know what she was doing. "I fixed you some meals to take home. You're working too much for being pregnant. And I can't imagine he knows how to feed you."

She didn't know if she should thank her mother or roll her eyes – Drew was actually trying. He learned to make meatloaf and mashed potatoes.

They hadn't discussed her mother's affair again. Claire swept up that mess and the two of them picked up like it hadn't ever been said, as if Amelia only remembered some piece of a conversation that had taken place in a dream. As time passed, Amelia found herself wondering about it again, needing to hear the whys, hows, and whens. The words her mother had said that day just didn't compute. They didn't seem to be enough. It seemed like it should be so unforgivable, yet from her own experience, she knew it wasn't that simple. Hadn't she forgiven men for just that same thing, many more times than she ever should have?

She would be listening this time, if her mother would say more. She was ready for it.

Amelia sat at the breakfast nook while her mother finished the dishes. "Is Dad over there because he's mad at you?"

"Oh, Amelia, your father loves his work and he always has." Claire had her hands in the dishwater still. She didn't look over. "Is he mad at me? I don't know. Perhaps he is."

"Are you guys getting divorced then?"

Claire exhaled, shaking her head. "My own mother divorced," she said. "I wasn't going to put you through that."

"And now?"

"I don't know, sweetie." Her voice drifted. She dried her hands on a towel. "Can I fix you something to drink?"

"No thanks. I am pretty tired," Amelia said. "I just wanted to stop by for a bit. I didn't mean to shout at you before."

Claire took a stiff breath then. "I don't mean to fight with you either, Amelia. I just don't want you to end up unhappy." There was so much weight hanging on that wish, on any of her mother's wishes for her. She all but said, *like me.*

"We're fine," Amelia said, glancing down at the inconspicuous wedding band next to her engagement ring. Her mother wouldn't notice so small a detail. Not quickly at least.

Amelia didn't know what to say. Nothing was what she thought it was. Her mother knew it too, but she wouldn't say so. All those ideas she'd had, that her daddy would come home, that her parents would be happy, that her baby would have a grandfather – it was all part of that lovely picture they'd created that was never going to be real. Amelia just wanted someone to say it out loud, that her daddy, the warrior, the bravest man they knew, the hero from all those stories, was never going to be what they'd built him up to be. "He's not coming home, is he?"

There was a short flash of terror in her mother's eyes then, hidden under the surface, a fear that Amelia rarely saw and hadn't understood in her youth. Maybe it had always been there underneath her prim exterior, the truth she hadn't wanted to admit for so long, that after waiting for someone for thirty-three years, a woman finally knows for certain whether it's going to work out or not.

Amelia blinked away obstinate tears, and Claire reached out to pat Amelia's shoulder with a stiff hand. "Oh, sweetie, I imagine he'll come home for your wedding, and he'd love to meet the baby, no matter where he decides to stay in the end. It just might not turn out the way we thought."

Amelia tried to smile, but she was sure it must have turned crooked.

"Being alone," Claire said. "I've done it for so long. I think I'm tired of waiting for my real life to start."

She put her hand over Amelia's, smiling cautiously at the idea of a new beginning. Hadn't it been just the two of them for so many years? Shouldn't they be ready for this by now?

Amelia had hoped for a name to place on this faceless man who destroyed her parents' marriage, some villain to point her finger at. But his name didn't matter anymore, and Amelia didn't ask. She listened to her mother talk about the spa, how she'd like to add something new to the class schedule – maybe martial arts, kickboxing. She had Amelia's hand clutched in hers and she patted it. "Have you ever thought about kickboxing, sweetie? I think it would do you good."

"No thanks, Mom," Amelia said, but Claire went on anyway, about learning to meditate, traveling to India some day, and maybe going back to school for a business degree. And of course, how it would never be too early to start buying clothes for the new baby.

WHEN AMELIA FINALLY MADE IT BACK FROM HER MOTHER'S that evening, having stayed longer than she'd intended, Drew had fallen asleep in front of a golf game while trying to wait up for her.

She wanted a hug from him, so she wedged herself underneath his arm. His eyes fluttered open for a moment, and he mumbled, "Mmmm," as her body folded against his, her curves filling his angled spaces, a perfect complement to each other.

She had a husband now. There was an inconspicuous wedding band on her finger that blended into her engagement ring, and she grinned at the idea of it. She ran a finger over the curve of his wedding band too, matching hers but thicker. No one had noticed his ring yet either – such a small detail to represent such a big idea. She hadn't remembered to brace herself this time. When all the decisions of her life happened in a continuous assault of worries and thoughts, she must have decided to marry him a long time ago.

Drew squeezed her, stirring lightly, but he eventually fell back asleep. It was late, but she wasn't tired enough yet to sleep. She slid out from under his arm and changed into some pajamas. She stretched out her yoga mat in the living room, facing the back yard windows which were covered in a thin coat of ice. Drew wanted to keep some bookcases in their living room. They were so bulky and packed full that Amelia felt inclined to organize them, preen them and add some candles or vases to open up the space. But she didn't. Except to straighten the edges from time to time. He'd grown on her, grown around and into her. His shoes were mixed with hers beside the front door, his little scraps of poetry were left around the house on shopping receipts, on junk mail, and the occasional paper towel. She picked them up sometimes and put them in a basket for him. She'd hate for him to lose one. He told her once about ideas – about how you got one single chance at them most of the time, and if you failed to write them down, they were gone. They would never come back quite the same way. They could never be remade or remembered. That tiny idea and its brief sliver of life here and gone, just like that.

Amelia eased herself to the yoga mat, her feet pressed together and her spine stretched tall. She took a breath in, deep and full, and let it out in a smooth blow. Somehow she heard Mindy's voice in her head, *Smile at your belly*. The way she'd said even just the word "smile" was long and lyrical, her voice rising and falling like a song. Amelia's belly was still mostly flat, a tiny pocket that looked like she'd eaten a big meal except it felt firm to the touch. *Talk to your belly, your voice is your child's connection to this world right now.*

"Hello, little one," Amelia whispered, looking around the room as if someone might be watching. Drew was still asleep and showed no signs of stirring. Her own voice sounded meek in her head, uncomfortable and unsure. Was her speaking voice really that tense? What if her baby didn't like it?

She didn't know what to say anyway. What do you say to a baby that's no bigger than a large raisin?

So she took another deep breath, letting it out slowly, a hiss at first, but then she started to hum, the notes ambiguous but eventually taking shape, a song. She noted to herself that she'd have to learn some children's songs, but no child was ever harmed by The Beatles either. With her eyes closed, humming in the dead of night with a golf game flickering color onto the walls, green, white, green, she pressed her feet to her thighs. She pressed her thighs to the floor and it grounded her to the earth, her spine rising higher, her hands resting calm on her knees. The deep breaths transformed into song in her chest, soft at first and then growing, her whole body pulsing with the abundance rising somewhere from the middle of her.

4.3: considering everything

JODIE AND EMMY GOT OFF TO A ROCKY START, BUT THEN, Jodie hadn't been giving her a fair chance. Emmy wasn't Piper, and it took her some time to allow for the fact that she wasn't supposed to be. Jodie didn't tell Emmy much about what had happened between all of them, and there was something refreshing about that. All she knew was that they'd all been friends once, and now they'd drifted apart.

Jodie regretted not telling her more one day when there was a knock at their door. From their living room, all Jodie heard was Emmy's voice, flirty and bright. "Hmmm..." She cooed, "Who are you, handsome?" Jodie wouldn't put it past Emmy to hit on anyone: the mailman, their landlord, the pizza guy, the landscapers, the electric company meter reader. At least she hadn't gone to the door in her underwear this time. Jodie didn't hear the other person's response, only Emmy, echoing back. "Drew? Like, *the* Drew?"

Jodie bounded from the couch, shooing her quickly from the doorway. Jodie's hair was tied up in a short sprig of a ponytail, and she had sweatpants on. This was the first time she'd seen him in three months. She wished she'd been wearing something else.

"Can you talk?" he asked her. His eyes were such a rich brown she could have sunk right into them. The last time she'd looked into his eyes had been the worst night of her life. Maybe his too. He began to smile – not quite as brilliant as he used to, but something more defeated and forlorn.

She slipped untied boots onto her feet and pulled a coat over her shoulders, stepping outside with him. It was still cold outside, though the sun shone stronger as the days melted into spring, the ground soggy underneath her feet, slushy puddles of muck. On the trees, tiny buds were just beginning to grow.

"I was just in the area," he said, waving to the street.

"Uh-huh," she said softly.

"I'm glad you found someone," he said. "Was she from my list?"

"No," Jodie said, sputtering out an abrupt laugh. "Amelia's! You mean you don't even know if that girl was your friend or not?"

"Heh," he chuckled, catching her laugh. "I don't know, she looked familiar maybe."

"Yeah, tell Amelia I said thank you. For the girl, I mean. Emmy, she's alright."

"I will," he said. His eyes turned to the ground. "I tried this once, months ago."

Why he was there, he meant. Piper had told her that he'd stopped by once. Nothing good ever came out of conversations that started like that. She waited, feeling the pit in her stomach deepen and churn. They were never actually together, and yet somehow she felt like she was about to be dumped.

"I thought we understood," he told her, searching her face for answers. "But I guess we didn't both understand the same way, did we?"

She didn't have an answer for that. She tucked her hands into her pockets. What did he want from her, an apology? To roll back and undo it all?

"I did care about you," he said. "But this is bigger than you understand." He was scared, nervous, a look of immense gravity on his face. "We're a family now," he said. "The family I always wanted, and I have to take care of that. If we were ever friends, then I hope you'll understand why I don't think we should talk or see each other, considering everything. I don't want her to have to worry about all this again."

Jodie inhaled and exhaled. She looked into his deep, gentle eyes which reminded her of how he had said she was *nothing*, but she knew that wasn't true. Because if that were true, he wouldn't be here.

"I know we haven't actually been speaking," he added. "I guess I just wanted to come here and say..." Then he laughed to himself, turning his head. "I don't know, maybe you never thought we were friends."

She still hadn't said anything. She had to say something. But she wouldn't say she didn't love him. She wouldn't say it didn't matter. And she wouldn't say she was sorry for letting him know that. "We were," she said, firmly. "Yes, we were friends."

He didn't quite turn his face to her, not enough that she could see his eyes again, but she thought she saw a smile before he nodded once and turned slowly to go.

His walk was calm – he didn't hurry away. He didn't sulk or hang his head. He lifted his face to the sky, heavy with clouds; he probably wondered if it was going to snow again before spring took over. He always liked the damn snow. Jodie stood there long enough to see if he would wave, if he'd even turn to look back to her once more before he rounded the corner.

He didn't.

CONSIDERING EVERYTHING, JODIE WASN'T IN THE MOOD to drive out to her brother's house for a proper, sit-down, family dinner. But she went. And she brought a date. Eric wanted to make this a regular thing, but she hadn't told Berges that yet. She wasn't sure what that would mean, to have a regular date to regular family dinners.

Jodie even brought a pie for dessert. Store-bought, but still.

"What's wrong with you?" Berges asked her, carrying her pie. "You're cranky for even you."

Jodie sneered at him. "What's wrong with *you*? You're wearing *chinos*!" He wore a buttoned shirt in dark gray, tucked into his pants with his sleeves rolled twice. She felt underdressed in her jeans and cardigan. "You don't have to try to impress him so much. He already likes you for some reason."

Berges got along with her brother. It boggled her mind how well they all got along. Ruth too, her sister-in-law, her new family, not the sister she thought she might have had one day, but the one she actually got. Ruth wasn't too bad. She was sturdy, honest, and a little bit funny, which Jodie liked. She wasn't graceful, or fashionable, or even exceptionally pretty, and Jodie liked her for all of that. She was glad her brother married this one.

After dinner, they sat around the table drinking wine. Ruth had fruit juice in her wine glass.

"So tell me about being a surgeon," Eric said to Berges. "It must have been weird at first – you know, cutting into people?"

"You've been watching too much *Dexter*, honey," Ruth said.

"You'd probably chop me up if you got the chance," Jodie said, immediately wishing she hadn't said that out loud. First, she hadn't meant it in the *Dexter* way, and second, if he honestly thought she needed nipping and tucking, she would probably rather not know.

Berges looked at the bunch of them strangely, but then he smiled. "Well your eyebrows are a little thick," he said to her. "But plucking isn't really my area of expertise." He kicked her foot lightly underneath the table as he started to tell Eric about his work. It made her grin.

After dinner, Eric and Ruth were being too cute for comfort. They all moved to the tiny blue living room with its covered couches. Sometimes they looked at her with too much concern, after patting Ruth's round belly, as if Jodie were about to embark on what might be the biggest regret of her life. She didn't need them to worry for her. It wasn't like their family line would die out. With all the marriages and siblings they had, there was no danger of that in the least.

A commercial on the TV showed plump, diapered babies dancing to KC & The Sunshine Band, and Berges started to bop his head where he sat. Jodie cringed beside him, thankful that her brother and Ruth were too busy canoodling to notice. She jabbed him in the side.

"Don't give me any more wine, or I'll dance," he threatened. "Don't think I won't."

Jodie believed him.

When her brother and Ruth had left the room, she felt the confession spill out of her. "I don't see myself ever wanting kids. Do you think that makes me a monster?"

She had no idea why she did that, why she told him that like his opinion should matter in any capacity. Or why she waited for his response like she actually cared what his opinion was.

"Why should that make you a monster? Don't have any, then. Hope you've been remembering your pills."

It was easy for him to say – he already had one. No matter what became of his romantic future, he had offspring out there. She wouldn't. But maybe she would have felt more secure about that decision if everyone in her life didn't keep telling her she was wrong.

"You'd be a tyrant of a mother anyway," Berges said, grinning.

"Screw you," Jodie said.

"Sure, if you want."

"You're foul." She laughed, not moving away from him. "No more wine for you. It's a ninety minute drive, and I'm tired, so you're driving."

"Fine," he said. "I'll drive. You can sleep if you want. I'll just put on disco and you can dream about us dancing."

They said their goodnights to her brother and Ruth, and Berges helped her into her coat, and then slid his on after. Eric stood at the door for a minute, watching them go, before he finally waved and disappeared inside. Outside, the night was cold enough that fat puffs of steam came from their mouths.

"Ice," Berges said, holding his hand out to her.

"Well hell, I've been called a lot of things before..."

"Not you, the ground," he said.

She looked over the pavement, but she couldn't see anything. She reached out a foot to test the ground. He still had his hand held out to her. "Dammit Jodie, I'm trying to do something nice for you."

"Oh, okay," she said, relenting, taking his hand.

"Okay what?"

"You know, thanks." She sneered at him. She took his hand and he helped her step over the ice. He was grinning far too eagerly, and she found it amusing. "Not like I was going to fall."

They came to his car and she stopped. "What, after all that chivalry, you're not going to open the car door for me?"

He still had her hand and he tugged her closer to him. "You're a big girl, you can open your own door," he said. He tried to lean in for a kiss, but she laughed out loud instead and reached up to ruffle his hair. It seemed the hair ruffling made him madder than the not kissing. It wasn't conscious, how she pushed him away. She didn't want to push him away. She reached her arms underneath his coat, around his back, so that the two of them fell into something of a stiffened hug. She let her face fall to his chest. He smelled of clean linens and the leather of his coat – the coat she liked on him. "Thanks for coming out with me tonight," she said.

Considering everything, Berges was kinder than he needed to be, still remarkably handsome for his age, and funnier than most, and she wouldn't hold his ridiculous dancing against him. The last time she'd been in the arms of a man underneath a cold, clear sky – however short it had lasted – had been a very long time ago. And the last time she'd been out on a date she left the guy cold on the corner of Eleven Mile and Main, and though that wasn't what she wanted to do here – she wouldn't do that again here – it felt the same. Pangs in her heart. Her *heart*. She couldn't believe it had come to that after all.

But Jodie looked up to his eyes, full of that victorious glow they had sometimes, the one that made her want to smack him and kiss him all at the same time. She scowled at him for a moment, then she softened. She didn't smack him. Jodie was no charmer – she probably wasn't even a good kisser at all – but he could have it if he wanted it.

No, that was only half of it.

The other half was, if she was going to be honest with herself, that she actually wanted it too.

4.4: unimaginable grace

ONE AFTERNOON THAT MARCH, PIPER'S SEWING ROOM was crowded with women trying on pastel dresses. In the few, short months she'd been using the room, the shelves had already gathered dust. Jodie knew Piper was too hopeless to dust her own shelves. With all that movement in the room, the dust flew up and scattered in the air, sparkling in the sunlight coming through the large windows. Piper wore the fluttering pieces of her own gown, which Jodie couldn't tell if it was strange because it was meant to be, or because it was still unfinished.

Piper turned to Jodie, a constipated frenzy in her bright eyes. "She should be here any minute now. You know, I asked you both to be in my wedding. I *want* you both in my wedding. My wedding that's in seven weeks. My wedding, which I'm already almost finished with the dresses for? Please, please be nice to her."

Jodie grinned. "When am I ever not nice?"

Downstairs, one of Piper's sisters opened the front door, and it was Amelia's voice that greeted her. Piper ran between her sisters and nieces, some of them dressed in lavender and buttercream, and some of them just helping out. Each of the dresses were in various states of being finished. Jodie's dress was in alternate colors and would be the last to be completely done. She had already wrangled herself into the gown, a rich lavender color that seemed to make her pale skin shimmer. In its current state, there was no zipper yet to pull the bodice together, so Jodie wore the mess of fabric hung from one shoulder and held the rest of it up with her own hands.

She waited for Amelia to finally make it up the stairs. Piper moved back to their spot near the window, making pleading eyes at Jodie to please get along. Just for an hour, her eyes said, not even that long. Just long enough to try on these dresses and take final alterations.

Piper hurried over to her first. There was a flurry of soft-spoken words between them. The only thing Jodie heard was Amelia, "I don't want to be too much trouble."

Then there was more whispering. Jodie tried not to watch them, as this conversation was clearly not meant for everyone. Piper was stunned first, but then her face broke out into a beaming smile that overwhelmed the whole room. She engulfed Amelia with a hug. "Oh, I'm so happy for you," she said.

Jodie was listening even more closely then, her eyes to the floor to look inconspicuous.

"But the dress," Amelia said. "I'm so sorry, it was hardly half-decided and I never expected it to happen so fast. I'll understand if you can't do it. Seven weeks from now, I'll be a boat."

"No, you'll be beautiful," Piper insisted. "How far along will you be in May?"

"Sixteen weeks, I have no idea how big that is."

A baby? That was what he meant, when he came to her that day, when he was so very serious about needing to protect his family?

Jodie was watching then, she couldn't help it. Piper held her hand out in front of Amelia's barely swollen belly. Piper would have known exactly what a sixteen-week belly would look like. She'd seen twelve of her nieces and nephews inside sixteen-week bellies, and she already had hand-me down maternity clothes from her sisters. She had tears in her eyes still, but they didn't look entirely happy. Jodie was the only one who knew Piper was actually trying, the only one who knew she had hoped she would be altering her own dress to accommodate a bigger belly. "It's okay," Piper nodded to Amelia. "I can do that."

"But if it's too much trouble..."

"No, it's not, I want you in my wedding too," Piper said. "I'll just let it out a little, it'll be no problem. Oh, a baby." Piper reached up and took a handful of Amelia's red curls. "I hope it gets your hair."

Jodie was stunned with more emotions than she knew what to do with, and not all of them were selfless ones either. Of course Amelia and Drew were having a baby. It was what people did – they fell in love, they paired off, they started lives together. Drew had written this into their fate the moment he first met Amelia. It wasn't like Jodie had ever wanted to have his baby instead, or be his doting wife, or roast his Sunday dinners, or fold and press his laundry, even in some alternate reality where Amelia had never existed. It was never meant to be Jodie's life. And Jodie wasn't losing, because Drew was never hers to lose. He was always meant for Amelia. Jodie had just borrowed him for a night, and she held on a little too long.

Piper stood there in her strange wedding dress. She had tears in her eyes, holding one of Amelia's hands and looking to Jodie as her sisters and nieces fluttered around the room in unfinished gowns. "I'm so happy, you guys. I'm just so happy right now."

Jodie tried to imagine they were happy tears and not sad ones.

"Well, okay," Piper said, swiping a hand across her cheek, gathering herself back together, speaking to herself more than anyone else specifically. "I was just going to work on Jodie a little, and I'll fix Amelia here in a minute." She began to run around the room again, fetching Amelia her dress, passing between her sisters and nieces, checking seams and pulling up zippers.

Amelia stood there by the door, working herself into her buttercream dress, a small bulge under her belly button, and she left the back unzipped where she'd already grown too much for the zipper to close. She slowly made her way into the middle of the room to wait.

Piper was headed for Jodie then, and Jodie held her arms out away from her body, the way she'd seen Amelia do before, only more awkwardly. Piper had ribbon in one hand and pins in the other, wrapping and sticking fabric to the gown. Jodie felt a pin in her side and squealed.

"Goddammit, Piper!"

"I'm sorry," Piper said, a pin still clenched between her teeth. "Can you hold the ribbon here? No, don't move your arm though, you're puckering the side."

Amelia stepped forward. "Here," she said. "Let me." She held out her hand, palm open to accept the ribbon.

Piper demonstrated the angle. "Like this," she said. "Thankies."

Amelia held the ribbon taut. Jodie couldn't look Amelia in the eyes, but just went silent while Piper wrapped the butter-cream ribbon around the layers of lavender tulle as she finished her pinning, and Amelia stood there in Jodie's peripheral vision, the fine point of her chin held poised, barefoot and pregnant with the back of her dress still undone. The unimaginable grace it must have taken for Amelia to stand there and hold that ribbon, not to spit in Jodie's face, not to grab a pin and prick her herself.

But then, despite her best efforts, Jodie glanced up. She found Amelia not poised, but glassy-eyed, her bottom lip quivering as she bit down on it, taking smooth, deep breaths of air. The two of them stood together in Piper's wrecked dresses, strewn pieces of fabric and trailing ribbons, lavender and buttercream, torn apart and stitched back together. It struck Jodie sharper and deeper than any pin could ever reach.

Jodie was not going to say she was sorry. But in her heart, it felt something like that.

Acknowledgments

Thank you to Dylan, for all the times I just had to go write something down. I think I got it all down in the end. Some day I will write you a book with pictures in it.

Thank you to my husband, Jim, for going to work every day, and for bringing home health insurance. Thank you for editing for me, even though there were not enough zombies and too many weddings. Thank you for being patient and persistent, even when it was hard to do. Thank you for feeding my heart, so that I might write these stories about love.

To my dear, brilliant, talented critique partners, Carla, Nina, Milena, Rachel, Jane, Van, and Ruth, thank you for enduring all the freak-outs, the pit stops, the questions and babble, the wrecked drafts that nobody should have had to endure, for the kind words, the infinite guidance, the brutal truths, for setting the bar as high as I asked you to and not letting me wiggle under it, for murdering commas, for calling me out on my fluff, for fixing my atrocious spelling mistakes and not questioning (out loud, at least) how I ended up a writer at all, for slaps upside the head, for not letting me doubt myself, and for beatings with theoretical dead fish. This novel would not exist without you.

To the rest of my Bistro Table friends, thank you for listening to me whine, change my title fifty times, change my cover art forty-three-thousand times, and for all the feedback and unfaltering support. (Thank you Shana, for answering all of my questions! And Vilde, for the long-winded rambles which are always useful!)

To my LH peanut gallery, thank you for being my very first readers and for being the best cheerleaders a girl could have.

To Michelle, thank you for the encouragement.

Thank you to the creators of Freedom (seriously, folks!) and Liquid Story Binder. Absolute genius.

For reference, thank you to Annie for the poetry advice. And though the Belle Haven lighthouse is fictional, I'd like to thank Todd R. Berger for *Lighthouses of the Great Lakes*, and to the authors of the website: midwestconnection.com. Thank you to Mark Stephens for *Teaching Yoga: Essential Foundations and Techniques*. Thanks to the uncles, dads, and families of my friends, whom I commissioned to ask thousands of questions about military life and careers.

And thank you to all the independent authors out there who blogged and tweeted, who shared their knowledge, gave support, and inspired, paving the way for new indies like me. You made this path possible for us, and I am endlessly thankful for the freedom to shape my own career.

Finally, to my readers, new and old, thank you for letting me share this story with you.

About The Author

Laura Rae Amos is a Michigan native now living near Washington DC with her charming husband and tornado of a little boy. After studying creative writing at the University of Toledo, she moved to the suburbs of Detroit to have a baby instead of an MFA. She is a blogger, web-fiction writer, poet, occasional musician, photographer, dabbling artisan, and all around creative distraction. She has nineteen books in her head and needs to learn to write faster. Or else focus. *Exactly Where They'd Fall* is her debut novel.

Please visit lauraraeamos.com or follow @LauraRaeAmos on Twitter to find out more about upcoming projects, to read more about the making of Exactly Where They'd Fall, or to learn about the other books in this "story web". Though this isn't a traditional series, you can be assured that you'll see many of these characters again in one form or another.

Suggested Musical Soundtrack

Thank you to the following musical artists for the kick-ass songs that played on repeat while this novel came into existence.

"Die Alone" and "Glass" by **Ingrid Michaelson**, and also most of the *Girls and Boys* album

"Fix You" by **Coldplay**, and also most of the *A Rush of Blood to the Head* and *X&Y* albums

"Skinny Love" by **Bon Iver**

"The Grace" by Neverending White Lights

"Fake Plastic Trees" by **Radiohead**

"Island in the Sun" by **Weezer**

"Someone Like You" by **Adele**

"Get it Right" by **Jets Overhead**

"Bluff" by **Pilot Speed**

"Colorblind" by **Counting Crows**

"Blackbird" by **The Beatles**

"Chasing Cars" by **Snow Patrol**

Book Club Discussion Guide

1. How are Jodie and Amelia alike in their reluctance to be a part of a romantic couple, and how are they different? What parts of their pasts do you think most contributed to their current state of mind?

2. What do you think the title might mean? What did you assume about the title before you read the book? Did its meaning change for you as you read?

3. How does each character deal with the prospect (or the reality) of "ending up" alone? Do you think a healthy and well-adjusted person should be able to live happily on his or her own, or is it human nature to want companionship?

4. Several of the characters in this novel have chosen to keep secrets from their friends, lovers, children, or parents, with good intentions. Some characters eventually chose to have those secrets known. What secrets does a person owe to his or herself to have known, and which should be kept closed for good? How much of a parent's private life is off-limits to even their children? Is it safe for friends and lovers to keep secrets from each other for the good of the relationship?

5. Can two people who have romantic feelings for each other ever remain just friends, without risk to their chosen partnerships? Alternately, can two people who have had sex with each other remain just friends, even if they don't have romantic feelings for each other?

6. Many of the characters yearn for, or dwell on things that could have happened (or almost happened) but didn't, sometimes influenced by circumstances that were out of their control. How does it affect a person to think about all the alternate paths their life could have taken? Do you think the choices we could have made, or did make, are governed by fate or by chance?

7. How do you think each of the main characters deals with the idea of perfection? How are they afraid to fail?

8. If any (or all) of these characters had a villain in their lives, who or what would that villain be?

9. Which character did you most identify with, and why? Which character is least like you?